ETERNITY'S BLADE

BOOKS BY WILLIAM COLLIS

STANDALONE NOVELS

Eternity's Blade

NONFICTION

The Book of Esports

William Collis

ETERNITY'S BLADE

BLACK
STONE
PUBLISHING

Published in 2025 by Blackstone Publishing
Cover and book design by Larissa Ezell

Printed in the United States of America
Originally published in hardcover by Blackstone Publishing in 2025

First paperback edition: 2025
ISBN 979-8-228-00374-3
Fiction / Fantasy / Historical

Version 1

Blackstone Publishing
31 Mistletoe Rd.
Ashland, OR 97520

www.BlackstonePublishing.com

I dedicate this book to all my family:
past, present, and future.

PART I

THE VALLEY OF THE LILIES

CHAPTER ONE

MURDER

"Hold the knife to my throat," whispered the courtier.

Just like everyone else in the Valley, Prince Soh'shoro had never seen Death. To the boy, this was just another ritual of silk and rough salt, to bury meaning beneath monotony.

"Be firm and quick." The courtier's breath reeked of lilies. "I tire of repeating everything."

And the boy, still trusting, drew his blade clumsily across the soft neck.

He didn't understand what happened then. Why a great stain of miracle crimson seeped across the lilac finery. Why the courtier jerked, again and again, like a prayer strip in a sudden wind. Why the disembodied Voice screamed hideously, bringing his attendant, Kenwu, running, and then Obajen-mahoe close behind. And the lord snatched the boy prince into his arms, dragging Soh'shoro away from his first murder.

"What have you done, my son?" Obajen-mahoe choked out, eyes rich with silver tears. "This was supposed to be your secret."

He fled with Soh'shoro swaddled like a precious gem. He ran higher and higher through the labyrinthine house, as if distance itself could cure the sin. Until at last he caught his breath on the great terraces, clutching the child against him as the two stared out across the entire world.

"Why don't you understand?" Obajen-mahoe begged. "This is the Valley of the Lilies." His arm swept across the Mist-thick hills. "Here there is no violence. No illness. No Death." Obajen-mahoe's voice dropped like a stone.

"And then there is you, Soh'shoro. And what you might do."

The boy shivered as he listened, for even then he felt the terrible burden of the power that belonged only to him.

The Valley began with the Mists, their ashen veils parting on a knifing snow line shot through by hoary talus and rockfall. Arête ridges cascaded into moraines of ice and scree, lifeless save for lichens clinging weakly to the frozen slopes. Among these highest peaks the Qu'en Shards rose, mute sentinels against gray oblivion, their angular geometries and luminescent patterns clawing back the limits of the world.

Beneath, the Valley's heights gentled into high scrubland. Here the taiga began, limber pine and black spruce rising hauntingly from the sparse landscape, unnaturally tall and majestically isolated. A little lower, and the forests deepened with elm and silver birch, ancient boughs tangling above bare yarrow and browning weed. Even here the Mists could reach on cold days, though, so settlements remained sparse: a disused shrine or an ascetic's cave.

And then the basin of the Valley blossomed: great rolling plains of grass, shimmering as light on water, translucently splendid even in the dark. Streams that started high in the Valley's walls pooled here, becoming rivers and ponds. Villages dotted these shores, and hamlets walled themselves into obscurity behind terraces of rice. And in the central depths spread the City, majestic and meretricious, silvered strings and lofted lanterns marking the last crèche of Man. The Mists were made here: starting skyward from the Emperor's Mausoleum, then drifting over the Valley like an endless cloud before collecting against its distant peaks.

The lilies grew most thickly in the basin. By high summer, the whole Valley floor lay blanketed as though with snow. They choked away the laurels and the reeds, strangling ponds and paddies alike, until all that survived was the beautiful white of the lilies.

"We must never speak of this," Obajen-mahoe commanded, splashing brine over Soh'shoro's bloodied face and hands. The courtier's gore ran off the prince's skin in a languid trickle. "*Death doesn't come into the Valley.* Understand?"

Soh'shoro nodded fearfully, as Kenwu patted him dry with devotional silks. The attendant then burned the same cloth in an open salt brazier, touching it only with the tips of his fingers.

"This can't be a coincidence," Obajen-mahoe remarked. "Not when the Onan'ji visits."

"We can still keep this secret," Kenwu countered. "The courtier was old enough for Rebirth. I will personally oversee Traders vanishing the body, so there will be no way the monk can know."

"Of course the Onan'ji knows!" Obajen-mahoe snapped, tongue darting over his painted lips. "Ever since her passing, he's stalked my son. This death is *his* doing."

Lantern paper refracted colors like spilled inks across the lord's face: amber and deep orange and teal. And in that beautiful light, Soh'shoro's saw Obajen-mahoe's tears, falling like gemstones against the iridescent patterning of his intricate double-sleeved robes.

"I'm sorry!" the boy gasped. "I didn't know."

And Obajen-mahoe hugged the panicked child.

"It's not your fault," he soothed, patting the grass charms woven through Soh'shoro's hair. But his fingers clenched white with fury. And Obajen-mahoe pushed the child away suddenly, deciding.

"What is it, Father?"

"Stay here," he commanded, before turning to Kenwu. "I'll meet the monk alone in the salt shrine. You deal with the body."

"Of course."

"Don't leave me!" Soh'shoro cried.

"I have no choice!" Obajen-mahoe snapped. "Be brave until I return."

The lord threw the chamber door wide, stalking outside like a rising storm. Kenwu hesitated a moment. He turned to Soh'shoro pityingly, forcing a smile. Then he too vanished into the mazelike Quo'dai-ma House, locking the latch behind him.

Soh'shoro waited until he was certain neither could hear. Then he fell to the reed flooring, burying his face in the silt-stained cushions beneath his salt box. He felt the rubbery flesh of the courtier's neck, the foreign warmth of his blood. He hadn't understood. But he had chosen all the same.

And the Voice still whispered, like wind through an ill-fitting screen.

Go away, he begged. *Not now.*

The boy shut his eyes, pressed his fingers to his ears. Yet these whispers always accompanied violence and danger, growing only louder the more he fled to his inner world.

Please.

Always his mother's voice. Always indistinct and indecipherable, more instinct than language. With each cry came snippets of her memories: a caress of veinless skin, a clash of crane-bright blades. Each impression compounded until Soh'shoro had no choice but to accept their warning. But safely locked in his chambers, what could be the threat?

The Onan'ji, the prince guessed. *My father is in danger. He needs me.*

Soh'shoro ran to the window, rolling up its reed blinds with practiced dexterity. Using them like a climbing anchor, he slipped onto the House's ceramic eaves.

Countless times before, the prince had snuck out to watch fireflies and paint moons, so these heights held no fear for him. Instead, the thin air and chill breezes soothed him, distracting from the Voice with the grandeur of his Palace. The ringed citadel unfurled like a painted scroll: sculpted gardens and ritual homes of osmium and cryptomeria, threading miniature landscapes like beads on a birthing charm. Beyond the inner bastion, residences for base nobility and epoxy priests faded into the first blush of the Pleasure District's floating lights. And always overhead, the great gray permanence, rising from the Mausoleum to smear away the sky, roiling ever outward to the world's edge:

The Mists.

Soh'shoro's entire life belonged within their hoary walls. To touch the Mists was to vanish. Or worse, to have one's mind burned away like impure glass. Mostly they remained confined to the Valley's distant peaks. But their roils could turn animal and alien, drifting with a will of their own. And the closer they came, the louder the Voice called, as if its source lay smothered in that silver oblivion. So the Mists marked the edges of Eternity, marking the boundary beyond which Death itself would not cross.

Two more steps, and Soh'shoro slipped through another open window and back into the grand halls of the Quo'dai-ma House. He landed soundlessly on its lacquered flooring, kneeling to catch his breath.

My father is close.

The boy ventured deeper into the reedy shadows of his House and its caseating splendor. Few servants stalked these inner halls. He passed only a solitary pair of courtesans, gossiping about the Emperor's gossamer entombment. Soh'shoro flattened himself behind a jadeite urn until they passed.

Already he could hear Obajen-mahoe's angry shouts ahead: "Never again, Onan'ji. Not in my House."

Reaching the salt shrine, Soh'shoro pressed himself low against its latticed walls, sidling to avoid casting shadows through the upper paneling.

"All the same," replied the monk's voice, pale and heavy as icicles. "You refuse him the rituals. So what purpose does he serve your House? You will grant me what I ask."

The boy reached a familiar tear in the mulberry paper. When he pressed his eye to the narrow gap, the rectory within sprang to life.

Pillars of bare wood glittered with Gi'en charms and tinted lanterns. Elaborate calligraphic myths covered the pulp walls: tigers and winter wolves, snakes and brilliant scorpions. Untold centuries had smoothed all the floorboards with countless polishings. And salt braziers smoldered everywhere, spilling their thick, acrid stench like quenching iron. Boxes and boxes of the white gold lay ready for processing on elevated, ceremonial bricks. Beside each container an angry needle gleamed, freshly blanched in lily water for lancing the cakes into dusty grains.

"You think your Order beyond Imperial law?" Obajen-mahoe countered fiercely. He stood directly in front of Soh'shoro, blocking his view of the monk. "Make whatever threats you want. The courts will never allow your Qu'su monks to steal my son."

"The courts will have no choice." The Onan'ji's voice quickened, like a river's current in the snowmelt of spring. "We Qu'su guard the Valley's slumber. Gentle its Mists. Prevent Outside. And all this your child threatens."

Soh'shoro pulled back from the paper tear, heart pounding. He had to see the monk who dared speak so directly to the lord of the Quo'dai-ma, without care for custom or station. He crept closer to the silk-screened door.

"You sent the courtier. Why?"

"Because I know what Soh'shoro did at his birth. But that could not tell me who lived free, the mother or the child."

Reaching the doorjamb, the prince peered through its joisting.

The Onan'ji kneeled calmly on the rush matting, head half bowed as if in meditation. His garments were simple: cloth robes and wood-stilt sandals. But the monk's hair fell in braided waterfalls of dyed silk, and his skin shimmered magnificently in the afternoon light, with an unblemished splendor, like polished gold.

"Soh'shoro is only a boy. Another Reborn flesh in the Eternal guardianship of our House. Nothing more."

"I will tell you what the child is." The monk smiled, slithering his head forward like a snake. "An Old Word we have almost forgotten."

The Onan'ji's legs unfurled, propelling him upright with unnatural rigidity. And now Soh'shoro saw what caused the monk's mysterious golden skin. Every vein across his body had been pried free. In their place gleamed artless purity, crawling across flesh like miraculous rot. Even the whites of his eyes blinked without blood vessels, unblemished as summer lilies.

And those lurid orbs stared right into the doorway's shadow, smiling at Soh'shoro.

"Death."

The prince gasped.

Obajen-mahoe heard the boy's cry, wheeling in disbelief at the intrusion.

"Don't run," the monk hissed, holding Soh'shoro's gaze through the narrow jamb. "I hoped you would come."

Obajen-mahoe threw open the door, seizing Soh'shoro by the shoulder. "Do not speak. Just leave and—"

"Bring him to me," the monk commanded.

"No," Obajen-mahoe spat back.

"Bring him. Or the Ang'soon will learn what their daughter must marry."

Something in Obajen-mahoe broke. Kneeling, he whispered quickly, "Don't do anything. Just be silent. This will be over soon."

Holding Soh'shoro tightly against him, he displayed his heir before the monk.

"Quo'dai-ma-na-Soh'shoro. We meet at last." The Onan'ji bowed deeply. "I am master of the Qu'su monks: the Onan'ji. Call me only by my station, for in service I forsook all other names."

Nothing made a sound, save the cicadas chirping in the afternoon heat, and the thin trailing of the Voice, growling like a predator in wait. Coldly, the monk surveyed the boy.

"Death," the Onan'ji repeated, savoring the syllable like a delicacy. "A forgotten thing, full of cold uncertainty. The Valley is permanent and everlasting. Everything you are not."

The boy's whole body coursed with fear. He shrank into Obajen-mahoe's layered robes and their rough scent of cherry incense.

"You want to know, don't you? What you really are?" Idly the Onan'ji drew forth a lily petal, chewing indifferently. A thin trickle of juice gleamed across his bloodless golden lips. "What our Corpse of an Emperor hides. All things are true to their nature, and yours is killing."

"How dare you!" Soh'shoro's bright eyes burned, running saline dye across his cheeks. His mouth ached with dryness. But still he stepped from Obajen-mahoe's shadow. "You insult our courts! You threaten my father and myself! Get out!"

"Brave." The Onan'ji sighed, golden face shifting, neither joyous nor bitter. "But bravery requires fear. And you are scared, are you not, Soh'shoro?" The Onan'ji folded his hands, as if unwinding a kite's string. "Unlike any other in this Valley, you know terror and longing and passion. Because you are Death. And so you can die."

The prince thought of the courtier, and the thrashing silence of that very morning.

"Watch," the Onan'ji instructed.

The monk broke into motion like a surging wave, a salt needle already balanced in his palm. The heavy metal lanced cruelly, bright as a harvest moon. But Obajen-mahoe leaped forward, throwing Soh'shoro to safety. The monk's strike pivoted, legs sweeping into a scissoring motion. Obajen-mahoe crashed to the floor, and the salt needle followed, driving for the throat, its sharpness glittering like starlight across a pond.

Then the same Voice that had called to Soh'shoro cried out again. But this time not for him. The thousand terrible whispers protested the Onan'ji's violence with a brilliant chorus of broken bells. Their screams blotted away thought, controlling instinct and twisting motion. Until the needle jarred harmlessly into the floor.

"I can't hurt him," the Onan'ji spat. "You see. Death is not allowed into the Valley. The Voice prevents it."

Obajen-mahoe gasped, staring at the danger so close it skimmed the skin of his throat.

The Onan'ji turned to Soh'shoro. The boy stumbled back, but in that half step the Onan'ji seized him with his free hand.

"Please!" Obajen-mahoe begged.

"But nothing protects you, does it?" The Onan'ji wrenched the needle against him. Soh'shoro's eyes widened with fear and pain. He thrashed to break free. And the Voice cried its warnings. But to Soh'shoro alone. Clearly the Onan'ji heard nothing, as he opened a fine line across the boy's throat. A single drop of blood ran from his bronze flesh.

"The child is Outside."

The monk let go. And streaming tears, Soh'shoro dove atop Obajen-mahoe's fallen figure.

"Get out!" the lord of the Quo'dai-ma screamed. "We are finished! You will never have my son."

The Onan'ji rose, like a falcon before its dive.

"We're past that, Quo'dai-ma. The Mists are coming free. Everything must change."

"Help!" Obajen-mahoe called. "Help!"

The monk pressed his head to the straw matting, in a formal bow.

"I am everywhere, Obajen-mahoe. So try everything in your power to keep Soh'shoro safe. Because I want you to learn that you cannot. To live, he must obey. He will scathe unless he serves."

The sliding doors burst open, so violently their wooden ruts buckled. Three courtiers rushed forward, surrounding the Onan'ji. But the monk merely raised his hands in supplication.

"Pantomime!" He laughed. "What can they do? How can we hurt each other? All who belong to the Valley hear its Voice." He grinned pointedly at Soh'shoro. "And the Voice prevents all violence."

"Out!" Obajen-mahoe spat. "Cast him out!"

The courtiers dragged the monk from the room by his wrists. The Onan'ji smiled ever wider, holding Soh'shoro's gaze with the same sinister hunger as when he had first looked upon him. The prince could still smell the lily juice smeared across the monk's lips.

"You will call me friend, one day, I think. One day soon."

And with that the Onan'ji vanished into the labyrinthine house.

"Father!" Soh'shoro sobbed. "Are you hurt?"

Obajen-mahoe rolled to his knees, forcing a smile. "He can't hurt me, Soh'shoro. Even the Onan'ji is bound by the Valley."

He clutched the child as tightly as he could, heart beating like thunder. The boy wriggled closer, comforting them both. Outside, a thin afternoon rain began to fall, waking the scent of bright grasses. Obajen-mahoe checked the cut on Soh'shoro's neck, but the blood had already begun to clot.

"My son." He wiped his finger over the wound before kissing it. "My son." Tears streamed down Obajen-mahoe's face. "We'll keep you safe."

Obajen-mahoe lifted Soh'shoro into his arms. He carried the boy from the salt shrine, out through its covered walkways, and into the murmuring rainfall.

The pair gazed beyond the grand gate of the House, where the Onan'ji staggered, pushed by the courtiers. His sandals were thrown after him, splattering onto the muddied earth. The monk picked up the stilted wood indifferently. Then he raised one hand to the storm, catching the droplets on his bloodless skin. He licked his hand between thumb and forefinger. Then, casting a shawl overhead, he vanished down the tree-lined path into the lower Palace.

"What did he mean, Father?" the boy asked softly. "What am I?"

"It doesn't matter," Obajen-mahoe whispered. "You're my son. Nothing more."

But even then, the boy knew it was a lie.

CHAPTER TWO

RITUAL

The blade slid neatly from its ossuary.

Soh'shoro's eyes burst open with waking terror. But only Kenwu looked down at the boy sadly, as if he already knew.

"Calm down," his attendant whispered. "It's days since the Onan'ji left. Now it's time we depart too. For the Gi'en."

Outside, dawn razored to life. A thin, reedy light slipped through paper windows, coloring Soh'shoro's grass sheets a miraculous amber. Kenwu held the family ri'shou'an aloft—a ring-hilted sword, its tempered edge patterned like beating wings, its once-broken spine recast with golden inlay—before wiping the weapon with clove oil for travel. Then he returned the ri'shou'an to its ossuary, sheathing the ancestral blade of Soh'shoro's mother beneath its scabbard's motif of silvered cranes.

Rubbing sleep from his eyes, Soh'shoro rolled up in bed. "I don't want to go."

Kenwu smiled sadly. "We have to. It's the oldest festival. To renew the Valley's bonds."

"You've never taken me before. Is Father scared of what the Onan'ji said?"

"A lot has happened, yes." Kenwu hesitated. "And I feel you would be safer by your father's side."

Soh'shoro crawled from bed, closer to Kenwu. Trying to be helpful, he handed a salt brush to his attendant. Kenwu nodded graciously, taking the ferrule and snapping it in its bamboo case.

"Will I see my wife? Like Father promises?"

"She's your betrothed," Kenwu corrected gently. "And the Ang'soon must attend. If all the Houses aren't present . . ."

"What happens?"

"Nothing, because it does not happen," Kenwu insisted. "Eternity, Soh'shoro, is nothing more than constancy. We don't need to remember why."

He glanced outside, then placed the ri'shou'an sword and its ossuary sheath inside a traveling strongbox. The copper latch clicked tight, sealing away the mysterious blade. "Come. A lesser courtier can finish the peace knotting."

Now Kenwu led Soh'shoro through the dim rush of the Quo'dai-ma House. Everywhere servants seethed, packing trunks and chambering cloth, like bees to their hive.

"Why did you take my sword?" the boy whispered. "What's wrong?"

"Nonsense." Kenwu shook his head.

"But Father says swords must stay sleeping in their ossuaries." The boy flinched with the sudden memory of the courtier's splitting skin. "What are they for, Kenwu?"

"I don't remember."

"You always say that."

"Because our memories fade, Soh'shoro. Each Rebirth blends with the next, until lifetimes become forgotten." The attendant smiled wistfully. "Be patient. The Valley is as it should be. Once you accept that, you won't need to wonder anymore."

The boy's eyes turned to the Mist-sick hills, peeking through joints in the papered windows. Clearly the conversation still bothered him.

"Would you rather I left the blade, young prince?" his attendant offered.

But Soh'shoro shook his head in reply.

The pair arrived at the Quo'dai-ma House's grand gate. Here, Kenwu made the boy change slippers three times, once each pace, last into the wooden stilts favored for travel. Then he wiped Soh'shoro's brow with bright grass, hard enough to smear juice across the skin. Thus purified, the pair stepped amid the waiting throng of palanquins beyond.

Each carriage reeked of lilies, jammed into great copper urns. The flowers pressed so tightly against their bronze stoppers that petal juice seeped free in brilliant ivory smears. The prince shivered, remembering the same ichor running from the Onan'ji's lips.

The palanquin's bearers waited at the edges of the courtyard: mouths silent, eyes glassy, sunburned skin bright with blue tattoos. The inked shapes were only lines and circles, repeating in an endless sequence of beautified randomness. Soh'shoro hesitated before the horde of mute men.

"They're just Traders," Kenwu explained. "Silence is their nature."

"Do they feel anything? Anything at all?"

"Who knows?" Kenwu replied dismissively. "It's not like you can ask them. The Mists burned all that away. Even their voices. Only the tattoos keep them from turning completely into husks."

He lifted Soh'shoro into the largest palanquin before leaping after with surprising alacrity. The pair settled onto a divan sandwiched between lily urns. Petal stench clung bright and brilliant, making Soh'shoro's eyes water and stirring hints of the Voice.

Obajen-mahoe appeared moments later, his broad nostrils flared with anxiety.

"The Mists," he barked at Kenwu. "They're angry."

"They're always unsettled before the Gi'en," the attendant replied.

"Use your eyes. This is dangerous. The Mists chase the shrines into the lower hills." Obajen-mahoe shook his head. "We need to start the rituals quickly . . ."

"We've barely dressed," Kenwu continued distractedly. "And the train is still packing . . ."

"Then the lily stocks join us at the Mausoleum," Obajen-mahoe countered, clambering into the palanquin with some effort. "We can't risk waiting. The ceremonies must begin tonight."

Bells rang fresh and bright as songbirds. Soh'shoro rubbed the last sleep from his eyes. Obajen-mahoe stroked the boy affectionately, settling in beside him.

"The Gi'en will fix this," Obajen-mahoe soothed. "It's your first time, but you'll soon see. The rituals keep the Emperor safe. Turn lilies into salt and welcome the spring. Just as our blood preserves His flesh." The lord reached his hand outside the bower, slamming its wooden poles. "Upward! We're ready! Now upward!"

Their bearers jostled to life, lifting the glamorous palanquin atop their backs. Soh'shoro bounced into the air, laughing raucously as he lurched into motion.

"We're flying!" he screeched.

Obajen-mahoe chuckled too. Even Kenwu broke a smile.

But as the procession pranced toward the Emperor's compound, the boy kept sneaking glances at the Traders. Even as their brows streaked with sweat and muscles strained with exertion, the palanquin bearers never made a sound.

"Where do the Traders go? When they cross?"

"What are you talking about?" Kenwu replied distractedly.

"The Traders. Where do they go when they walk into the Mists?"

Kenwu glanced at Obajen-mahoe before replying. "Nowhere. There's nothing Outside."

"But they have to go somewhere."

"Why?" Obajen-mahoe interrupted. "What is above the sky? Or below the stones? You might as well ask why rain falls or grasses shimmer. The Traders leave with lilies and return with salt. That's our cycle. If there is anything beyond the Mists, we will never see it." His face darkened. "Nor would we want to."

The Emperor's Mausoleum loomed ahead, a spire of gilded metal and reinforcing wood. The tomb looked like a giant shard crashed to earth, puncturing its lantern-strewn sky at alien, arbitrary angles. Lily gardens surrounded the spire, swelling artificial ponds and snowing pollen. The Mists poured from the Mausoleum's peak, fountaining their hoary plumes to hide the sunlight and mute the heavens. From here they drifted over the Valley's skies before descending to cap the distant mountains.

"The source of the Mists," Kenwu reminded Soh'shoro. "The Emperor's gift."

The Mausoleum's grand, alloyed doors ground open, petals fluttering from their maw. The bowers rocked into that waiting half light. Kenwu disembarked first, footfalls echoing strangely on the tungsten tiles. Soh'shoro followed, almost tripping as his gaze spiraled the chamber. The inner Mausoleum glittered with aluminum composites and lithium polishings, metals Soh'shoro had only seen as tools. An enormous duramen staircase split the chamber, helixing both deep into the earth and heavenward toward the dark. Alabaster-swathed epoxy priests stumbled back and forth, muttering the strange, rotten chants of untaken Traders.

"I'm scared."

"What is there to be scared of in the Valley?" But Kenwu pulled the collar of his robes over his mouth, as if the very air here were distasteful.

Soh'shoro gazed up the spiraling staircase, grafted to the shard's steel ribbing. Its upper floors vanished into chipping paint, creaking metal, buckling arches, and leaking spores.

"Is that where our Emperor sleeps? The upper tomb?"

"You're too young to go there." Obajen-mahoe clapped the boy's shoulder with nervous enthusiasm. "A few summers yet before your blood work begins."

Epoxy priests drew close, waving lanterns held aloft on heavy, obsidian staves. Their colors sparked vividly into the darkness, flaring metals in a riot of oranges and teals.

"Come, yes, come," the first priest rasped strangely, each syllable discordant between smearings of lily paste. The man offered a hand, skin covered palm to sleeve in the faded, viridescent tattoos of the Traders. But this art lay aborted, the litany of characters trailing into unfinished stains. "Welcome to the Quo'dai-ma House. Welcome, all."

And lit by the refracted rainbows, the nobles descended into the depths of the Mausoleum.

Here the waterfall gardens blossomed: a mosaicked cupola of white marble and polished soapstone, their cavernous limits extending far beyond lantern light. A vaulted ceiling of glass suspended lily ponds overhead like a lapis twilight. Artificial channels carved in their crystal fed cascading cataracts, spilling petal-flaked foam and saturating the entire chamber with fog. Everything smelled strangely of old iron.

Obajen-mahoe stripped naked at the glassy banks, strolling into the icy waters. Waves crashed about his pale form, laving him with froth. Lily petals caked his skin like bandages.

"Come, my son!" he cried, his face beaming. "Once a year!"

He smiled to himself. "Glorious!" And he dove headlong into the waters.

Soh'shoro stripped too, eager to distance himself from the epoxy priests. But two strides in, the prince paused. "It's freezing!" Lily petals congealed about the boy's shins like rime.

"Snowmelt. A sign of spring," Obajen-mahoe explained. "You'll warm once you're in."

Swallowing his fear, Soh'shoro dove into the flows. The bracing waves broke across his skin, until his teeth chattered and his lips burned blue. Obajen-mahoe swam over, lifting the boy into the air and laughing.

"Another year!"

But as they splashed, Soh'shoro plunged his face playfully into the frigid waves, opening his eyes to the dark beneath. And in that briefest moment, he glimpsed them: Hundreds of metallic ovules lined the waterfall basin, like ants swarming to the defense of a colony. Their fogged glass glistened silver, obscuring bamboo-like hollows within.

And Soh'shoro jerked his head up above the waves, sickened.

"What are they?"

"What are you talking about?"

"The shapes in the water. The metal pods."

"Dolls," Obajen-mahoe answered cryptically.

"What do you mean? What's inside?"

"Just the work of the epoxy priests, Soh'shoro. Best ignore it."

But the prince shivered, consumed by dread. He swam as quickly as he could to the banks of the pond.

"Easy." Kenwu soothed the boy with a salt brazier, laving its smoke to warm his bare flesh. "What's wrong?"

But the prince merely dressed in silence.

A new light entered the waterfall garden, a lone lantern suspended from a purple parasol.

"Quo'dai-ma-na-Obajen-mahoe!" a voice called warmly.

Obajen-mahoe waved the figure closer, stepping from the waves.

"Ang'soon-na-An-go'yi'ki." He brightened. "Where is your sister?"

The man drew near, until his light bathed both lord and child. "This is the best part of the Gi'en. I wasn't going to let her retinue slow me down." He swallowed strangely. "Besides, you know she can't bathe here anymore."

Soh'shoro stared at the Ang'soon prince with amazement. The serenity about him was like a warm breeze in autumn; the thin curves of his pale face were barely visible behind dark, straight locks. He wore a chrysanthemum robe, bound in triplicate with slatted string. The cords folded like clasped hands, pale and beckoning.

"Can it be?" An-go'yi'ki wondered. "Is this Soh'shoro's Rebirth? The prince you've kept secret for years? My brother-to-be?"

Obajen-mahoe nodded, pulling on fresh robes. "At his first Gi'en."

"An honor." An-go'yi'ki kneeled before Soh'shoro.

"Answer," prompted Kenwu. "You're going to marry this man's sister."

And Soh'shoro bowed too, as best he could within the stilted robes of the court.

"Is she here?" the boy asked with sudden eagerness. "Will she help with the rituals?"

Obajen-mahoe gently squeezed Soh'shoro's shoulder, warning him.

"He doesn't remember?" An-go'yi'ki glanced at Obajen-mahoe for the briefest moment. Then he kneeled before Soh'shoro, smiling warmly. "We must be careful with the princess. She is closest to the Emperor. And for that, she rots."

"We all have burdens," Obajen-mahoe interrupted.

"Then you know I am not here solely for swimming." An-go'yi'ki darkened. "I've warned for years this is wrong. That ever since Soh'shoro's Rebirth the rituals weaken . . ."

"Not in front of the boy," Obajen-mahoe snarled.

"Besides, the prince has pressing matters," Kenwu interjected smoothly. "Come, Soh'shoro. You can see the whole City from our pagoda. You've never beheld such beauty."

Kenwu took the boy's hand firmly, dragging him from the waterfall gardens. Soh'shoro glanced backward, watching the Ang'soon prince pull Obajen-mahoe aside in the gloom.

The Mists are coming free. The Onan'ji's words.

"Is this my fault, Kenwu?"

His attendant paused.

"Eternity will tell," he replied cryptically.

The lanterns of the epoxy priests gave way to the lily ponds outside the Mausoleum, then the Palace courtyard. Hints of ancient asphalt peeked between its freshly set cobblestones, and two mirrored pavilions dominated its center. Salt vats surrounded these pagodas, twice as tall as men and many times as wide. Their troughs stood empty now, protected by purple tarps until the festival exchange.

Soh'shoro was sweating by the time he reached his pavilion's upper terrace. Still, the view left him breathless. The whole City swept beneath him: the gabled finery of the Palace, the riotous lights of the Pleasure District, the bronze row houses of the Trading District, and the dilapidated thatching of its reed-walled slums. And the Gi'en bells, chiming loudly as their shrines crossed the plinthed bridges of the City gates.

But always Soh'shoro's gaze rose to the Mists. They churned angrily, tumbling down the mountains and across the hills, creeping in ravenous tendrils over rice paddies and terraced hamlets. Stretching deeper and deeper into the basin, as if drawn back to their source. He watched tirelessly as the sun turned, sipping opalescent brine tea, trying to understand. For those veils stirred the Voice, and with it snatches of his mother's memory. Black sails, glimpsed through the smoke of a narrow pipe, settling as the dusk did now atop the City.

"The Mists are monstrous this year," Obajen-mahoe called from between winded gasps, as he crested the staircase. He had changed into a brilliant robe of polychromatic purple, so long fifteen men followed, some crawling on all fours, to hold the train. His face was buried behind no less than three heavy veils. "But we will be safe in the City. It's why almost all come for the Gi'en." He moved to a sumptuous coach overlooking the salt vats below. "Once the Emperor is renewed, this roil will cease."

But Obajen-mahoe sounded as if he were trying to convince himself.

Now roars and cheers erupted from the City, glee and revelry spreading like wildfire. Rainbow streamers and banging drums swarmed the streets. The cheers of onlookers blended with merchants hawking ghost-rice cakes, with pleasure courtesans flirting, with mercers trailing reams of freshly spooled silks for their final decorations. This was the heart of Man—the treasure of the Valley—as blindingly bright as the lilies.

And Soh'shoro thought of the Onan'ji. *Will he be here too? A faceless shadow in the crowds?*

With dusk came the shrines' final approach. The impossibly bulky shadows reached the Imperial gates, leaving crowds of commoners straining against the Palace walls for a final, parting glimpse. The procession lumbered onward, snaking single file through ring after ring of the Imperial compound.

"And now they come." Obajen-mahoe beamed.

What Soh'shoro saw then stayed with him into dreams: the swarm of shrines dancing atop the backs of burdened Traders. Each was built like an intricate house, with terraces and gables and thousands of bells jangling the same, repeating notes. They crowded into the Imperial courtyard, dancing in a tangle of sculpted wood and osmium charms, lit by brilliant candles hanging from their bows.

"They're gorgeous," Soh'shoro gasped.

The procession advanced beneath the pagodas. Now the fireworks began, igniting the darkness with cacophonous bursts of beauty that swallowed the stars. Color rioted everywhere: deep-pastel banners, viridescent and niveous in the half light; cerulean and indigo kites; hanging lanterns flickering violet and tangerine. The shrines jerked atop the heavy sweat and suffering of their bearers. And the first drew close to the salt vats, jangling with chaotic ferocity, as Obajen-mahoe cast a fistful of lily petals down upon it in welcome. Next Traders opened a lower hatch, and salt poured from the structure's innards. The grains spilled into their waiting trough, announcing the season's crop. Crystalline dust scattered with the rising wind like seeds from a dandelion, sending the crowds of onlooking courtiers screaming.

"For Eternity! To fight the rot!"

Emptied, the shrine retreated from the salt vat. More Traders waited nearby, carrying urns of lilies. They stuffed these inside its cavernous bulk, restocking the idol for its next journey. Soon the shrine swelled with the new white of languid petals, even as another emptied its grains into the salt vats, continuing the ritual.

"This is our cycle," Kenwu instructed. "Lilies for salt. Salt for Eternity."

Soh'shoro looked above the shrines, to the mirrored pagoda of the Ang'soon House. Atop its upper terrace he noticed

An-go'yi'ki. The prince lay swarmed by pleasure courtesans, massaging his chest and shoulders through his unlaced robe. His lips shimmered with rice wine.

And in his shadow waited frailty and elegance, a smearing of dark hair and pale silks.

"You mustn't stare," Obajen-mahoe chided.

A huge firework broke overhead then, larger and more luminous than all before it. Its brilliance burned away both light and dark, until there was only an elegiac glow of falling sparks. And now he first fully saw the Ang'soon princess.

She sat swaddled like a doll, beneath reams of medicinal charms and heavy silks. Her pitch hair was swept up in a tangle of ornaments and candy-colored clay beads. Her skin, where it peeked from the folds of her indigo robes, was the transparent white of winter frost. But her face fascinated him most because it was hidden. Layered away behind a mask of lacquered wood, purple as summer grapes and smooth as pearls.

Soh'shoro could not look away.

The shrines bled salt and bore lilies. The heat and brilliance of the City overwhelmed like a hand drawn close to fire. Night stretched its endless revelry of fireworks. And the Ang'soon princess coughed. Blood painted her mask's breathing hole, quickly licked away by a soft, pink tongue.

Soh'shoro shivered with a sensation he did not understand. A twinned desire of curiosity and sympathy. And an instinctive need for what must come, and what he alone might do. He shut his eyes, listening to the thrumming drums. His whole head hummed.

"Rest," Obajen-mahoe whispered. "It's late. And the last ritual is not for you."

"It's to take our blood, isn't it?" Soh'shoro asked. "The Emperor needs it."

Obajen-mahoe nodded. “It is the bond of our Houses. Transfusing Eternity.”

“I want to help . . .”

“Not this ritual.” Obajen-mahoe’s voice darkened, searching for the right words. “Not until I am certain.”

“Of what, Father?”

“That answer is not for pleasant dreams.” Obajen-mahoe lovingly stroked the boy’s brow. “Rest, young prince. There is all Eternity before us.”

Soh’shoro shut his eyes, smiling at the warmth of Obajen-mahoe’s hand.

But it was the bloodied smearing of the Ang’soon princess’s mask that tumbled with Soh’shoro into sleep, like a fistful of discarded salt cast across the ritual-bound world.

CHAPTER THREE

ROT

"She asked for you."

Soh'shoro pulled silks from his bleary eyes, revealing a stormy dawn. He did not remember falling asleep. Even now the jangle of the shrines persisted.

"Who asked for me?"

"You know." Kenwu smiled.

The boy stood eagerly, bracing himself against the pagoda's railing. Below spread the detritus of the night's festival. Shrines slept like slumbering beasts in the courtyard, their strangely silent bearers shielded from the rainstorm by makeshift tarps. Loose salt drifted like froth on a flooding river, blending with broken streamers and discarded silks. Cicadas hummed and crows called, blending with the Pleasure District's roaring laughter, so raucous it seemed as if the dawn were dusk.

And still the Mists clung low on the Valley's hills, retreating only slowly.

"The princess rarely accepts visitors. And we only have a brief moment before she must escort the shrines from the City." As if to punctuate the remark, a peal of thunder trembled the wooden scaffolding. “Hurry. They’ll start the caravan when the storm breaks.”

Soh’shoro was still half-asleep and his preparatory rituals blurred together: a bath of rock salt; censers smoldering with sweetly acrid incense that tinted the rainy morning shades of yellow and lilac; brine-based gruel so sour it puckered the boy’s lips; and a fresh robe patterned with silvered cranes, mimicking the designs of the family ri’shou’an.

Next Kenwu led Soh’shoro to the betrothal pavilion. Paulownia and miniature maples framed the open structure, rain pouring from its osmium eaves in a furious hum. And every whisper sounded her name: the beauty whose eyes rotted with phage.

The Ang’soon princess waited, kneeling on bare reeds. Her ceremonial robes, twelve in all, alternated brilliant shades of indigo and cherry, like the ridges of a fan. But the rumored beauty of her face remained hidden behind another lacquer-wood mask, this one deep crimson and melanized blue.

Kenwu pushed the prince forward before retreating obsequiously. So the boy found himself alone before his bride-to-be.

“You’re very kind,” Soh’shoro began. “Like your brother.”

The princess made no reply. Instead, her eyes flitted beneath her mask. Soh’shoro just barely made out rot eating their ciliary muscles. The hideousness took his breath away.

“What should I call you?” The prince tried again. “You cannot only be called ‘princess’—”

“I am only my title,” she snapped. “Particularly to you.”

“But every person has a name.”

“Exactly.”

Soh’shoro felt suddenly unsure of himself.

“Do you know why I asked to meet?” she continued. Her blackened teeth lurked beneath lips brightened with pastes of powdered reed and lead.

The boy nodded. "Because I watched you. At the festival."

"Everything can be turned to purpose," she replied, her voice high and hollow, like wind through clay chimes. "Even this marriage."

"I don't understand."

"Then ask."

The boy was silent.

"I said ask," she commanded. "You've wanted to since you laid eyes on me."

Silence.

"Ask!"

The prince could no longer contain his question: "Why do you rot?"

Her whole body tightened, lips curving into a black smile behind her mask.

"It fascinates you, doesn't it? My suffering."

The boy nodded.

"It fascinated me too, those first years after I awoke. Not caring how it weakened my body. Thinking no sickness could chase me into Eternity." She laughed, almost casually.

"I don't understand."

"And that's why I am certain." She snaked forward, sending her jeweled hair singing. "No wonder Obajen-mahoe keeps you hidden."

"You're speaking in riddles."

"Did he not tell you? Flesh is little more than a mask." She stroked the twisted, gorgeous lacquer of her own. "But Rebirths rarely transcend gender."

This the boy understood. "You're talking about my mother?"

The princess nodded. "I know your secret. You are not her. You are not the Rebirth of the real Soh'shoro."

"I am."

"Then why do you remember so little of her? Why make our marriage? The Houses interbreed to keep bloodlines pure. But so young?" She shook her head. "Your father is trying to use my blood to blot out your stain."

Soh'shoro blinked in horror. "I am the true prince of the Quo'dai-ma."

"Just as Obajen-mahoe expects us to pretend. As if this is all Eternity's design." She leaned closer. "But I knew your mother for more seasons than the beats of your heart. We all did. And you are not even her shadow." She smiled thinly. "So what are you?"

The boy's quick mind flashed between revulsion and fascination, strange and searing, for the haughty, sickening beauty before him. In that moment, his mind first broke from childhood. Fear gave way to opportunity.

"You're scared of me," Soh'shoro stated flatly, holding his tone steady. "That's why you say such hateful things."

The Ang'soon princess recoiled.

"Yes," she admitted carefully. "But not of you." Her fingers trembled. "I am scared of what you make me want, Soh'shoro."

She tilted her mask slightly. Just enough that the purpling spores on her lower face lay exposed, like gorgeous smears of lilac polish. She ran a single, slender finger along her gums.

He could not stop himself. He reached out to her, body coursing with anticipation.

"Your mother did not fear the rot either."

"It's beautiful." The boy spoke without thinking. Because those trails of Death called to him, almost like the Voice.

"It hurts. Each day into forever."

In reply, Soh'shoro took her hand. He had the strange sensation of touching a mirror.

"I don't care what is wrong with you."

The princess swayed before him, like newly split bamboo.

"You are a child," she replied sternly. "You don't care because you know nothing of this world."

"I know I must marry you."

She hardened beneath his grasp. "And I must marry you. So I will keep your secret from my brother and his court. But you will do something for me in return." Her rich perfumes spilled over the boy as she leaned forward and kissed his forehead. A thin bead of saliva remained afterward.

"What?"

"There will be others, after. And I tire of enduring, and nothing more."

"But what do you want me to do?"

"Kill me."

The boy froze with dread. Before he could reply, the Ang'soon princess stood with regal finality. She glided to the pavilion's edge like a playing piece drawn across its board. Attendants swarmed with indigo umbrellas, shielding her from the storm.

"Please!" Soh'shoro called. An ache spread in his throat, as if he was waking from a lurid dream of thirst. "I won't. I won't but I need your help. You remember. You can tell me of my mother!"

But she remained silent, floating away like lily petals borne by a summer breeze.

Soh'shoro lay down. He smelled her on the reed mats, a mixture of dried honeysuckle and wood shavings. Tears welled in his eyes. The rainstorm eased.

"What did my sister say? To make you so unhappy?"

Soh'shoro wheeled, gazing up at An-go'yi'ki's smiling face.

"You knew I'd be here?"

The Ang'soon prince nodded. "I'm to escort you to the Rebirths, if you'd like? They mark the closing of the Gi'en."

The boy nodded carefully, brightening slightly with

An-go'yi'ki's company. Together they passed from the betrothal pavilion, making for the Palace's outermost ring. The Ang'soon prince unfurled his purple parasol, shielding the pair from the final raindrops beneath its lustrously oiled canopy.

"I brought you a present. I can give it now, if you'd like?"

Soh'shoro could not stifle his smile. The last of his tears faded.

"Please!"

An-go'yi'ki unfurled a paper sash from his robe. Soh'shoro greedily tore back the wrapping, revealing a brightly painted doll, its arms of intricately woven string. He shrieked with joy.

"I take it you know how to dance a puppet, then?" An-go'yi'ki laughed.

"Kenwu taught me. But Father thinks it vulgar."

"Well, he'll have to let you play now." An-go'yi'ki winked. "Even he can't turn away a gift from the Ang'soon."

The pair passed beneath a wide, arched gate. Here rose the epoxy temples, in bare-raftered long houses, yawning beneath crenated eaves. Everything stank of boiling sealant and clinging moss.

"Just ahead—" An-go'yi'ki pointed.

In the temples' courtyard, hundreds of bowers waited. Each carried a body, wrapped with lilied bandages covering all except their eyes. The mummified figures breathed only occasionally, in sudden hisses like air escaping a kettle. Epoxy priests moved among the silent faces, laving them lovingly with bright oils and unctuous ointments.

"Rebirths?"

An-go'yi'ki nodded. "The priests restore them for the Mists. Making the bodies as perfect as they can for the journey."

Soh'shoro grew curious. He drew as close as he dared, until he smelled the sweet scent of age on their flesh. Almost all were ancient, their seasons clear in every wrinkle smothering their clouded eyes.

"Flesh cannot last forever. We age. But then we slumber." An-go'yi'ki drew near too. "The Valley calls, and Traders take us into the Mists. To remake our minds."

"Then why are there children?"

For underneath the awning of the nearby temples, swaddled in cloth, lay nurseries. Thin-blanketed infants gurgled at birthing charms or mouthed at the inky fingers of disinterested priests.

"They are the vessels, Soh'shoro. Nothing more. Awaiting the return of their rightful minds."

"They're newborns . . ." Soh'shoro protested.

"Each paired with a Rebirth," An-go'yi'ki continued. "Carefully planned and foretold. While their elders pass into the Mists, the children sleep inside the Qu'en Shards." Soh'shoro envisioned the massive, sloping metal of these relics marking the edges of the Valley. He had only ever seen them as inked paintings. Because he had never left the City.

"And then?" Soh'shoro asked breathlessly.

"And then the Rebirths wake anew. Reincarnated as children."

Soh'shoro clutched his new puppet tightly. In its curving wood, he imagined himself snapping suddenly to life, inspirited inside the doll. His stomach twisted at the hideous thought. *I am my mother's Rebirth*, he told himself. But after the Ang'soon princess's haughty reproval, he could no longer make himself believe it.

"What if the rituals aren't honored?" he asked hesitantly.

"What do you mean?" An-go'yi'ki replied curiously.

"If there are too many births, for example."

"We always have need of more Traders." An-go'yi'ki smiled. "Not all return each season."

"And too few? Could a Rebirth wake without its vessel?"

"I don't know." An-go'yi'ki frowned. "The Mists remake the mind. But without a new body . . ." He kneeled to face Soh'shoro, grasping his shoulders gently. "You really are curious, aren't you? Always asking questions." He hesitated. "It's why I brought you here. So we might speak, just the two of us." His voice dropped. "Away from your father."

Soh'shoro grew guarded. "What do you want?"

"To warn you."

A chill shot down his spine. "This is about what you told Father in the waterfall gardens, isn't it? That something is wrong with the Valley?"

"Our paradise is Eternal, Soh'shoro. But Eternity is maintained at a cost. With carefully repeated rituals like these." He swept his arm across the silent figures and their cooing futures. "For a long time now, I have feared there are those who want to destroy this balance. To break the Valley itself." An-go'yi'ki leaned close, whispering into Soh'shoro's ear. "You must be careful, Prince. There is a traitor in the Quo'dai-ma House. One who . . ."

"Soh'shoro!" A sharp call came from across the courtyard. And Kenwu sidled between the pair. "There you are! Always sneaking off! Why didn't you wait at the betrothal pavilion?"

"It's my fault," An-go'yi'ki soothed. "I thought to spend a little time with the prince."

"He should not be here!" Kenwu snapped. "And you should not be traveling without your retinue!"

The boy glanced curiously up at the Ang'soon, realizing his earlier lie.

"Remember your station," An-go'yi'ki warned the attendant imperiously. But his anger quickly melted. "Though you are right, Kenwu. I should not leave my sister unattended for so long." He turned once more to Soh'shoro, pale face creasing. "Remember what I said, will you?" He winked. Then his bright parasol flashed wide, burying his face beneath its twirling violet. "Be careful, prince."

And An-go'yi'ki strode back toward the Palace gardens.

"We must return too, Soh'shoro," Kenwu insisted. "Your father doesn't want you here."

But the boy hesitated, imagining the courtier's corpse among the waiting Rebirths. A sudden hope dawned.

"The courtier I killed. He'll be all right soon, won't he? He'll wake in a new body, like everyone else?"

"Keep your voice down!" Kenwu caught the child's gaze, paralyzing him. Now he spoke barely louder than a whisper. "You think Obajen-mahoe didn't look? He prayed every day she'd return, like the rest. Every day, Soh'shoro."

The prince did not understand.

"What you do . . . It's not part of our cycle. You take, and Eternity itself dies." Kenwu shook his head. "So no, prince. That courtier will not be Reborn. Nor will anyone else you cut. That is your power. And your burden."

What am I? Soh'shoro's jaw tightened with new resolve. For he was tired of not understanding, of being cloistered inside the Palace and kept from the Valley's secrets. The princess's words reverberated in his mind like the beat of a festival drum: *You know nothing of this world.*

And Soh'shoro decided. "Father doesn't know I'm here, does he?"

Kenwu nodded carefully.

"Then I want to follow the Rebirths. I've never been outside this Palace, let alone the City."

"What did the Ang'soon say to you?"

But Soh'shoro ignored the question. "Please, Kenwu. Just

as far as the City gates. Just for a moment. So I can see a little of the Valley . . ."

Kenwu shook his head. "With the Mists this unpredictable . . ."

"We can take my palanquin. Please!"

"Your palanquin would be noticed, prince." But then Kenwu smiled conspiratorially. "A shrine, on the other hand . . ." And he pointed to one of the grand monuments, shuffling now atop bow-backed Traders into the outer courtyard, ready for its return to the Mists.

"Thank you, Kenwu!"

"I don't like it." The attendant held the boy's gaze. "But you'd sneak off eventually anyway . . . You'll say you ran away again, like with the courtier, if we're caught?" The attendant waited for Soh'shoro to nod. "Come on then. Before I change my mind."

More shrines danced into the courtyard, mingling with the Rebirthing litters. Soon bronze drums sounded, and a vanguard formed just before the Imperial gates. Kenwu guided Soh'shoro into the eerily silent crowds of Traders.

"I'll follow just behind on foot," Kenwu whispered. "Be quick. And ride only to the City gates, understand? You leap out, and I'll get you." But then he pressed Soh'shoro's ri'shou'an into his childish hands, the silvered cranes of its locked ossuary flaring in the watery sunlight.

"You brought this?" The boy's form bowed with the heavy weight of the blade's ringed hilt. "You knew I'd ask this, Kenwu?"

His attendant looked away angrily. Twice he started to say something, then stopped. His face fluctuated between regret and fear.

He will change his mind.

And before Kenwu could say more, Soh'shoro vanished into the mass of jangling shrines. It took him only a moment to find a temporarily unattended structure and clamber inside. Here he crouched down between lily urns. The desiccated petals looked eerily like sloughed skin sealed away, but the scent dizzied him.

Soon Traders approached, accompanied by an epoxy priest. The holy man inspected the tattoos of the mute men carefully before noticing a blurry, chartreuse oval. He grabbed the Trader by the wrist, stretching his limb to inspect the fading ink more closely.

"Not clear enough," the epoxy priest muttered. "Must fix for Mists."

With practiced routine, he unsnapped a ritual satchel from his waist. Next the priest squeezed a gauze of petals, dripping its lily juice over a heavy needle. Last he lanced the tincture under the Trader's skin. The Voice cried sharply, protesting this violence, and the boy winced. But the Trader seemed only to calm as the character on his arm sharpened into fresh definition.

"Good," the priest concluded. "Enough ink now to leach slowly under skin. Hiding you." He smiled. "Go! Go! Ready for Mists!"

Now the Traders swept up Soh'shoro's shrine, gliding toward the City. The great gates of the Palace ground wide, almost one hundred hands tall, revealing only revelry beyond. Throughout the streets, onlookers danced, string music jostled, laughter and drinks spilled. The City blurred past, in row houses and slender gardens, bright hearths and silver chimes. In the distance, Soh'shoro could even make out the glimmering bronzes of the Trading District's capsular domes. So he marveled and marveled, through stolen glances from the shrine's narrow windows, at the joys of his expanding world.

At the limits of the City, wide bridges spanned the great rivers of the Valley's basin. Beyond, the horizon stretched into ice-slick hills; next the cold stones of lower passes; then the slow ascent of rice paddies and terraced villages; last and always, the Mists. Everywhere, lilies glimmered like fresh fallen snow, their petals drifting with the wind.

Beautiful, Soh'shoro thought, gasping. *And huge. The Valley would take countless days to cross.* The vast expanse called to him. *Just a moment longer. I must see more.*

The shrine processed onto a massive, sloping bridge of polished tangerine lacquer. Great ritual arches sloped overhead in reversed crescents; their crossbeams settled thickly with crows cawing softly into the morning sunlight. The waters beneath raged with the angry currents of melting ice. Soh'shoro took one last look at the open roil of the grasslands beyond.

And then it was too late. The Voice cried out.

Like falling awake, Soh'shoro's eyes rose to a figure poised atop one of the arches. Already the man was in motion, sliding down the sloping crest so lithely his arc reminded the prince of a shooting star. Then the figure leaped impossibly high, soaring across the gap to slam atop Soh'shoro's shrine with the airy ease of a summer tern. The Traders buckled with the impact, panicking soundlessly as their grip on the support poles faltered. The bower twisted awkwardly.

With preternatural grace, the monk remained balanced atop the tumbling shrine, his ri'shou'an carving through its latticed window like a ray of sunlight. The man snaked a hand inside, seizing the boy. The structure crashed against the bridge moments later, almost knocking Soh'shoro senseless. Still, he recognized the veinless, polished skin of the Onan'ji.

"You came for me," he gasped.

Without answering the monk struck him full force in the face, nearly blinding him.

Outside, Traders swarmed the upturned bower, but the Onan'ji had already pincered the child's body beneath his arm, levering him outside. And like a mythical tiger waking, the Onan'ji leaped from the upturned carriage and over the bridge's edge.

The pair plummeted. Air buffeted furiously. Then the monk and the boy vanished beneath icy foam.

Impact and cold shocked Soh'shoro awake. He tried to scream, forcing water into his lungs instead. He spasmed. But the Onan'ji's confident hands surfaced the prince, even as they locked against his throat.

Above came shouting, then scrabbling footsteps. Soh'shoro was certain he could make out Kenwu's voice, loudest of all. But none could make that leap, let alone risk the churning waters.

Already, the prince was lost.

Currents washed Soh'shoro and the monk against a wooded embankment. The Onan'ji released the boy here, letting him vomit the last of the water into the rocky shallows.

"You don't need to fear. The violence is over."

But Soh'shoro still clutched his blade.

Without hesitating the child drew the ri'shou'an from its crane-kissed ossuary, the sword glinting brilliantly like a gibbous moon. It was the first time he had ever unsheathed his mother's blade. The brilliant symmetry of its wing-patterned tempering curved effortlessly into its narrowed edge, flaring the webbed gold patching its spine. And he struck with the same gesture, as fast as his small hands could manage. All he knew was that this might be his one chance to save himself.

The Voice cried, trying to guide him, priming his reflexes. But Soh'shoro was too young. He did not know how to listen. Nor could the prince balance the ri'shou'an's heavy ring guard, which twisted his wrist awkwardly. The Onan'ji batted away the sword bare-handed, as a cat might toy with string. In the next instant, he struck Soh'shoro with the back of his hand, dashing the boy's spine against rocks and sending his blade clattering aside.

Soh'shoro lay gasping on the stony banks, tasting blood. The sour iron flavor somehow reminded him of the Ang'soon princess's rot. The monk stepped over him, holding the prince's own ri'shou'an to his throat. He held the sword with strange affection, almost as if the weapon were a lover's long-lost hand.

"Don't kill me," Soh'shoro begged.

"Kill you?" The Onan'ji smiled like a painted jackal. "I will never hurt you again . . . so long as you obey. Now get up."

But Soh'shoro remained frozen on the ground.

"Get up! They're coming for us."

The prince remained paralyzed by fear. Yet, in that instant, mysterious kindness took the monk. With monolith-like insistence, he offered his hand.

"You must get up," the Onan'ji persisted, gazing pleadingly into the prince's eyes. "If you want to truly save this Valley. If you want to see your mother again. Please, you must get up."

Everything balanced on that moment. But it was the Onan'ji's honesty, worming and dangerous, that made Soh'shoro take his hand.

And so the prince's childhood came to an end.

CHAPTER FOUR

PURPOSE

Soh'shoro and the assassin traveled for days, bridging the rivers on the western side of the Valley and then ascending through finely dusted snowfields toward the mountains beyond. The receding Mists above loomed cruel and angry as a storm. They spoke little—the rhythm of their paces replaced words, and silence became more potent than any conversation. Terror passed into endurance. Only the passage of the moon marked their journey: glinting out in the darkening sky just before rest or sliding away as it was time to rise.

They kept to secret paths, barely-used roads, and overland thoroughfares cutting brush and bracken. At night they camped in wild places, beside brooks hidden beneath boughs of tangled leaves. Though Soh'shoro found broken respite in sleep's oblivion, the Onan'ji never seemed to rest. Indeed his gaze watched constantly, chaining the boy as surely as any bonds. The prince knew he could not run, so he lost himself to regret and disbelief and anger, ceaselessly trudging toward the mountains and their Mists.

"Before it begins," the Onan'ji purred one morning, "I must show you what threatens the Valley—why I stole you."

Their path led straight into the heart of a highland village.

At first, Soh'shoro thought he might escape here by calling to its peasants for aid. But the thatched houses stood empty as kettles after a feast. The muddied roads grew thick with new weeds and untended bamboos. Everywhere clung the legacy of life interrupted: an axe tumbled beside unsplit wood, threads tangling on abandoned looms, drying lines bleached by countless suns.

"The Mists have been here, haven't they?" Soh'shoro asked. These were some of his first words since the abduction.

"Correct." The Onan'ji smiled. "They took this village during the Gi'en, when the Valley is weakest." He stopped stock-still in the middle of the ghostly settlement, staring at the boy. "Have you seen a husk before?"

The boy shook his head.

"They are like Traders, Soh'shoro. But without any protection, the Mists eat their minds completely. Look here . . ."

He cracked open a door to a meager house. Inside, the light came thin and watery, like the radiance of stars through the Valley's Mist-thick skies.

"I hear breathing," Soh'shoro gasped.

"See the bodies." The Onan'ji pointed to sparse litters. Across them spread a family—mother, father, and son—eyes wide and lips mouthing. But they remained catatonic otherwise. "They are gone, Soh'shoro. Their minds burned away by the Mists."

Soh'shoro drew close to the child. The boy clutched a rotten doll, far baser than An-go'yi'ki's gifted puppet. Soh'shoro still carried the present, smuggled in his robes. He rubbed its polish now, out of either comfort or sympathy he could not be sure.

"What is the boy looking at?" he gasped. "Is he hallucinating?"

"Remembering," the Onan'ji purred. "The thoughts are not his own."

Soh'shoro didn't understand.

"He'll recover, won't he? With their next Rebirth the family will . . ."

"There is no Death in the Valley, Soh'shoro. But there is oblivion." The monk's lips kissed that last word lasciviously. "Priests will visit this village soon enough. They'll bear the bodies back to the Trading District, entombing them beneath their bronze domes. Then these husks will simply exist. If they are lucky enough to find new flesh, their next life will be much the same. Our cycle cannot be broken. But our minds can be lost."

The boy gasped.

"This is the danger to the Valley, Soh'shoro. The more the Emperor weakens, the more his control over the Mists fades. The more our world verges on oblivion."

The boy's sharp eyes narrowed. "You're threatening me. Aren't you?"

"Very clever." The monk's veinless lips shimmered like river foam in storm light. "The same will happen to you if you disobey. I won't kill you." Strange affection smeared his face. "I won't need to. Do you understand?"

The Voice shivered to life at the danger. For a moment, the prince felt its cries match the mouthings of the husked child.

"I will run . . ." the boy stammered back.

"Then why haven't you?" The monk laughed bitterly. "Our lessons have not even begun, Soh'shoro. And yet you learn."

The pair returned to the ghostly streets. But the sight of the child's pathetic doll, caked with mud and dust, chased the prince well into that evening's slumber.

They reached the Qu'su temple four nights later, jutting from the Valley's forested slopes. The sprawling complex rose partly atop outcroppings of rock, but mainly on tall, wooden pillars. Chanted prayers drifted down from their heights with the wind.

"The Qu'su dwell among the edges of the Valley, to better hear its whispers." The monk pointed to the Mists, roiling just above the temple as though poised to smother it in intangibly beautiful, deadly whiteness. "This place will be your home, Soh'shoro. You are Qu'su now."

The Onan'ji led the boy beneath the crimson arches of a winding stair, into the main compound. Here sprawled black briar shrines and sweeping terraces, rising in bleached pillars of banded oak. Smoked stone pathways conjoined the structures, ribbed by veils of draping moss. Chir pines clustered so tightly to these walks that only thin slices of moonlight slipped through. The air tasted sweet with altitude.

Dozens of monks tended the temples, praying before pyre smoke or polishing bronze tools. Their earthen robes blended into veinless hands, their patchwork markings not nearly as smooth or golden as the Onan'ji's blemishing. A girl almost Soh'shoro's age smiled; he flinched away in disgust.

The monk led Soh'shoro into the main temple's gloom. Here the Onan'ji relaxed, sinking onto its reed matting. But Soh'shoro hesitated before the shrine's threshold, recoiling from the timbered innards' pungent scents of baked polish and boiled rice.

"We will speak now," the Onan'ji promised, "about what you will become."

The monk gestured to the mat before him. "Do you know what I am?"

"Qu'su," the boy answered, unmoving. "A guardian of the Valley."

"But why, Soh'shoro? Why does our Valley need protecting?"

"I don't know."

"What *do* you know, then?" The Onan'ji leaned forward in the gloom, like a cocoon birthing its butterfly. "That all life is Eternal? That there is no violence, no sickness, and no Death?"

The monk's face creased with facetious mimicry. "But if everything is perfect, why does our paradise need my monks?"

"I don't know," the boy repeated, joining the Onan'ji on the bleached-stalk mat.

"You, Soh'shoro," the Onan'ji hissed. "The answer is you. We walled your kind away. Your Death." The Onan'ji inhaled, funneling mint incense into his nostrils. "We Qu'su guard the Valley from Outside. From its influences and its dangers, ever snaking through the Mists." The Onan'ji's face passed into shadow. "From those idle blossoms that slip free."

Fear twisted Soh'shoro's stomach. He pressed his hands to the mat, steadying himself.

"You are rare, Soh'shoro. But not special." The Onan'ji leered, a cavernous jackal's smile. "Over Eternity's course, I have taken countless lives like yours. Because you are aberrant: catalysts of uncontrolled reactions that draw Death itself through the Mists. It is for this pruning that my Order, the Qu'su, exists. To kill the killers."

"Please," Soh'shoro begged. "I don't want to die." And he remembered the courtier, choking on his own blood. "I won't use my power again. I want to be like everyone . . ."

The Onan'ji raised his hand for silence.

"I already told you: I won't kill you, Soh'shoro." The monk scowled. "I could have done that a long time ago." He paused, licking his lips idly. "I'm sure you feel it too. As I have shown you, something is wrong with our world. The Mists hunger. The Houses rot. Because our rituals falter." The Onan'ji rubbed his fingers against each other, like centipedes scuttling over rocks. "We made life Eternal in the Valley. But to do so we also chained its mirror. And Death longs to escape. Not as men want, understand, but as water seeps from cracks." The Onan'ji's eyes sparkled. "The power of its hand is invisible. It compels by potential, not by brute force. And we choose as it wishes, because in time all paths are chosen."

"You're speaking in riddles."

The Onan'ji opened his palms. "I will speak plainly then. There is a conspiracy to destroy the Valley."

The boy froze. The Onan'ji's golden skin glimmered in the temple's pitch hollow.

"Who?" Soh'shoro demanded. "Who turns against our world?"

"One of the Houses. Perhaps even yours. We are not yet certain."

Soh'shoro's mind raced, remembering An-go'yi'ki's warning... *Who could work against the Valley? Obajen-mahoe? My bride?*

"Someone would stop such a traitor—"

"How?" The Onan'ji leered. "Remember my sword against your father's neck?" His lips twisted strangely on the word *father*. "All lives are Eternal. We Qu'su exist to purge Outside. Those born of Death, like you. But we are powerless against the Valley's own." The Onan'ji cracked his jaw. "Rot in the bones spreads, Soh'shoro. We must cut it out."

"What are you saying?"

A lone firefly blinked mournfully in the upper rafters of the temple.

"Normally, I would have murdered an anomaly like you at birth. You are an aberration to this Valley and anathema to its Eternity. But now I have no other choice. The Qu'su cannot protect our world without help. You are of Death, Soh'shoro. You can kill those the Qu'su cannot. You can protect our paradise."

He spoke the secret at last: "You can be Eternity's Blade."

But all Soh'shoro could do was long for Obajen-mahoe's warm touch, and his own grass bed. And perhaps strangest of all, the quiet rot of the Ang'soon princess. He pictured her then, though he did not know why: an apparition of fearful cruelty, luring him with her perfectly bloated eyes. His hands ran the curve of An-go'yi'ki's gifted doll, still hidden in the fold of his sleeve.

"You sound like a demon."

The Onan'ji smiled into the wafting incense.

"In time you will come to realize that Man himself is a demon. And only Death keeps him civil."

The boy marveled at the meticulous curiosity of those words. The Onan'ji terrified him. But he was equally fascinated with his tangled musings of the Valley's secrets.

"Go," the Onan'ji commanded. "We are done here. This next lesson you must teach yourself."

The boy hesitated, then rose. The Onan'ji shut his eyes in meditation, raising something narrow and silver and cruel. The motion frightened Soh'shoro terribly, and he rushed from the temple's darkness into the argent void of the night.

Upon the outer steps of the shrine he knelt, fighting back tears and moaning softly. At last the full magnitude of his abduction struck him. He could not believe it was real. He kept imagining a veil falling away, and with it all his misery and terror, until he lay again amid the warming lacquer of his stolen home. But here, everything felt cold.

"Did he tell you what you're going to do?"

Soh'shoro startled at the girl's approach. The young acolyte who had smiled before looked down at him now with the same wide, bright eyes. Her short brown hair looked like another shadow cast across her tanned skin.

"Go away." The boy's voice trembled between hatred and fear.

In answer she offered her hand, darkened with mountain dirt.

"It's not horrible here. At least it doesn't have to be."

"Stop. I don't want to talk to anyone."

"You can't live like that." She crouched beside the boy, hugging her knees to her chest and rocking back and forth slowly, almost playfully. "Eventually we accept. Or else we can't endure."

"He sent you, didn't he?" Because already Soh'shoro glimpsed the depths of the Onan'ji's designs. "You were told to say this."

"Of course." The girl's honesty caught him off guard. And for only the third time he looked at her: silver eyes looming brilliant and bat-like. "We all have our roles in the temple. But that doesn't mean I can't help."

"I don't want help like that."

"You sound as I used to." The girl stretched her arms playfully. The veinless markings of the Qu'su glimmered from elbow to wrist, like an elegant wrap of gold. "But then come the lessons. My first was that desire does not matter. Only outcome."

Soh'shoro's loneliness swelled unbearably then, and so he spoke. "These lessons, how are they taught? What will the Qu'su do to me?"

"You'll do it to yourself," she whispered sadly, her eyes welling as if suddenly fighting back tears. "That's the power of our ways. You'll come to want what we are. Because of what that means for the Valley."

She crawled sideways on her knees, fighting past his sidelong glance. The tops of her thin breasts shone tan and rich with starlight. Her scent of winter bur and honey filled him. "I'm Yei'an. And I already know what you are."

Her full, round cheeks reminded Soh'shoro of the sloping mask of his princess. And seeing the boy soften, the monk weaved a little closer.

"I won't be kept here."

"Everyone runs," she said. "I did. You will. It's part of the training. It's what the Onan'ji wants."

"I won't need to run. My father will find me."

Only now did Yei'an look away.

"You're not a prince anymore, Soh'shoro. You're his."

"When the courts come . . ."

"How?" Yei'an snapped. "We live among the Mists, at the edge of the Valley. On cold days, we're swallowed whole." Her face flashed fearfully as she glanced up at the tumescent veils. "No one can find us here. No one outside our Order knows the Qu'su's secret places. And even if the Quo'dai-ma discovered this temple, there are others. Endless havens in which we hide." Yei'an bit her upper lip. "You're Qu'su now. Accept it."

"And what will they do to me?"

The girl grinned, feverishly wide. "Everything."

He ran.

As soon as Yei'an left him in his temple cell, Soh'shoro searched for escape. Chains girded the oak door, and the only window was ribbed with winding iron. But the boy smelled mold, fresh with the evening rains. First Soh'shoro checked the weather slats and ceiling tiles. Then he set to work on the floorboards, prying at their joins until his knuckles bruised. At last he found a plank softened by rot. Working his fingertips raw, he popped a nail, then a second. Time wore on. Eventually the floorboard loosened, then bent free.

He poked his head through the narrow gap. Beneath his cell, the massive wooden stilts elevating the temple vanished into the tree line, then the Mists. Soh'shoro guessed the fall at five times his height. But he didn't care.

The prince's sharp hearing detected footfalls of a Qu'su outside his cell. He counted steps, tapping their rhythm with a rusted nail. When he became certain the guard had vanished, Soh'shoro did the same.

Wriggling and squirming, he lowered himself onto the cross-beams underribbing the temple.

He tested the stilts for descent, but the columns were worn smooth with age and overspanned his grasp. Soh'shoro's only chance was to jump for the nearest tree. Below, the Mists churned eagerly as dawn kissed the hills.

And before Soh'shoro could doubt himself, he leaped into thin air.

He fell just long enough to stifle a scream. Then he struck the upper branches of a pine hard. His fingers snatched bark. Air rocketed from his lungs. The bough bent awkwardly with his weight, thrashing needles like startled larks. The boy fell, twisting, onto a lower limb. He caught its spur, breaking the worst of his momentum, even as his fingers slipped on old knots.

And he tumbled below the canopy. In that moment the Mists swirled closer, as though driven by sudden wind. One rolling veil stretched, buffeting over the boy. And everything vanished into its cool kiss.

No! I've touched the Mists!

The world split apart in an instant. Distance stretched into itself. The force of his fall was muted, as if bent to a foreign orbit. Soh'shoro heard the Voice, crying with avaricious eagerness far more clearly than ever before, and through its call came memory:

Dark hair and fearful features like his own, choking bile onto black cloth. Putrid powder and metal rods spitting open flame. A tiger's mask carving bone with wicked, narrow knives. And last and most incredibly: water that ran on forever, so far it kissed the sky.

My mother's memories.

And they hurt. Her thoughts overtook Soh'shoro's mind,

disjointing his own. The Mists snarled tighter. Something skeletal stalked toward him, a tangle of hollow wings and eyeless emaciation. It spoke with his mother's voice, terribly clearly, as if soothing a child in its womb:

Soon, she begged. *You will find me. Trust the Mists.*

But a first lance of daylight split the sky. The gray veils and their horrid shape recoiled, as heat burned back moisture. And Soh'shoro tumbled free of that white world in total disorientation, slamming onto the mountain slope. His leg cracked hideously. He gasped in spinal pain. The fog swirled a hand's breadth from his face.

I survived. I touched the Mists and survived. But Soh'shoro did not have time to marvel at his escape, nor the mystery he'd glimpsed within those roiling banks. *I have to move.*

His leg aching terribly, the boy crawled toward a small ravine, then slid down its loose stones. Here he glanced at his knee: Blue patches had swelled into angry spotting; blood seeped from a fleshy tear, staining naked bone.

Just run. I have to run.

Soh'shoro made himself stand, biting his lip against the pain. Then he began his long, slow limp to freedom.

The chilling slopes of the high mountains brightened into full dawn. His feet dragged on rocky ground; his cheeks reddened with exertion; his heart thundered away all other sound. Soh'shoro shambled as fast and far as pain would let him; then farther, until his eyes felt numb and glassy. Always he descended, deeper and deeper, dreaming of his reed sheets. He couldn't say how much time passed. But it wasn't long until his leg gave out in the shallows of a mountain stream.

Soh'shoro coughed bubbling foam, then rolled onto his back. He lay until his breath quieted and the heat leached from his muscles. Then he turned his head and drank, gulp after gulp.

But no matter how much he swallowed, his throat remained gummy and dry.

Everyone runs. It's part of the training. Now the boy turned Yei'an's warning over in his exhausted mind. The words wouldn't leave him because he felt their kindness. *Are the monks watching? Is that why I've come this far?*

The boy struggled upright. Now Soh'shoro forced himself to climb against the stream's current. If anyone followed, he hoped they'd keep descending, never realizing their quarry had doubled back for the hills. But to make certain, he discarded his only possession, An-go'yi'ki's gifted puppet, to mark a false trail. The sight of the bright doll and its intricate strings lying lonely beside the riverbank somehow hurt more than his exposed bone.

The boy struggled on. His fingers clutched for balance on bare branches overhanging the stream like watering animals. His knee torqued painfully as he slipped on shallow pebbles. When at last he stopped to rest against a cracked boulder, he saw his toes had turned blue in the frigid stream. Only then did he leave the brook, stumbling horizontally across the mountain, coughing with phlegmatic exhaustion. Sleep claimed him in some glacial pad, his eyes dusted with dry tears.

He awoke with dusk. Overhead, early bats snaked above banks of Mists. Soh'shoro listened to rustling spruce leaves in the thin, high wind. Then he rolled over, prodding the muddy bruises on his leg. *Freedom.* The boy forced himself up, staggering toward the lowland hills of the Valley at last.

Morning. Slopes gentled, and the air tasted rich with lilac and lilies. Glancing upward, Soh'shoro scanned his descent for trackers, but there was only bare rock and snowcapped peaks. He relaxed, moving slower now. The ground opened from boreal forest into glacial glades, rare with yarrow weed. Soh'shoro cut across the open ground, heading for a lowland hillock. In the distance, he could see the smoke of a hermit village, rising with the day.

And as he reached the center of the dell, a figure stepped from the other side of the clearing.

"I will not punish you for running."

Soh'shoro shuddered as if struck. His hands fell open at his sides.

"Running is your nature." The Onan'ji advanced steadily, raising the prince's discarded doll. With a single callous gesture, he snapped its strings and tossed the broken puppet to the ground. "The chained seek freedom. One does not despise a fish for swimming upstream to breed, or flowers for blooming with the sun."

The boy tested his leg for a sprint. But his knee spasmed, and the tinny ache of fatigue thrummed ever higher in his spine.

The Onan'ji grinned, drawing close. "Why should I hold you in contempt for what you are?"

"Let me go, please. I don't care what I am. I just want to go home. I'll help you in the courts. I can find the traitor for us. Please?"

"No." He held out his hand to the boy. "Take it, as you did before. You have a new home now."

Soh'shoro refused to move.

"I said I wouldn't punish you for running. But I will punish disobedience."

Soh'shoro shrank backward, digging his heels into the sharp rocks. His body tensed with a final, sagging burst of fear.

"This is your choice, Soh'shoro," the Onan'ji said menacingly. "You are free to accept just as easily as fight." The monk then drew his ri'shou'an in a flash of electric silver, flaring the dawn like fireworks. Soh'shoro had never seen such fluidity, except in the ancient inkings of wolves keening to their prey.

The Onan'ji flipped the blade, offering its ringed pommel to the prince. "Take it."

Soh'shoro stared in disbelief, reading the calculated softness of the Qu'su's veinless eyes.

"What?"

"You must learn. Freedom does not mean you are free."

The boy didn't hesitate. The Voice screamed to help him. And as fast as he could, he snatched the blade and struck with all the might of his failing form, in anger and helpless fury. But in one smooth motion, the Onan'ji weaved outside the slash.

"Do you see? Desire is its own prison."

Soh'shoro swallowed his cunning. He centered the sword, feigning weakness by shifting weight onto his wounded leg. The Onan'ji's face creased with pity, like a craftsman surveying amateur work. And Soh'shoro slashed into that sympathy, with piercing alacrity.

It was over then. In three swift motions, the Qu'su stepped against the strike and locked the ri'shou'an away as he shattered the boy's collarbone, then twisted his charge to earth. Soh'shoro lay stunned, gasping the warming air of spring.

As the Onan'ji knelt beside the boy, his eyes softened.

"Clever. You have the instincts of a killer." The monk frowned. "But not the understanding. Don't you see, my child? Man's nature is limitation. You may choose, but that does not mean your choices are meaningful. The hungry dream of food, but that does not mean they eat. The cold wish for fire, but that does not mean they find warmth. There is a difference between desire and the power to achieve it. We are bound as surely by nature and logic as Eternity itself." He smiled wistfully. "So you may wish to kill me. But you cannot do so."

He then gently helped the boy stand, taking the prince's full weight with the very arm that had struck him.

Soh'shoro gasped. The throbbing of his fractured bone sent him retching into coughs. The Onan'ji waited patiently, holding him almost lovingly, while the boy suffered the blinding white sharpness of the spasms.

"Why hate the Qu'su? Why resist?"

Soh'shoro rolled his head, staring through blurring tears into the unblemished face of the golden monk.

"I won't be a murderer."

"Then you didn't understand the lesson." The Onan'ji's eyes glimmered like a thousand stars falling to earth. "You already are, Soh'shoro. You became one the moment you took my blade."

CHAPTER FIVE

TRAINING

At first, the boy split firewood until his back ached, carved warding charms until his fingers blistered, and sharpened practice blades until they gleamed. Each action fell away as both repetitive and mundane, connected to the coming violence only through rote obedience.

Finally, when the scars of his escape faded with the heat of summer, the bladework began. The Onan'ji gifted Soh'shoro back his sword: the ancestral ri'shou'an from the Gi'en, its razor edge swirling with tempered patterns of wings, its ancient breaks set with leaded gold. Even its crane-carved ossuary had been lovingly preserved, glistening with fresh polish and protected by cushioned silks. The boy's joy at recovering a relic of his past blinded him, so he practiced striking the thresher dolls without so much as a word of protest.

Days bled away in silence. Soh'shoro slept in the same wooden cell. Ate alone the same meals of wet rice and mountain mint, or seared shoots and fresh nuts. And he dreamed the same dreams: of Obajen-mahoe, of his bride, and of escape. But he ran only once more, this time barely making it beyond the temple grounds. In his quiet moments, the boy knew this was because he no longer believed in his freedom. Not as he used to.

Fall arrived, and with it, new skills, presented merely as extensions of boyhood pastimes. Soh'shoro chased fireflies once more, but now he did so across temple walks that creaked with each misplaced step. He played memory games with the sounds of dusk, testing senses beyond sight. And with the first snow, swimming in the shallow ice of the mountain streams turned to meditations of endurance. The Onan'ji never asked too much of him, and always it seemed he who yielded to the boy's protests. Yet all the same, he shaped Soh'shoro: delicately, coldly, and with terrible purpose.

Yei'an visited rarely, and each encounter seemed stolen: a late-night feast of shared winter berries, a gentle voice whispered through a paper wall during afternoon rains. Though he was wise enough to see the manipulation, the boy still grew to need her. When she was assigned as his dueling partner—even though he knew what it meant—Soh'shoro could not resist. Isolation was worse than submission.

From dawn till full daylight, and then again from dusk to deep shadow, Soh'shoro learned at last the true skills of the Qu'su: joint locks and countertumbles, balancing arts and sword mantras. Soh'shoro and Yei'an wielded wooden blades, but the other monks at the temple fought with real ri'shou'an, moving with impossible ferocity, like forests catching fire.

"Our Order masters combat because we may practice it without restraint," the Onan'ji explained, as the pair watched the monks spar.

It was early winter now, both master and student swaddled in heavy cloaks to keep back the icy winds. "Our duels are real. Each cut is one that aims to kill, because the Voice protects us from Death." The Onan'ji pointed out a blade, whispering terribly close to a novice monk's throat. But his veinless skin shimmered to countermotion, letting the cut slide barely wide. "The Voice is the Valley's greatest guardian, Soh'shoro. Abjuring violence in all who hear it. But it can be so much more. For its whispers do not merely prevent danger. They anticipate it. The more we Qu'su study the Voice and meditate upon its cries, the more it guides our motions. Speeds our reactions. Quickens our senses," the Onan'ji mused. "A pity your kind cannot hear it."

He does not know I can hear the Voice. It took all the boy's control to hide his amazement. *He thinks because I can kill, I must also be deaf to the Valley's whispers.* Soh'shoro was not certain how this secret would help him against the monk. But he vowed to keep it all the same.

"Soon you will train as they do," the Onan'ji continued. Almost distractedly, he unwrapped a snack of leaf-rolled rice soaked in vinegar. "We will need to be careful, and that will slow your study. It may take seasons to attain merely a shadow of our mastery."

"Then why must I learn such things?"

"Even a young wolf is enough to hunt the lambs of the Valley," the Onan'ji mused, offering the rolled rice to Soh'shoro. "But talent is not the lesson I seek to teach." He swallowed the last of his own meal, in a gulping, hungry mouthful. "Instead, it is I who wish to learn. To discover how alike we truly are."

The boy slept little that night, puzzling at the Onan'ji's words. What similarities could he share with such a monster? The monk sometimes acted as if he cared for the boy, his cruelties tempered by compassion. Yet more often he treated him as a tool. Two natures warred within the Onan'ji. *But why?* Was this another tactic to break him, or something more?

The next morning, instead of the training halls, the Onan'ji led his student to a grove of ancient bamboos. Yei'an waited here, atop a snowy rock shadowed by dwarf pine. Winter rain pounded against the hollow fronds. The spatter vanished into blankets of deep moss, covering the grove's stony bedrock and icy shale.

"Yei'an!" the boy called eagerly.

But the girl looked at him sadly as she rose from her rock. In her hands were two metal blades. She tossed Soh'shoro his own gold-laced ri'shou'an.

"Duel her," the monk instructed.

"I know your test," the boy intuited immediately, "and I won't hurt her."

The Onan'ji laughed a terrible laugh, welling up like the humming silence of a deep cave. "You think that is the lesson?" There was a glimmer there—a hint of what would come. "You think you stand a chance against her?"

"Then what are you trying to teach?"

"Suffering."

Soh'shoro's eyes widened.

"He is not asking." Yei'an's blade rose, glimmering in the rainy light of the bamboos. "You can't stop this. Please, just do as he says."

The boy looked to the Onan'ji in panic, then back to the girl.

"I won't." He lowered his hands. "I don't know what you think, but I won't . . ."

The Onan'ji laughed again, this time a rushing sound like dry leaves thrown to fire. Yei'an's steady steps drew close.

"I am not making you do anything. That is part of your lessons too."

And the boy dropped his blade to his feet. "No."

The girl didn't hesitate. Instead, she charged, her ri'shou'an singing a clean slash through the rain. Soh'shoro froze for a precious moment in disbelief. The Voice shrieked, but he stumbled back too late. And the blade's tip caught his shoulder, fountaining blood.

He screamed. Then he weaved, trying to run. But the girl's

sword arced like a diving bird, opening his lower back with searing agony. Soh'shoro fell to the ground, crying out again.

Yei'an refused to stop. She pounced atop him, locking his arms away beneath her legs and slamming her ri'shou'an's ringed pommel into his skull. The world split. Her sweet breath kissed his bloodied face. Soh'shoro tried to roll, as he had trained to do. But pain made every motion slow, and Yei'an resisted with easy confidence. She struck again, breaking his nose. His vision sparked. Agony turned to animal anger, and somehow Soh'shoro torqued his arm free to protect his face.

The Voice cried once more. But for the first time, Soh'shoro truly listened. He didn't resist its cry or revolt against its terror. Instead, he held its instinct, letting the mysterious whispers guide his motions. He caught Yei'an's next strike. She lunged again, and once more Soh'shoro trusted the Voice, easily locking the blade away.

But then a deeper realization struck.

You must keep this secret. The monk mustn't know you hear the Voice. For he guessed the Onan'ji's lesson was also a test: to confirm the boy's deafness. In that moment, wisdom outweighed pain. He let Yei'an's next strike land.

The world exploded. She pounded again and again, now slamming his collarbone and snapping the old wound. Soh'shoro heard only the beating of his heart, smelled only the iron of blood, thought only of suffering. He could endure no longer. At last, he struck back, with a mixture of instinct and muscle memory, driving his palm against Yei'an's face.

The monk rolled off him, gasping.

"You didn't even try," she whispered, wiping blood from her teeth. "I gave you so many openings to . . ."

"It's over," Soh'shoro pleaded. Gore poured from his head and back. His hands trembled.

The Onan'ji kneeled beside the boy, smiling his veinless smile. "I was wrong." He raised a hand to the rain, in the same curious gesture as when he had been cast out of the Quo'dai-ma House all those seasons ago. "Yet still you learn. Survival is as natural as a storm. This is why all men, given a choice, will choose violence."

He rose, looking disappointed.

"She hurt you badly. It will be a season at least before you can train again." The Onan'ji gestured toward the main temple. "But your suffering will continue to teach."

With that callous remark, the monk stalked away, vanishing into the rainy bamboos.

Yei'an cocked her head, making sure the Onan'ji was truly gone. She then lay beside Soh'shoro, still breathing heavily. Rain pounded from the sky as if the world itself opened. Somewhere in the distance, a branch snapped.

"You didn't even try," she repeated.

"How could you?" He forced the words through agonized gasps.

Her eyes flared. "You think I have a choice? You think he doesn't have ways to hurt me too?" She swallowed. "Your wounds are very bad. Let me help."

Soh'shoro curled defensively, gathering his knees to his chest. The sharpness in his ribs spread like fissures.

"Please," Yei'an insisted, drawing closer.

"I know what you're doing. You're his. You're just pretending you aren't."

The girl's dark lips turned into a quizzical smile. Idly, she licked away the last of their blood. "I told you before. That doesn't mean I can't care." She reached into a pouch by her side. "He's like a river, Soh'shoro. Wearing down a stone. That's all we are to him."

Yei'an withdrew an unctuous paste, wrapped in a thick layer of wild spearmint. "Lily salve," she explained. "Only Qu'su keep the recipe." She hesitated briefly before adding, "Because there are wounded, when hunting your kind."

The boy pushed the medicine away. So she leaned over him, forcing back his shirt. Gently, her willowy fingers rubbed salve into skin.

"I won't give in to him," Soh'shoro forced out defiantly.

"Yet you give in so easily to me?" She flashed a wide smile, almost an invitation. The richness of her scent blended with the tang of fresh blood.

"He has forever, Soh'shoro," she continued, smearing paste across the boy's face. The balm worked quickly, and his breathing eased. But as the anesthetic strengthened, the Voice returned. Not as before, panicked and desperate, but instead as subtle whispers, like leaves rustling in a summer wind.

The lilies call to it, Soh'shoro realized. *The Voice and the lilies are connected.*

"He doesn't have forever with me," Soh'shoro replied, for the first time admitting that truth to himself. "I'll die too. I'm not like this world. I'm temporary."

"And that's why you're wrong." Yei'an's hands felt along the slash on Soh'shoro's lower shoulder. "It's not you he needs, just your kind. If you won't break, he just waits, until the next child of Death is born."

Now the Voice snarled hungrily through the salve.

"You resist, and your burden merely falls to another. He wanted me to say that. Tell you that you should be selfless, that you should do this duty yourself."

"He's a demon, Yei'an."

"That doesn't make him wrong." Without cleaning her hands, the girl brought the same smearing of lily paste against her own split lip. She touched the wound curiously, as if seeking pleasure in it, pushing harder and harder until a tear ran down her face. "This killing. Your talent. It protects the Valley. How is that wrong? How is that not something you want?"

The boy ignored the question. Instead, he pulled Yei'an's hand away from her split lip.

"Stop. You'll make it worse."

"That's the point," she sneered. "We don't feel much pain in the Valley." She squeezed her lip until another tear ran down her cheek. "That's why I want you."

"Want me?" he asked.

"To make him suffer."

And Soh'shoro stared wordlessly into her bat-like eyes.

"The skills he teaches can be turned," Yei'an continued. "I saw it in you clearly today, even if he didn't." More tears, like the evening stars, glittered down the girl's bright cheeks. "You are my escape."

Yei'an brought the uncture one more time to the boy, and now there was love in her touch. She massaged the ointment deeper and deeper into his cracked collarbone, blending pain with gentleness.

"If you won't learn for the Valley, learn for me," Yei'an finished. "But please, Soh'shoro. *Learn.*"

At that, he reached out and held her hand.

It took two seasons for Soh'shoro's wounds to heal, but injury was not the reason the prince relented. The logic of the Qu'su now consumed him. He felt like a drifting leaf, borne gradually away atop the yawning waters of the Valley's potential. He could not fight against that current. But he could choose how far it carried him.

So he clung to Yei'an's promise: *Make him suffer.*

Soh'shoro still longed for his lost life of royalty. But now he accepted the Qu'su's tutelage, like a prisoner accepts a sentencing. The Onan'ji sensed this obedience, and so began a new phase of Soh'shoro's instruction.

"Careful," the monk warned their first night in the mountains. "We are terribly close to the Mists here. Closer than even I prefer to dare." He waved a hand across the winding path, its strangely patterned cobblestones bleeding tar. "Just a little farther."

White veils swirled on either side of the trail, each tendril interlacing like tangled string. Occasionally Soh'shoro glimpsed a shape in the Mists, always ill-defined and distorted. The Voice echoed with its strange motions, as if whatever lurked inside the veils was its true source.

"You lied to me," Soh'shoro said at last. "You said the Mists are oblivion, but there's something inside them, isn't there?" He thought of his mother's memories, when he had tumbled from the temple and the skeletal shape that had spoken with her voice.

"Of course." The monk kept his eyes focused on the path ahead. "The Valley is not just a paradise, Soh'shoro. It is a prison."

"A prison for what?"

The Onan'ji turned back to face the boy. "A question needs more than an answer, Soh'shoro. It needs understanding. And acceptance." He continued with strange affection. "But you have neither. If I told you what I believe is inside the Mists, my words would be as meaningless as pebbles cast into a pond."

A flash of memory flitted across the monk's face, like a bright thrush darting amid undergrowth. Soh'shoro felt certain that the Onan'ji was crying, though no trace of emotion crossed his face. The monk turned back to the path.

The pair fell silent for a time as they climbed higher into the peaks. But suddenly the Onan'ji shouted:

"Joy!"

"What?"

"That's your answer. The one you won't understand." And the Onan'ji picked up his pace.

Night deepened. The stars blazed in brilliant, yawning stretches. Something dark and heavy broke the twilight ahead, at the summit of the trail.

"The Mists can't touch the Qu'en Shards," the Onan'ji explained. "It is safe to camp here."

He opened his travel pack, spreading reed mats for sleeping. Soh'shoro simply stared at the monument. It was his first time seeing a Qu'en Shard, outside of paintings in the Palace.

The menhir curved smoothly into flowing, frigid metal: the same material that the Emperor's Mausoleum was made of. Grooves in its alien polish caught the wind, occasionally singing like the bells of a Gi'en shrine. Soh'shoro thought of the Traders' tattoos, for the monument was covered with the same endlessly repeating sequence of lines and circles. A strange hum purred from a glass hollow at its center. The cavity was wide enough to fit a curled-up person, or a young child.

"This is where they put the newborns for the Rebirths, isn't it?" the prince gasped.

The Onan'ji nodded.

"You know something of the Qu'en Shards, I see." As he spoke, the Onan'ji split twigs for a fire. "There's one on almost every peak. Marking the limits of our world."

Soh'shoro drew closer. A clotting sheen spread across the lightless metal, rank with humidity. Even the ground felt damp. He kneeled, pressing his hand to the mire. When he pulled it away, the scent of iron clung to his newly smeared palm.

"Blood?" the boy gasped, in both disbelief and revulsion.

"Not exactly. But the Shards are a kind of open wound."

Now the Onan'ji struck stones, and the first sparks of flame took their campfire. "Their moisture is from the Mists. The metal deflects the veils, protecting the Valley."

And Soh'shoro realized he had seen these metallic pods before: in the lilied waters beneath the Emperor's Mausoleum. But the sunken Shards of the waterfall gardens had held something inside, hidden behind their fogged glass.

What was it?

The flames crept higher. The Onan'ji nodded with satisfaction. He reached into his pouch, unwrapping a seeded bean curd for dinner.

"Who made these Shards?" Soh'shoro asked almost reverently, still staring at the metal.

"We called their kind Qu'en. No one remembers what they were. Not really. Nor what broke their world." The Onan'ji set the bean curd in the metal pan before holding it over the flames. The fare sizzled pleasantly. "But their remnants linger, like wood scrapings from a miscut carving, ever weakening with distance. Man built the Valley, Soh'shoro, but we used the Qu'en's tools. Scavenging Eternity and chaining Death with promises we did not understand." The Onan'ji tested the curd's heat with the back of his hand. He seemed almost as interested in his cooking as in his tutelage. "There is only the Emperor, now. And even he is barely enough, little more than a woken copy. A desperate attempt to keep their dying race enfleshed. The last of his kind."

Soh'shoro tried to hide his shock at the words. He had never heard such open talk of the Valley and its secrets.

"I've never seen the Emperor," Soh'shoro confessed. "I've entered his Mausoleum, but . . ."

"I'm cold," the Onan'ji interrupted. "If you want more secrets, make us tea." He gestured to a lingering snowpack.

Unsteadily, the boy set about gathering fistfuls for the melting pot the monk set beside the campfire.

"You've never seen the Emperor because your courts hide him out of shame," the Onan'ji continued. "He is more corpse than child, so rotted as to have lost all defining features. That's the point of the Gi'en and its blood. To renew and preserve him. All a last, desperate attempt to seal Outside."

Soh'shoro pressed another fistful of snow into the melting pot. "Is there something beyond the Valley, then?" he asked fearfully.

"Of course. That is where we came from. In the beginning."

Soh'shoro's hands grew careless with the revelation, and the pot clattered to the ground.

"Careful!" the Onan'ji snarled, and Soh'shoro risked asking no more.

They ate in silence, gazing at the Shard. But soon the Onan'ji turned unusually talkative once more. As Soh'shoro bedded down on the wet earth, the monk stared into the firelight, holding something wicked and narrow.

"It's called a shurishi," the monk explained. "An ancient tool of the Qu'su."

The slender dart glimmered in his hand, like light on a single strand of hair. It reminded Soh'shoro of the needles used to tattoo the Traders. But it was far lighter and more delicate, like a razor's whisper. "A weapon to study alongside the sword."

As the monk spoke, he pressed the needle against the exposed flesh of his arm. The thin metal lanced with confidence and calm, deeper and deeper into waiting softness. As it vanished beneath the skin, the Voice rose with it, protesting the violence. A low hush at first, rising angrier and colder as the monk dug the needle completely beneath the skin.

"This is how the Qu'su learn to listen. How we bait the Voice and master its mysteries: by calling it with gentle violence." With a sudden tug, he pulled the narrow steel from his skin. Beside the smattering of blood, a tiny tangle of capillary remained.

At last, Soh'shoro understood the veinless miracle of the Onan'ji—why the golden, unblemished stain spread across his whole body. He had spent his whole lifetime in such bloody meditation.

The monk wiped the needle across his sleeve before thrusting its tip into the fire. A moment later, the heated metal glinted like a red ribbon. He spun the shurishi playfully, sending its molten point twirling like a miniature dancer.

"This is why you can never defeat me, Soh'shoro." The Onan'ji's voice cracked with terrible sadness. "Your kind is deaf to the Voice, but I have listened for lifetimes to secrets and to horrors. All revealed to me in the mutterings of the Mist. And those darknesses amount to a single truth, another answer you will not understand."

The boy leaned close. The shurishi slithered into the monk's arm as his face creased with the pleasant focus of pain.

"This Valley . . ." His voice trailed off for a moment before returning. "It is haunting because it is unfinished. True paradise is not merely the absence of Death." He swallowed hard as the shurishi completely vanished beneath his skin. "True paradise must be shared."

The questions that riddle raised within the boy would take a lifetime to answer. But whether the Onan'ji had meant to or not, he had given Soh'shoro a gift. The power to question the Valley.

Joy.

The night deepened. The Qu'en Shard hummed. And as Soh'shoro slipped into slumber, still he wondered at the monk's strange words, and what truly lay beyond the haunted Mists of his home.

CHAPTER SIX

ASSASSIN

Years passed unnoticed, like all years in the Valley. And with them Soh'shoro learned, practicing until he moved cleanly and cut coldly—shaped at last into the Onan'ji's dark desire. His fury found form in every swipe and counter, every block and jutting slash.

He embraced the arts of the Qu'su. He enjoyed the violence. He had for seasons.

Perhaps he had all along.

"You are ready to kill," the monk promised. "This summer will be your blooding."

Yei'an came to him most nights now. She sat whispering beyond his door. Soh'shoro smelled a new perfume of anise and pampas on her skin, blending with her familiar scent of winter bur and honey. But fear kept the walls between them.

After she left, in the depths of each midnight, he practiced listening in secret: taking a smuggled shurishi, teasing the veins above his elbow, where temple robes hid his golden scars. The Voice cried and pleaded, and he focused, then discerned, breaking apart its discordant murmurs until he felt, rather than heard, instinct twitching across his skin. Gradually the beginnings of mastery came, and with it a sharpness he had never known of the world. The more he learned to listen, the more even nature's smallest details became wells of profundity, and time itself slowed beneath the weight of miraculous, instinctual understanding. Lost in the Voice's calls, he felt much more than himself, as if quickened by the accumulated intuition of uncountable lifetimes.

But within those cries also lurked his mother's memories. They pleaded thinly through the Voice like the scent of long-extinguished incense. He still did not have the talent to tease them together, so the fragments they offered haunted him even more. Again and again, he saw bright knives and obscene masks beside strange rods of silver. Then endless waters and whitecapped waves. More and more, Soh'shoro became convinced his mother had known something terrible.

Something of Outside.

So each night he searched for her secrets, and the great golden stain of the Qu'su spread, brightening his flesh.

Everything felt balanced on a precipice. Blood and force as inevitable as the heavy heat. And beneath that atmosphere of anticipation the Traders arrived, part of an unseasonal caravan bound from the Mists, accompanied by a lone epoxy priest.

"What business do these men have at our temple? How did they even find us?" Soh'shoro wondered.

"I led them," the Onan'ji replied. "Because we will have need. Everything in the Valley is of dual purpose: the one noble, the other dark." He frowned. "The Traders are no different. They bring salt into the Valley, but they also bear away Death's stain. When your killings begin, there will be need of such cleansing."

The Onan'ji forbade Soh'shoro to follow the Traders and their priest into the main temple. But the prince often turned his training against the monk now. It was easy enough for Soh'shoro to mantle atop the structure's wide eaves, crawling to a smoke hole. And through its grooves, he peered down at the monk and the sunburned men.

The Onan'ji pointed to a calligraphic sheaf, sprawled on a low table between polished shurishi and a thick uncture of lilies. Soh'shoro remembered as a child watching the Traders receive their tattoos, and immediately recognized the same intent. The Onan'ji took up a lily-blanched needle. But when he lanced it underneath the Trader's arm, he did so with cruelty and depth, not artistry. The Voice ached angrily. The shurishi wormed deeper, digging for something.

Suddenly a small metal sliver emerged, coated in dark blood. The Onan'ji dropped it distastefully into a waiting pan.

"Not pure." The epoxy priest shook his head. "Must be washed with salt."

"There should be bright strings," the Onan'ji insisted. "And slates like bronzed emeralds. We are so close to completing the *machine*." Soh'shoro did not understand the Old Word.

"Soon, maybe."

"Not soon enough! I must deliver these myself, to be certain of progress."

"This evil work." The priest hesitated. "Such relics should never cross the Mists."

"You fool! Such relics *belong* to the Mists," the Onan'ji snarled. "We looted them after the Mausoleum fell, scavenging all we dared from that detritus to seal the Valley! I am not violating your faith. I am repairing it!" He tossed the calligraphic sheaf to the priest angrily. "You speak the code. Now hide it on the flesh. Conceal my work with fresh tattoos."

"How much longer?" The priest glared as he took up the lily needle. "We tire of dark services."

"The blink of an eye!" the Onan'ji snarled. "We are close

now. The metal already hums. The prince is ready. Soon we will have no more need of your kind's work. You will all be free."

The Voice warned Soh'shoro, with a quick and sudden hiss. He dropped away from the smoke hole just before the Onan'ji glanced toward him.

Why conspire with such Traders? What was that metal fragment? Why speak of freedom and machines?

That night Soh'shoro mulled over these mysteries, as he bathed in a mountain stream. By the time he returned to his cell for the cold comforts of sleep, he still had no answers.

And then he heard Yei'an at his door. But this time, she pulled its latch and slipped inside.

Neither spoke.

Yei'an ghosted over to his bed, squirreling down beside him. She smelled fresh and bright and dangerous. He didn't hesitate to kiss her.

She responded furiously, pushing him against his reed bedding and pinning his hands above his head. Her lips ran against his neck and chest. He shut his eyes as she bit him gently.

"I'm sorry," Yei'an whispered.

"What do you mean?"

"He's broken you. Like he broke me." She ran her fingers through Soh'shoro's hair. "What's the point?"

Soh'shoro glimpsed another figure in that darkness. As shadows played across Yei'an's thin face, her eyes faded as if with phage-black scars. In fantasy Soh'shoro reached for her lacquer-wood mask. The prince pulled Yei'an closer, kissing her harder. They rolled over, onto the bare floor. She crawled on her knees above him, forceful and eager. A salt dish clattered from its nearby table, shattering.

Yei'an took him. As she rocked, her pink tongue rolled Soh'shoro's fingers over and over in her mouth. The broken ceramic cut into his back, beading blood across the floor. Her hands pinned him down.

"What's wrong?" he asked, because the Voice cried its soft warnings.

"Nothing's wrong." Her silver eyes stared deeply into his. "I want this."

She bit his lip, harder and harder, until he tasted iron. But he pushed her away, wiping the blood from his mouth, still breathing heavily.

"What's wrong?" he insisted.

"I do want this." Yet bit by bit Yei'an withdrew, her legs balling defensively. "But I can't have it."

He stroked her short hair. "Why not?"

"Because he wants it too."

Any lingering pleasure vanished beneath jolting fear.

"The Onan'ji trusts me. He asked me."

"Asked you what?"

"To do this." Yei'an pulled farther away, a sob welling in her chest.

"Why would the Onan'ji want this? For us to be together?"

"Because you will risk your life." She spoke between rising tears. "And if you die, he would have to wait. But he doesn't want to wait anymore. He is impatient now. His plans begin."

"Yei'an, calm down," Soh'shoro insisted. "I don't understand . . ."

Her eyes filled with wounded anger. They glowed more brightly for all her weakness, like a full moon in a storm, electrifying him.

"He thinks your stain spreads from parent to child."

Soh'shoro looked away, disgusted with himself. Somehow he smelled a strange scent of honeysuckle and wood shavings.

"That's why he commands this. That's what I don't want

to give him." Yei'an grasped Soh'shoro's cheek, forcing him to turn to her. But the dark of night had deepened, and her form seemed little more than shadow.

"This isn't loneliness. If he hadn't asked . . ." She stroked his face slowly. "You understand me. And I understand you."

She stood, pulling her robes tightly about herself.

"But I won't help him anymore." Her figure looked like a rigid shard of metal thrust from the earth. "I know what happens now. At least it was my choice."

Then Yei'an vanished into the dark.

Soh'shoro did not call out, nor try to follow her. Instead, he stayed awake all night, watching shadows lengthen into dawn, fighting back terror at the pressing sense of inevitability closing about him.

I know what happens now . . .

The next morning, he arrived late to practice. Like always, Yei'an waited among the sparring monks. But she looked away when he stared. Even in profile, her face was swollen and heavy. She, too, had spent the night crying.

The Onan'ji approached Soh'shoro, handing him his ri'shou'an. The pale metal glimmered like a slice of moonlight.

"This will be our last practice. Real cuts come next. Show me you are ready."

The monks sparred, and the day's heat rose. Soon Soh'shoro partnered with Yei'an. Each time their bodies brushed close, he tremored with memory from their evening.

But her ferocity never broke.

Still, Soh'shoro was easily her better now. Partly it was how deeply he had embraced his training. Partly the Voice's whispers, though he worked constantly to hide their guidance. But mainly, it was his nature. Soh'shoro had only begun to admit it to himself. But he had a talent for Death.

So he had little trouble slipping Yei'an's guard, or tripping her to the mossy ground. His every strike came fluid and fast, vanishing like shadows flickering across a screen. Soon sweat streamed down Yei'an's brow as she gasped for air, while Soh'shoro breathed calmly and steadily. Had he been more experienced, he would have questioned why the Onan'ji held their pairing so long, or why the needle-thin strokes of their blades clattered against each other with such perilous fragility.

But he wanted to see her.

Then Yei'an's weapon drove in luridly overhead, and Soh'shoro caught its downstroke against his guard, twisting as he had been taught to throw the monk off balance. Both swords sang a final time as the combatants stepped past each other, but instead of their ri'shou'ans' cobalt sparking, there spat a sound like breaking bells. Before he understood what had happened, Yei'an fell to her knees, blood spilling from her neck and mottling the parched summer earth a rain-drenched brown. He was so stunned, it was only when Soh'shoro cut his palm trying to stem Yei'an's bleeding that he realized her sword had broken, and its tip now lay wedged firmly in her throat. Even as Soh'shoro fought the metal free, he felt the Onan'ji's unflinching gaze upon him, cruelly patient as his charge struggled to save the monk's life.

Soh'shoro barely processed those next moments. He clutched Yei'an's fading body to his chest, tears streaming down his face.

"It was my choice," she forced out through curdled breaths.

The milky horror of her bright eyes rolled empty. A final, reflexive gasp twitched across her lips like a smile. And suddenly, Soh'shoro found only a corpse in his arms, rigid and heavy as corded timber. In its pristine gore, he held Death, even as he begged and begged for it not to be so.

"Leave," the Onan'ji instructed the other monks. Then, like a heron to its perch, he drew himself over Soh'shoro. "Do you see?" He placed his hand firmly on the prince's shoulder. "Do you see how frail the world? How life ends by your hand?"

Yei'an's gore caked against his flesh, drying painfully turgid in the summer heat.

"You have killed before. But for the first time, you understand your power's pain." The Onan'ji smiled. "Everything after this will be easy."

"You wanted this." Soh'shoro gazed up in fury. "You planned this."

The monk nodded. "She was a tool that refused its purpose." His eyes flared, baiting Soh'shoro. "Are you the same?"

In that moment, the prince was ready. The ri'shou'an lay beside him. Anger rose with the purity of revenge. But then the Onan'ji stopped him with a single word.

"Purpose."

Soh'shoro felt his insidious control, like a kite pulled by its string.

"Killing me changes nothing, prince." The Onan'ji had never used his title. Not in all his seasons at the temple. "Yei'an will still be dead. The Valley will still rot." The monk smiled. "Your vengeance is as snow in summer to our Eternity . . ." The Onan'ji's voice trailed off as he saw Soh'shoro soften.

Yei'an had been right. Soh'shoro had changed. He had been broken. But not because of weakness, rather because of sympathy. It was goodness that chained Soh'shoro in that moment. A belief that the taint of his birth might yet mean something to the world.

"This is the final lesson," the Onan'ji continued. "Even

paradise has need of Death. Do grasses not wither with winter? Are trees not felled for shelter? Are lilies not plucked for trade? At its deepest root, existence is predicated on violence. You, Soh'shoro, must bear this burden for the Valley so that others need never know it at all."

The sun pounded through the trees, so angry and hot it seemed a star falling fast to earth.

"It is time to cut out the rot. To save our home."

Soh'shoro swallowed. "I want her sent into the Mists. She deserves that much."

The Onan'ji nodded. "I told you we had need of Traders." His voice turned. "I will honor your request, as you honor mine." He pinched his fingers into the deep tissue of Soh'shoro's shoulder. "Now bear her body so we might wash it clean."

Gently, the Qu'su helped Soh'shoro stand, leading him toward the main temple. Yei'an's corpse sagged in his arms, simultaneously painfully light and viciously heavy, as if the physical weight failed to reflect the magnitude of its emptiness.

"You hate me now. But when our work is done, you will understand." The Onan'ji knelt beside Soh'shoro on the reed mats. He splashed a damp cloth into the prayer room's cleansing font before gently wiping Yei'an's throat. Diluted blood ran through cracks in the floorboards. "You will give her death meaning." Then he added cryptically, "We will all be together again."

The Onan'ji laid the first lily petal across Yei'an's split neck. It made Soh'shoro sick to watch the monk touch her. Still, he let the cartonnage climb, swelling and distorting, until her face lay bandaged like those of the Rebirths. Soon she might be among them, an empty corpse smuggled out among the waiting brightness of other, returning futures.

"Show me your hand."

The Onan'ji cleaned the deep gash on Soh'shoro's palm

where he had cut himself pulling Yei'an's broken blade free. He was certain now that the monk was crying. The same shallow tears from that strange evening in the mountains among the Qu'en Shards.

"Tell me who I must kill. This needs to end."

The Onan'ji wrung out the bloodied cloth with metered harshness.

"For this next work, the less you know, the easier your task shall be." The whites of the Onan'ji's eyes gleamed bloodlessly, their every capillary tortured free by years of needled questing. "Trust me. This is what the Valley wants."

"It's not what I want," Soh'shoro replied.

"Then remember the lessons. Desire is its own prison, my child. Unless . . ." His voice trailed off curiously. "Unless all that you desire shares the same cell." He offered his hand to Soh'shoro. The same hand that had struck him so many times. But now the Onan'ji held it forward lovingly, like a parent to a child. "Take it. We will not begin if it is not your choice."

And one last time, Soh'shoro accepted the monk's hand.

The days grew hotter. And into that miasma the pair traveled toward the staining grandeur of the City, day after day, moon after moon, for the killing. Soh'shoro's heart beat faster with each step, as the magnificence of his childhood returned. For the first time in years, he considered running.

They rented a teahouse room. Over a dinner of seeded shoots and rice wine, on a veranda overlooking the mighty rivers flowing through civilization's heart, swelling hideously with lilies, the monk told him of his next killing.

"It will be here, in the Pleasure District. But this murder will be different, Soh'shoro." The Onan'ji spoke softly, almost respectfully. "Your mark will, in many ways, be a test. This man is noble. He is guarded."

Soh'shoro nodded. What did it matter who he killed?

"Three more lives is all I ask. Just three."

"Four," he replied fiercely.

The monk nodded. "When it is done, our time will come, if you still wish it. That I promise." With sudden ferocity, he leaned across the teahouse table. "I brought you myself because I know you might run." He licked his lips. "But I will always be watching. If you fail or flee, there will be no forgiveness. The lessons are over now."

Soh'shoro felt fury. The seething desire to strike now, and end everything that would come. But the years of servitude still weighed him down, and he only sipped his wine in silence.

"I will send word when it is time."

And the monk left Soh'shoro alone.

He waited two days in the teahouse, each night full of laughter and drink. Blossoms blazed across the courtyard trees, their bright summer flavor mingling with scented torches. Everywhere swarmed the gorgeous colors of the courtesans: thin crimson robes, vermilion fans, and stylized golden veils. But Soh'shoro felt apart, just as his simple mountain robes clashed with their silks. He tried not to look at the dancers, but always the temptation lingered. Their painted skin and scented hair reminded him of his cruel princess. Each glass of rice wine tasted worse, sour and overly salted.

Then the note came. He knew what must be done. Soh'shoro left the teahouse without so much as a word, paying his fare with the mendicant beads the Onan'ji had given him.

At the gate of the nearby pleasure-house, Soh'shoro watched from an alley's shadows. It was almost dawn now, and men and women shuffled home, shawls pulled tight against the soft, dewy rain. Shops and teahouses were boarded shut. A courtesan struggled to fend off an amorous suitor, at last losing him when he tripped, obviously drunk, on her discarded scarf. Then the streets truly emptied. A first blush took the sky, colors warming into a pantomime of early grays.

At last, the honor guard arrived to collect his mark. Calmly, Soh'shoro counted their number. His eyes played over their blades, ceremonially sleeping in disused ossuaries. The pleasure-house door opened to greet them, squaring light into the darkness. And for one moment, his mark stood silhouetted in that radiance, bowing his leave, then testing the rainfall from beneath the low-hanging roof. Soh'shoro couldn't make out the man's face: Cloth wraps and a heavy shawl hid his features for the brothel visit. But then a guard stepped close, opening a parasol of brilliant violet—the sign he watched for.

Soh'shoro rested his hand on the ring of his ancestral blade.

The noble and his honor guard shuffled into the dark avenue, their way lit only by a hand-lamp and the sky's thin color. Soh'shoro waited until they passed, then slipped onto the muddy street behind them. He discarded his shawl, tapping his sword's ossuary to clear any rainwater. Still he watched the light of the hand-lamp grow faint, waiting.

He had to best seven men, including his mark. But not one of them heard his dash over the rain.

In what seemed an instant, Soh'shoro ghosted across the gap between himself and the rear guardsman. The man wheeled achingly slowly, not even drawing his blade. Soh'shoro bent low, steps wide, driving his shoulder into the guard's chest. His body jolted airborne, even as the prince snatched the man's face and twisted it to the cobblestones. Its thud was barely audible over the driving rain.

In the Valley, no one anticipates violence.

As Soh'shoro rose from the unconscious body, the remaining guards merely gasped, their faces caught between disbelief and complete uncertainty. Wide eyes and parted lips told of impossibility and denial, as if watching a living dream. But Soh'shoro did not hesitate. He lunged at the nearest man, striking three quick, unarmed blows to the chest and face that flattened him against a teahouse door, splintering its wooden frame.

The four remaining guards freed their weapons, screaming for Soh'shoro's mark to run. The noble took off down the street into the driving rain. The sentries circled the assassin, closing off pursuit.

When the first honor guard struck, Soh'shoro answered with his own blade, bursting from its ossuary like a star streaming through the heavens. The Voice whispered its guidance, but the sentry's slash was so inexperienced Soh'shoro barely needed its cries to deflect the sword. Locking the blade away and twisting, he snatched the man's wrist and torqued him to the ground.

But still Soh'shoro did not kill. Instead, his ri'shou'an drove into the cobblestones beside the fallen man's throat.

"Run!" Soh'shoro shouted at the remaining guards. "Death is not yours today."

The protectors glanced at each other, then the rain-soaked assassin. The youngest sentry dropped his sword, sprinting for a nearby alley.

Only two guards remained.

They lunged at Soh'shoro together, trying to confuse him, but their motions were achingly slow and inept. In the Valley, guardianship involved more ritual than reason, so the prince effortlessly weaved beneath the first slash, even as he caught the second, letting its blade skid against the hilt of his ri'shou'an. And with a sudden push, he jarred the weapons together. As the guard lost his grip, Soh'shoro caught the falling blade and slammed its ringed hilt furiously into the man's face, splintering his nose.

He turned to the last defender. The guard slashed protectively, maintaining space. The Voice needled, and Soh'shoro stepped into the cut, catching the blade and throwing it wide. His knee shot into the man's stomach. As the guard buckled, Soh'shoro continued his advance, vaulting onto the sentry's back and jumping free. He caught the overhang of a roof, scrabbling up onto the tiles. Behind him the guard collapsed to muddied earth, gasping.

Soh'shoro chased his mark across the eaves, leaping rooftops and ducking lantern strings. The Voice grew louder now, from both violence and anticipation. But the cries turned sorrowful, too, begging him to notice. Because the prince did not understand the bright parasol's meaning. And overtaking the noble, he leaped from the roof, rolling onto the muddy street below and cutting off his mark.

In the thinning light, Soh'shoro could almost make out the man's eyes from between their cloth wraps. The jet-black hair spilling from beneath its pale silk shawl seemed strangely familiar. But too soon the noble drew his own ri'shou'an, falling into an amateur sword stance used for dancing.

Soh'shoro rushed his mark, slashing viciously. But his opponent timed a lucky parry, sparking the razor edge of both blades before pivoting his own ri'shou'an into a lunge. Soh'shoro easily sidestepped the strike, then countered. The noble leaped backward, dodging just beyond the blade, and Soh'shoro followed like a comet, slashing as the man landed off balance. Blood spat into the morning air. Twisting painfully, his mark leaned on his own weapon to avoid falling. Soh'shoro kicked the blade out from beneath him, kneeing his stomach, sending the noble crashing against a slatted wall.

Then Soh'shoro expertly flipped his ri'shou'an for the killing stroke.

But the Voice screamed louder than ever before. Soh'shoro's whole body froze. In that instant he could do nothing but listen. He did not understand why his mother begged for him to make an error. He could easily have dodged the strike. But he trusted her cries of sacrifice all the same.

And Soh'shoro felt the other ri'shou'an slide neatly between his upper ribs, even as his own pierced the noble's chest.

The Voice shuddered silent. There was only the drum of the rain. The cloth wraps fell away from the noble's face. And in horror, Soh'shoro stared at the brother of his bride.

"An . . ." The prince's voice trailed off, eyes never leaving the Ang'soon's face.

"Why . . . ?" An-go'yi'ki choked out with terrible fragility, blood dribbling from his lips as he fought to free himself from the prince's blade.

Soh'shoro had no answer.

An-go'yi'ki fell backward, his body weight pulling Soh'shoro's ri'shou'an free to collapse onto his hands and knees in the mud. Gore fountained into a narrow, cobbled gutter. Soh'shoro's ancestral blade had split the Ang'soon's heart.

"How could you?" An-go'yi'ki's fading voice begged.

"I didn't know it was you."

Already the Ang'soon's noble features clotted purple; his trembling fingers scraped mud; his eyes ceased their rakish flickering.

"I'm sorry," Soh'shoro began.

But An-go'yi'ki was already gone.

Soh'shoro reached for the Ang'soon's sword, buried in his own torso. Trembling, he tried pulling at its hilt, screaming as metal scraped bone. But the ri'shou'an remained burrowed far too deeply in his flesh, and pain brought him to his knees.

It happened in the spaces between moments: the Onan'ji

flashing like a storm. In one impossible motion he blurred over the rooftops and onto the thoroughfare before Soh'shoro.

"You fool," he sneered. Soh'shoro had never heard such an empty tone, so spiritless and devoid of vitality. Only the Onan'ji's eyes revealed his betrayal, deep and uncomprehending. "You hid it from me. You understand the Voice."

Soh'shoro burbled gore. Down the thoroughfare, shouts of approaching guards punctuated the beating rain.

The Onan'ji kneeled beside his assassin. "Leave the sword but keep pressure on the wound's edge." His own hands forced Soh'shoro's against the bloody gash, showing him how to hold his innards. "Tell anyone who will listen to clean the cut with rice wine and salt. When they remove the blade, you'll need an epoxy priest to stitch it, just as they do for the corpses. If—"

"Are you crying?" Yet again, the Onan'ji's face was streaked with silent tears.

The Onan'ji deflected the question. "You'll bleed to death if you move."

"You're letting me go?"

"I don't have a choice." The monk clasped the prince's face with his hands. "Mark my words, this is not kindness." But his tears streamed more fully now than ever before. "If you survive, you will still serve. I will hunt. I will force our work upon you. And you will not know its glory, because it will no longer be your choice."

"What glory?" Soh'shoro jerked his head toward An-go'yi'ki's silent form. "Murdering my family?"

"The Houses are the darkness, Soh'shoro! The Ang'soon and Quo'dai-ma are the stain on the Valley." The Onan'ji shook his head. "How could I tell you? How could you believe?" His golden eyes glimmered in the dawn. "They keep us chained. Limiting how our world might blossom."

Then, in one easy motion, the Onan'ji helped Soh'shoro to lie flat on the muddy cobblestones. The tenderness and love in his touch seemed more alien and horrible than all the violence before. And he hugged Soh'shoro close, whispering through heavy tears:

"You were magnificent."

Then the monk was gone.

With a last, desperate burst of strength, Soh'shoro looked to An-go'yi'ki's corpse. But all his eyes found was the blinding white of lilies.

PART II

THE GRAVEYARD OF THE ANGELS

CHAPTER SEVEN

TOMB

Soh'shoro's next memories were a blur: the humming silence as the dawn bled out, the skewing hues of motion beside his stillness, and the inevitable, rushing cold of sleep after the slicking of the sword. In the tranquility of those next moments, Soh'shoro dreamed of Yei'an and her lilied form in the Mists. But as he tasted her, the rot crept in. And with it slithered the Ang'soon princess, now without her mask, face an impossible petal white against the smoking ruin of her eyes. He seemed eternally unmade beneath those naked, shriveled orbs.

Incredible storms raged, as if the Valley itself mourned An-go'yi'ki's death: bright lightning and driving rain, screaming winds and bursting thunderheads. And the Mists spread with the gale, daring deeper into the Valley like an animal circling the limits of its cage.

It was dawn when the screen whispered open. Soh'shoro knew where he lay by memory alone. The cool smoothness of silk bedding; the watery luminescence of dappled rays filtered through filigree screens; the scent of grass, now mixing with maple and saffron, now little more than an illusion beneath the thick stench of salt smoke. The chambers of his youth smothered him as surely as the cloying embrace of his cloth bandages.

"My child." Obajen-mahoe's voice came soft and sad. Wraithlike, he shuffled beside the prince, waiting. But Soh'shoro could not even turn his head.

"I escaped them," was all he could say. "I escaped."

"I know." Obajen-mahoe smiled sadly. "I know."

Later that morning, attendants brought ghost rice and brine tea. Soh'shoro's wounds were very deep, and he struggled even to sit, constantly enduring the soft agony of torn muscles.

"We searched everywhere for you." Obajen-mahoe tried to smile. "But the Qu'su temples are secret even to the courts."

"I tried to find you as well." Soh'shoro's own voice cracked. "I fled. More than once. But always they brought me back. The Onan'ji . . ." Anger seized the prince. "I know where his temple is. We can find him, stop him . . ."

"Shh," Obajen-mahoe soothed, cooling the steaming tea between cups. They were lined with leaded gold to seal their ancient cracks, using the same art that reforged his mother's sword. "You have been too long in their world." His voice trembled. "If we march a thousand men to their temple, what good would it do? This is the Valley, Soh'shoro. There is no violence." He swallowed. "Your horror is over now. All that remains is to protect you. Nothing more."

"You can't mean that!" Soh'shoro protested. "He stole your son! And all you can answer is that there is nothing to be done?"

"And what would you have done, *my son*?" Obajen-mahoe enunciated the last words with strange emphasis.

"The courts . . ." Soh'shoro forced out through shallow

breaths. "If not violence, they might banish him. Discover his schemes by . . ."

"And what do you think the courts will find, if they hunt the Qu'su?" Any joy in Obajen-mahoe's voice faded. "After all, it was your sword that lay beside An-go'yi'ki's corpse. Not the Onan'ji's."

Obajen-mahoe let the implications hang: *You would be as guilty as the monk in their eyes.*

"You don't know how the Onan'ji preyed on me. Hurting, threatening, lying. Using people I loved against . . ." But there seemed no point in remembering then, and Soh'shoro quieted. In the silence, Obajen-mahoe handed him the tea.

"I want to hear it from you, Soh'shoro. What happened to An-go'yi'ki?"

He saw the dream of his princess's silk then, of her soft cherry robes and acrid stench of salt.

"You already know," Soh'shoro answered quietly. "Only I am of Death."

He did not have to look to know Obajen-mahoe's disappointment.

"We must lie to the courts, then," Obajen-mahoe replied tearfully, standing to go. "Claim it was the Qu'su who killed and you who were hurt protecting your brother. His corpse has already been committed to the Mists. And the mad monks have few friends among the nobility. Such deception buys time, at least, to decide what next must be done."

Soh'shoro raised the gold-threaded teacup to his lips, savoring the brew's saline heat. Obajen-mahoe did not understand. Perhaps no one could. The Valley, with all its engineered parasitism and repetitious glory, might endure this murder. But what had been its purpose?

And the Onan'ji's strange words echoed, sowing wicked doubt: *The Houses are the darkness.*

Obajen-mahoe soon returned with a brazier of salt and an unctuous paste for the prince's wounds.

"Can you walk?" he asked gently, as he massaged Soh'shoro's injured hand.

Soh'shoro sensed his unease. "Maybe. Is something wrong?"

Obajen-mahoe pulled back a bandage before gently swabbing the prince's cut. Soh'shoro flinched but did not cry out.

"An epoxy priest arrived, I thought to stitch your wounds. But he requests our presence at the Mausoleum. Immediately," Obajen-mahoe explained.

"Is this about An-go'yi'ki? What happened to . . ."

"I don't know." Obajen-mahoe cut him off. "But I think it best for my son to take this audience by my side." A pause. "We may need to defend more than mere reputation."

Soh'shoro nodded, slipping free of his grass blankets with Obajen-mahoe's help.

"In the upper Mausoleum, you will see things," he warned, "things that are difficult." He paused. "I hid these from you as a child. Now you will understand why."

Soh'shoro nodded. "The Qu'su warned me of—"

Obajen-mahoe winced. "Not this."

He waited while Soh'shoro struggled into his split-toed sandals. Then together the pair walked in lantern light through the cherrywood corridors of their House.

"We'll skip the preparatory rituals," Obajen-mahoe commanded, as courtiers swarmed to attendance. "I want us there immediately, before anything is said."

"At least take the salinity charms!" a familiar voice shouted.

Soh'shoro turned to see Kenwu, framed in the rainbow light of the House. Tears of joy streamed down both their faces. In that moment, all memory of the Qu'su felt undone: Soh'shoro was still a boy, born to peaceful ritual and nothing more.

"Time enough for remembrances later," Obajen-mahoe interjected bitterly, pulling him away from his old attendant before shuffling the prince angrily down the corridor.

"Why isn't Kenwu coming with us?"

"He no longer attends the main House," Obajen-mahoe replied curtly.

Soh'shoro understood: Kenwu, after all, had lost him as a boy.

In the courtyard, Obajen-mahoe helped Soh'shoro atop their palanquin. He panted heavily now, sweat running down his brow. The bandage at his side lay damp with fresh blood.

"You're hurting yourself."

"I can manage," Soh'shoro replied. "Give me a moment." But when the bower jerked to life, he gasped.

"This is too much . . ."

"It's just pain." Soh'shoro's jaw set. "I mastered that long ago."

And the procession set off amid dreadful silence.

"As far as tradition is concerned, you are still of the Quo'dai-ma," Obajen-mahoe explained as they jostled onward. Placid streams, sculpted boughs, and the bluish glow of the morning lanterns floated outside the palanquin's windows. "Whatever the courts or the Ang'soon princess has guessed—of your abduction by the Onan'ji, of your time among the Qu'su, even of your return beside An-go'yi'ki's corpse—your station obscures it. Until the priests bring a formal charge, you will . . ."

"That's what this is, isn't it? My judgment."

"Judgment for what?" Obajen-mahoe's tone remained calculated. "Why would a prince murder the brother of his bride? Let alone how?" Obajen-mahoe pressed his hand against Soh'shoro's, squeezing gently. "You are my son. I accepted that long ago. Despite what you are. Or what you become. We will endure it together."

Ahead, the Mausoleum gates yawned open, their mechanical grinding like snakes slithering to rut. Inside, no festival lanterns or lily strings awaited. The tomb lay bare except for rotting salt vats and the priests' rainbow lanterns. Only a distant drumming, marking the nobles' return, recalled that bright festival of the Gi'en.

"We have to bathe. That ritual cannot be broken. It is too dangerous otherwise," Obajen-mahoe explained. "Can you manage? Like when you were a child?"

Soh'shoro nodded.

They descended the winding stair, into the chill of the waterfall gardens. At those icy banks that had once terrified him, the prince now merely caught his breath. He had not truly appreciated the garden's beauty before, how the glass ceiling suspended the lily pond reflections overhead, sunlight sparkling between each ghostly petal. Despite the pain of his wound, Soh'shoro found himself wading trancelike into the leaded waters, the flowers congealing about his skin like half-remembered kisses.

As a child he had floated here. But now he was tall enough to stand, and his feet merely slipped against the basin's smooth glass. He looked down, finally noticing the sequenced pods, honeycombing the depths, like shoots of new bamboo. *Qu'en Shards*. He waded deeper, eyes narrowing, peering into their fogged ovules. Within the closest he caught a face: hers.

The Ang'soon princess.

The Houses are the darkness.

Soh'shoro splashed to the banks only half bathed, in shock and confusion. Already it became easier to doubt. The waters were clouded with lily scum, the pain of his wounds deliriously sharp. He could not be certain what he had seen. That could not be his princess.

Attendants swarmed him, distracting with finery: first a great robe of amber, each seam tightened to force the rigid, narrow motions found so beautiful by the courts. Then salt for his hair, followed by delicate, chalky tinctures to flush his skin and freeze his eyes from blinking. Through it all, no one commented on the veinless markings of the Qu'su, so plain and hungry on his arm.

"I missed you, Soh'shoro." Obajen-mahoe stared with pride at the prince's newfound regality.

And forgetting everything, the prince smiled too. "I wanted this. So much."

Now the Quo'dai-ma nobles ascended the helixing stair into the upper tomb. Here, the Mausoleum's forbidden reaches tangled with rotted wood and repatched scaffolding. The air lay heavy with mold and waxy incense. Soh'shoro remembered Kenwu masking his face as a child, and now he did the same with the collar of his robes. But the more he breathed in the tomb, the more it enticed him. The stain clinging here reminded him of a rare scent, one he had only smelled once before: the rot of the Ang'soon princess.

Scaffolding gave way to a metal corridor, polished repeatedly yet still thick with spores. Brocade funerary reliefs hung from sconces brown with mold. Next, the hallway curved upward, funneling into a series of twelve massive lacquer steps.

At each pace, fresh slippers awaited. Soh'shoro and Obajen-mahoe changed shoes a dozen times, slowly and methodically approaching the vast osmium portal beyond. The ache of An-go'yi'ki's sword wound worsened, until Soh'shoro leaned on Obajen-mahoe for support.

"You're almost there."

Soh'shoro kept his gaze fixed on the gateway. "This all protects him, doesn't it? These rituals of cleanliness and salt?"

"Protects him," Obajen-mahoe replied, "and us."

Motion broke out in the fetid corridor behind. The Quo'dai-ma glanced back. And like a firefly winking awake, the Ang'soon princess ascended the lacquered stairs. Grand trains poured behind her in sweeps of indigo and sapphire and cherry, carried by crawling attendants. As always, her great melanized mask waited, sparkling with plum lacquer. When the princess joined them at the highest step, she bowed only to Obajen-mahoe before turning on Soh'shoro.

"I hope you die here," she spat, saliva flecking the narrow gash in her mask's mouth. As the honeysuckle-and-wood-shaving scent of her perfume filled his nostrils, Soh'shoro imagined he could also taste her sweat.

But older now, he felt a new awareness awoke in him. He questioned why he was drawn to this rotting beauty, and what about her ethereal weakness aroused him so much.

"He is prince of the Quo'dai-ma," Obajen-mahoe interjected. "You will respect my son, even if . . ."

"I will do what I want with him," she sneered. "And you . . ."

But the osmium doors ground wide, obscuring speech beneath their mechanistic whirring. A deeper hum joined from the chamber beyond: an insectoid, wheezing vibration, like waking cicadas. And the Emperor's chamber revealed itself at last.

The heart of the Mausoleum hung in a metal void, suspended by lancing wooden beams. Its massive dais bristled with ossuary charms fumigated by salt smoke, pouring from venting doors and vaulted terraces. Everywhere epoxy priests scrubbed with pearlescent silks soaked in brine. Only faint, soggy light touched the central catafalque.

It was here that the Emperor waited, hanging amid tangled lines of silver wires. Soh'shoro gasped audibly. For steel grafts bloated the body, needles and glass bristling from milky veins. Multitudinous robes sutured the figure like tourniquets, masking skin glistening with the translucent paleness of great time. Soh'shoro could not tell whether it was a man, a woman, or something more. For the face lay completely hidden beneath a heavy, purpling shroud. But always, rot crept over it. It tunneled down neck and shoulders, pitting the flesh with craggy spores, leaking pustulating masses onto the floor to be swept away speedily by industrious priests.

It's a Corpse.

The phage lay worst on the Emperor's back. Here lumpy, fetid flesh widened spine and shoulder blades, swelling into moldering pinions. Their stretch intertwined with the gelid lines pumping through the thing's body, holding the spans aloft in a twisted network of desiccated bondage. Had the protean wings once been feathered like the birds of the Valley, before the rot? The prince could not guess. Only a swollen structure remained, achingly gutted in its emaciation, impossible to differentiate from the relic above, thrumming constantly.

A Qu'en. Soh'shoro remembered the Onan'ji's words. *The last of his kind.*

For the Emperor's ichor fed ever upward into the mechanical mass of his Throne, suspended overhead like a metal sun. This relic dwarfed the Corpse, a dozen times in size, widening as it rose, vanishing into the shadows of the upper tomb. Seething and boiling hinted at some transmogrifying, alien process within. And from smokestacks at the artifact's summit, venting into the highest, darkened reaches, burst the first tendrils of Mists.

Made from the Emperor's flesh.

But something seemed wrong with the device. Cords hung too loose. Rent metal dulled with rust. One upper segment of the sphere seemed entirely missing, torn away as if by sudden impact. The Emperor's Throne still served its purpose. But barely. Either incomplete or damaged, Soh'shoro could not say.

Now the three nobles drew near the humming horror. All the prince could smell was salt, as if the entire world baked in its sour, acrid stench. Epoxy priests scrubbed before and behind their every motion, obsessively cleaning away the drifting spores of the Qu'en's sickness. Obajen-mahoe and the Ang'soon princess bowed to the creature, then fell to their knees. Soh'shoro hesitated. But at last he did the same.

"The Houses, before the Gi'en." An epoxy priest's voice ululated through the fog, and the fat, stumbling form of the holy man stepped from behind the relic. His eyes roved madly and angrily. His lips sieved spittle through strange, colored ribbons stitched between his gums. Bright medallions marked him as the eldest of his kind, the head of his priestly Order. "Welcome," he continued. "Our council begins."

The Ang'soon princess rose instantly, ready with anger.

"We know why we are called. The murder of my brother." Her steely gaze rounded on Soh'shoro. "Someone must pay for this crime. Someone . . ."

"Yes, Princess," the eldest soothed, gently raising a swollen hand. "Anger like heat and sunrise. The priests know such tragedies." Silent shame made Soh'shoro look away. "A Quo'dai-ma stolen and returned. An Ang'soon murdered in our City's splendor. And more . . ." The eldest's voice trailed off, like rocks sinking into deep water. His black eyes flashed. "But all this must wait. Must wait, yes. Today is not for judgment."

The Ang'soon princess tensed with frustration.

"What could be more important than my brother's death? The ending of an Ang'soon heir?"

The eldest shut his eyes, steadying himself. His ribboned lips tremored with both fear and anticipation. "Perhaps the true source of these miseries," he began. "Long feared, longer forgotten. A darkness from beyond the Valley." The strange speech of the priest wove each word into the next, with only awkward pauses for breath. "The Houses are called because the Mists are breached." Those words flared like a lightning bolt. "Something comes from Outside."

The eldest raised his hand, signaling, and the doors to a

venting terrace slid wide. A caravan of Traders entered the chamber. Each shouldered a litter pole, their free hands swinging great bronze censers of purifying salt. The Voice, frantic and cold, began screaming through Soh'shoro's mind, and a greater darkness fell over the tomb, sterile and starving.

The Traders laid their litter on the bare cherrywood floor, before the Emperor's Throne. Carefully, one drew back the plain cloth covering. A body rested within, bound by bandages soaked in brine. Even through the wrappings, Soh'shoro could tell the man had been terribly burned. Black boils charred his exposed skin. His empty eyes gleamed hauntingly, wide and clouded.

"This is foreign," continued the priest. The salt smoke thickened, and Soh'shoro's stomach quieted. The Voice remained, though, scratching like claws against glass. Through it, the prince glimpsed something in the dead face he was certain the others could not: familiarity.

Hold the knife to my throat.

It was impossible to be certain beneath the horrific burns. Yet to Soh'shoro, the foreigner looked identical to the courtier he had killed all those seasons ago as a child.

It cannot be the same man.

Carefully an attendant shrouded the corpse's face, leaving Soh'shoro to wonder what he had truly seen, just as he doubted his glimpse of the Ang'soon princess in the watery darkness of the waterfall gardens.

"Traders found this foreign body at the edge of the world," the priest explained. "At first, we hoped he was merely a husk. But he carried"—the eldest's voice caught for a second—"*things* with him."

The litter bearers unwrapped brine-cloth packaging beside the foreigner. Inside waited a twisted wooden pole, banded with thick metal worn orange with rust and age. The device was hollow at one end, a trigger mechanism on the other. Cartridges of black powder, bound in wax paper, rested against it, smelling faintly of fireworks despite the salt haze.

"This powder takes flame violently," the priest explained. "Like firework primer, but far fiercer. The burns are all across the corpse's skin."

But Soh'shoro had glimpsed these artifacts before. *My mother's memories . . .*

"Do we know the foreigner poses a threat?" he risked interjecting. "Could these objects merely be gifts? As we send Traders, might foreigners try to answer us in kind?"

"Outside is sealed for a reason, Quo'dai-ma." The eldest paused. "War." Even enunciating the syllable strained the priest. He reached a fatty hand to the Emperor's Throne, steadying himself. The Ang'soon princess blanched too, the pale flesh peeking from beneath her mask somehow losing its remaining color.

"Impossible," Obajen-mahoe whispered.

"Only because you do not remember it," the princess interjected forcefully. "But Soh'shoro knew such secrets. The Rebirths never eroded her mind. Until now." She stared at the prince pointedly. *My mother.* "She often spoke of a fight to forge the Valley. How we stole secrets because others saw them as sins. How some might still seek to smother our home."

The princess touched her mask, stroking the wood obscuring her lingering rot. "The eldest is right. If one foreigner passed the Mists, more may come. We must make ready." She seemed about to say more. But a coughing fit seized the princess then, silencing her. Attendants swarmed, cajoling and caressing, wiping spittle, then steadying her.

"Make ready for what?" Obajen-mahoe replied, indifferent to her suffering. "The Mists have never failed before. As long as we protect the Houses . . ."

"You merely protect your son!" the Ang'soon princess countered between spasms. "My brother is dead because of your House! He must be—" But her threats faded into hacking breaths.

"How dare you cast such aspersions!" Obajen-mahoe sneered. "Upon the Quo'dai-ma or its prince! What of yourself? Have you ever joined our rituals? It's true your kind is only for breeding . . ."

"Enough!" Soh'shoro surprised himself with the force of his words. The chamber fell into shocked silence. "Enough," he repeated, tone softening. Now he turned to the eldest priest. "I have seen it myself: The Mists are angry. Perhaps that is how the foreigner slipped through? When our walls weakened with roil?"

The fatty figure's ribboned cheeks tensed with consideration. He nodded.

"But we have rituals to renew our Mists, do we not?" Soh'shoro pressed.

"What does the Quo'dai-ma propose?" The eldest leaned forward with curious thirst. "What exactly?"

"Perform the rites of the Gi'en." Soh'shoro had no idea what those words meant. He merely guessed at their truth.

The priest smiled. "It's not spring. The shrines have not returned. There is no festival or . . ."

"All the same."

The eldest rubbed his flabby jowls. "Recent rites have been"—he selected his next word carefully—"unusual. Perhaps our Emperor is not fed"—again a pause—"sufficiently." The priest pressed his hand to the Corpse's metal plating, stroking it hungrily. "But An-go'yi'ki is dead. His sister sweet with sickness. And Obajen-mahoe has never allowed his son to join this ritual before. Without more blood, I fear our Emperor must remain ill-nourished."

Obajen-mahoe's eyes widened in fear. Soh'shoro recalled words from his distant childhood: *Not this ritual. Not until I am certain.*

"Besides, we have another option," the eldest priest continued. "When the Corpse's power fades, there is always fresh rot. Though that carries its own risks."

Now it was the Ang'soon princess's turn to shiver. *What does her sickness have to do with the Emperor?*

Soh'shoro stood torn between two terrors: Obajen-mahoe's and his bride's. And in that moment, he decided, again without thinking.

"I will join the ritual."

Obajen-mahoe glared back angrily. "You will not. You are badly hurt."

"I will manage."

"He is of your House." The eldest priest brightened, as if waiting for this very moment. "His blood will serve, will it not?" His tone twisted dangerously. "What possible reason could there be for turning down such a gift?"

Obajen-mahoe stood conflicted. He cast his eyes to the foreigner's body, then to the prince. Something in him shifted. "I see no other choice," he whispered pathetically. Then, louder, for all to hear: "My son is just as noble! His birthright just as bold!" He paused. "His blood will serve."

"What say the Ang'soon?" the priest asked.

The princess's eyes flicked dangerously to Obajen-mahoe. "It is clever, using ritual to prove your son's worth. To forestall his judgment." Yet here she hesitated, her gaze wandering back to the Corpse. "Does It feel anything?" she whispered. "Would I feel anything?"

As if in answer, the gelid lines piercing the Emperor shivered.

"His blood will serve." Her voice trembled.

"Then it is decided," the eldest priest called. "Blood the Corpse. Renew the Gi'en!"

"Get it over with," Obajen-mahoe declared.

Epoxy priests materialized from all corners of the smoking chamber. One by one they stoked the Corpse, setting its wires and untangling its lines, preparing some hideous, lancing arm of the humming Throne. Soh'shoro recognized these wicked points: shurishi. Or rather, the devices shurishi imitated. There were no words for the perfect, narrow smoothness of the tethered needles. Their art lay beyond any smithing the prince had seen, like fragile hairs of glass, nearly invisible in the salt smoke.

"Step forth," the eldest called. "Father and son."

Without hesitation, Soh'shoro reached for the proffered needle.

"I lead." Obajen-mahoe interposed himself between priest and prince, taking the instrument himself. "You follow. Understand?"

Soh'shoro took up a second needle in answer.

"Yield when it is too much."

Obajen-mahoe breathed deeply, relaxing his arm muscles. The Voice cried at the coming of violence. And in one quick gesture, he lanced the needle beneath his wrist.

"Bleed the bond," the eldest called. "Forge the chains."

Soh'shoro, too, pierced a rich vein in moments. He had much practice, divining the Voice's secrets beneath the Qu'su's shurishi. *A mirrored ritual.*

"We're just dolls," the princess muttered airily.

Now crimson seeped from both wrists into glass tubing. The carmine flows twisted through the elastic wires, entering the fluid exchange. Soon the milky darkness of the Emperor's ichor blended with fresh blood, spearing its coagulating brilliance inside the Corpse.

But the prince realized something was wrong. For as their blood bubbled into the cadaver, black smears seeped slowly down the tubing. As if the donation were too thin, or the fetid fluids of the Emperor too heavy. The chalky ichor slid icily, ever lower, approaching the needles lanced into both Quo'dai-ma wrists.

Soh'shoro met Obajen-mahoe's gaze. He saw fear there, but also deep trust. The Voice begged and cried. But Obajen-mahoe shook his head. "A moment longer," he whispered to Soh'shoro. "We will both know when the Emperor is sated."

Blood pumped deeper. Soh'shoro felt diminished with each thrum of the Throne's perspicacious hunger. Aches started with light-headedness, quickly stretching deeper into his body. His heart sped. His breathing shallowed.

"By our blood are You bound. As life binds Death," the eldest epoxy priest chanted, eerily repeating numbers threaded through the words. "As endurance feeds Eternity."

Soh'shoro's spine tingled, and his chest thumped painfully. He watched his blood mix with Obajen-mahoe's, cycling into the artifact. And in return, the pallid onyx of the Corpse's rot descended dangerously close to their veins.

"Gentle, my Eternity. Be gentled," the eldest slurred, his hand hovering curiously close to Soh'shoro's wrist. "More. A little more."

The prince's eyes flashed to the Corpse. At last, something rotten rolled beneath the funeral cloth covering the cadaver's face, where eyes should have been. Fresh crimson dribbled from the Qu'en's lips, as it uttered a single, guttural cough.

"It's not dead," Soh'shoro gasped.

"It's not alive either," Obajen-mahoe replied. "It is like the Valley. Caught between."

The Voice cried louder. At its warning, Soh'shoro's eyes snapped to the rotten seepage trickling down the tube. The prince tore the needle from his arm, just as viscid darkness skimmed his flesh. Then too late, he snatched the instrument from Obajen-mahoe's vein. Fetid fluid spurted from the open lines. In panic, an epoxy priest fell to smother it with brine.

"It is over!" Soh'shoro shouted. "It must be over!" His body shuddered with exhaustion, as if the relic had drunk something more vital than mere fluid. His wounds seared. His head swelled. "I am spent."

Attendants tried to steady the prince. But unfamiliar with the ritual, he had given too much. And Soh'shoro swooned to the Mausoleum floor. Obajen-mahoe loomed over him, squeezing his hand. Even the Ang'soon princess knelt nearby, tensed with newfound worry.

"Are you all right?"

The prince nodded slowly.

"Then we leave this place," Obajen-mahoe declared. "Now."

Behind, the Emperor pulsed with new vitality. Epoxy priests bundled its lines and cables, as a great bifurcated sarcophagus descended from above. In moments an outer coffin swathed the Corpse, its halves sealing shut with a hideous hiss.

Without hesitation, Obajen-mahoe took Soh'shoro into his arms, carrying him from the dais. The Ang'soon princess swayed slowly behind. Soon the osmium doors ground closed. And the horrid fantasy of Death returned to its exclusion, amid its rotting spores.

On the lower floor of the Mausoleum, Obajen-mahoe left Soh'shoro alone beside the helix stairs, shouting angrily for a palanquin. In that distraction, the princess drifted close.

"Why did you help me?"

"What are you talking about?" The prince's head still swam. His thoughts came too slowly.

"You donated blood in defiance of your father. To spare me."

"Spare you from what?" Soh'shoro countered.

The princess's eyes, purple with rot, swelled alluringly. "If you want truth, earn it with your own. Why did you kill my brother?"

Soh'shoro remained silent.

"Why?"

"I didn't . . ." The ache in Soh'shoro's skull fountained down his spine.

"Don't lie to me. Why?"

"I didn't have a choice," he snapped.

The princess didn't even flinch at his admission of murder. Instead, she looked miserably up at the Mausoleum's heights and the Emperor beyond.

"But I do." Her thin lips tightened with acceptance. "I won't wait forever for my fate." She seemed about to say more. But then the palanquins arrived, swarming with attendants and pillowing silks. The Ang'soon's retinue crashed over them both like a tide, bearing her away.

"When you wake," she called gently, fighting down a cough.

Soh'shoro's wounded side throbbed unbearably. He needed the help of Obajen-mahoe and two courtiers to clamber into his own bower.

I didn't have a choice.

Soh'shoro mulled that thought over again and again as the palanquin fled the tomb. Because he could not escape the feeling of a terrible mistake, one somehow worse than An-go'yi'ki's murder. Nor the sense of dread in those final, furious cries of the Voice.

For though Obajen-mahoe tried to conceal it, still Soh'shoro glimpsed the unmistakable mark on his bloodied wrist: a thin seepage of rot.

CHAPTER EIGHT

MARRIAGE

Cold joy held Obajen-mahoe's features transfixed between nervousness and anticipation as he woke Soh'shoro the next morning. "Even in such times, there is always tradition," he offered cryptically, and strode off coughing.

Soh'shoro could make no sense of Obajen-mahoe's frantic, sleepless eyes until he rose to find ghost rice porridge and plum-skin cakes beside his bed. He stared at the meal for some time, unsure what to feel. He knew its significance:

Marriage.

"The courts will not let the Ang'soon wait without an heir," Obajen-mahoe explained over a second breakfast of clear soup. "Without An-go'yi'ki, the princess must bear a child."

As effortlessly as he skirted the implication, Soh'shoro understood it: The murder of the brother had earned him the bride.

"Who makes this marriage?" Soh'shoro asked hesitantly. "The epoxy priests?"

"The princess herself," Obajen-mahoe clarified. "I was summoned to the Ang'soon House at midnight for the news." His hands tremored, as he scratched at a silk bandage covering his wrist. "I could barely move, Soh'shoro. The courtiers carried me, the ritual sickness hurt so. But I would not wait." He coughed. "She's forgiven you."

"No, she has not."

"What do you mean?" Obajen-mahoe's elation abated slightly.

"She has a use for me." But the prince's head remained foggy from the transfusion. Everything swarmed with lethargic pain, and it was too difficult to wonder.

"You fear too much. This is about the courts, and tradition. The Ang'soon princess still protects the Valley. If this is not her forgiveness, it is her duty."

The Houses are the darkness.

But Soh'shoro smiled, hoping.

"Marriage also protects you, my son, from both courts and priests. Perhaps that guides her choice as well. With the ritual and now a wedding, any claim of murder—"

"Do I deserve this?" Soh'shoro interrupted, almost to himself.

"This is the Valley." Obajen-mahoe rested his hand against the prince's shoulder, shaking uncomfortably with the exertion. "We don't *deserve* anything. It merely is."

That evening the Quo'dai-ma House moved into marital seclusion. In the Valley, weddings were treated almost as a Rebirth, for the two were inextricably linked. So Soh'shoro found himself sequestered in spartan chambers deep within his House. Daily conveniences, from painted lanterns to grass bedding, were forbidden. Even his family ri'shou'an, recovered with his wounded body, was sealed first in its ossuary, and then within an elaborate storage box of scented clay. The prince could only smile as its golden seams and leaping cranes, alongside their dark reminders, vanished beneath marital seals. That night, atop hard rice-straw matting, Soh'shoro slept deeply.

Tradition forbade Obajen-mahoe from visiting now, so the

next morning, Kenwu's bright face awoke Soh'shoro, smiling eagerly.

"There was no one else," he said, beaming, "who knew the proper ways. Your ways. Like I do."

The prince hugged his old attendant. The world, it seemed, was righting.

Kenwu shepherded him through what seemed a new purification ritual every moment: salt baths upon awakening, offerings of threaded lilies before sleep. Each act blurred into another, until Soh'shoro lost himself to the monotony of rote obeisance. Peace claimed him.

So he ignored Obajen-mahoe's constant coughing, echoing throughout the House each night.

The marriage occurred barely a dozen days later. The Ang'soon princess came at dusk without attendants, beneath the osmium pavilion where they had first met after the Gi'en. She stood simply before him, draped in plain silks and lavender brocade. By now, Soh'shoro's vigor had returned. He reached out eagerly to take her hand.

But she pulled away with the ferocity of a trapped animal. "Do not think this is what it seems." Her whole body tremored, only more beautiful because it was soon to become unrestricted.

"I won't hurt you."

"Like you hurt my brother?" Her voice came high and thin. "Your mother understood, Soh'shoro. She was brave enough."

"What do you mean?" he pressed. "Whatever it is, let me help."

"Then marry me."

The pair kneeled on the podium, sharing gilded salt to mark the union. Soh'shoro watched her small tongue brush lithely against her mask, the thin hints of slender, lily-painted lips flickering behind the hard black lacquer. The curve of her white skin, the raven falls of her hair bound tightly with small purple ribbons; all of her flowed so delicately, so smoothly. And she was now his.

"The rite is finished," the princess concluded, swallowing the salt. "Our lives are joined."

Soh'shoro smiled. "I have so much to tell you. I know you don't trust me. But I also know that you do not understand me. You see something of Death, and nothing more."

She nodded.

"But there is good in me. I have tried to make sense of this world, and my role in it. I have only done . . ." He hesitated. "You asked for honesty. So I will tell you everything. How the Onan'ji stole me. How the Qu'su seek to . . ."

"Do you expect me to find sympathy in your story?" Her eyes flashed regally. "Do I look like a piteous thing to you?"

Soh'shoro's breath caught in his throat. "I am telling you that I care. That your brother's murder was an accident. That I tried . . ."

"Are you going to force yourself on me?"

"What?"

"We are married. There is a duty. So tell me: Are you going to force yourself on me?"

"No. Of course not."

In that moment, he remembered that strange Rebirthing crèche An-go'yi'ki had shown him. And its newborns, bound for the Qu'en Shards that would remake their minds.

"Then as far as I am concerned, our ritual is finished. We shared our salt. And you have declined your privilege."

She rose scornfully, more ethereally beautiful than Soh'shoro had ever seen her: a paradise undeserved. She opened a purple parasol, the last relic of her brother. Its bright color tremored weakly in her thin hands.

"Why even marry me then?" he shouted.

"Because it will be easier if you hate me," she replied both cryptically and tenderly, then left the pavilion unescorted.

Soh'shoro remained, wiping tears from his eyes. He had planned to tell her everything that night. Now he was alone, without uttering a word of it. He sought her forgiveness, or at least understanding. Instead he merely found the scent of her hair, just as he had as a child.

"I'm sorry."

But only the ghost of her memory remained, smoldering.

A rich bed had been prepared in the marital chamber, where Soh'shoro returned alone. If the courtiers judged, they did so only in the softest of whispers as they left him unattended. Even now he could hear the Ang'soon princess, isolated in her adjacent bridal suite, coughing softly. She was as close as the thin paper wall. And still an Eternity away.

So that night he dreamed feverishly of her rot, as rainstorms swept over the Palace. For at last he knew why he craved her. Of all the Valley, she lived closest to Death. She alone might truly accept him. And in turn, he might help her accept her sickened self. That fantasy played over and over again, as he chased her ghostly sufferings through sleep.

So it came as no surprise when a gentle strand played across his face, soft and slow. At first he thought it the princess's bejeweled hair, stoking his desires. *Has she changed her mind? Has she come for me?* But the figment smelled strangely of mountain smoke.

And suddenly Soh'shoro knew this was no fantasy.

He did not panic yet. His Qu'su training kept him still, even as the thin strand of silk slid across his cheek.

A burst of lightning came, and in that flash, he caught the figure above him, all in black, crouched atop the ceiling's wooden crossbeams. A silk cord dangled from the intruder's hands, a dark bottle pressed against it and tilted slightly. A ri'shou'an gleamed at his waist. The Voice whispered. Soh'shoro mastered his fear, shutting his eyes before the assassin noticed him awake.

The cord ran past his lips, slipping gently into his mouth. *Think*, Soh'shoro begged. *Think.* But anything he might use to defend himself lay secreted away as impurities forbidden during the wedding. Even his ri'shou'an remained sealed in clay. Perhaps the Qu'su had watched him all along, waiting until Soh'shoro's own passion left him virtually defenseless.

Think. The cord—the poison must be swallowed.

When the first drops of the liquid touched his lips, Soh'shoro recognized the smell: lily juice. The same sweetly sour mixture the epoxy priests blended with ink when tattooing the Traders. By the acrid stench, he could tell this tincture had been further concentrated. *To numb the mind*, he guessed. *To knock me unconscious.*

Soh'shoro had almost no time.

Calmly, he moved his tongue around the cord, forming a kind of cup inside his mouth. He felt the slow, irregular drops of lily poison blur into a consistent trickle, cool and herbal, pooling between his tongue and cheek. In the space between moments, he faked swallowing with tiny gulps of saliva. The stream stopped, and Soh'shoro waited. The cord withdrew slightly. He had expected the assassin to approach now, but he heard no sounds of motion above.

He intends to wait for the first signs of the drug's effect.

Soh'shoro knew what had to be done. And what did it matter who the intruder who waited in the rafters was? Either way it was one more life, his own or another's.

He pretended to toss, letting his hand rise to scratch his cheek where the cord disturbed it.

Breathe.

Everything happened at once. Soh'shoro pulled the silk strand as hard as he could, eyes snapping open to see the assassin lose balance on the beam. The form plummeted out of the darkness, blade whistling through the pitchy gloom. Soh'shoro rolled sideways. There was no sound when the assassin's feet hit the matting, but his ri'shou'an sang a thin note as it drove through reeds into wood. The figure spun, striking again. Soh'shoro fell backward to avoid it, spitting the poison violently across the assassin's face and eyes. Whether or not the liquid struck, it distracted the killer.

Soh'shoro charged the assassin, even as he screamed for help. His hand wrapped around the hilt of the killer's blade, the other driving coldly into the man's face. His opponent was quick, however, and even unbalanced, he slid beneath the blow, shouldering the prince away and freeing his ri'shou'an.

There was one clean cut, but, stumbling, the assassin swung his weapon far too high. In an instant, the Voice screamed its insight. And Soh'shoro listened, locking wrists and pulling his attacker down. Then came a soft sound, like a bucket of well water overflowing, as the assassin fell atop his own blade. Lightning broke once more, and Soh'shoro now saw his face.

Kenwu's eyes looked up in shock, lips frozen open in confusion.

"Actually . . ." his attendant forced out, almost smiling, "I'm glad you came back . . ."

In the horror of the moment, pulse pounding in his ears, Soh'shoro could offer nothing in return except disbelief. So he merely held Kenwu, as his old friend died in his arms.

The chamber door jerked open, so violently it bucked its ruts. "No!" Obajen-mahoe cried, rushing to the prince.

"I'm safe," Soh'shoro managed. But all he could think, looking down at Kenwu's body, was how hollow the words sounded against the endless drive of the rain.

CHAPTER NINE

REPRIEVE

Just before dawn, the downpour intensified. Huddled against a cracked screen, Soh'shoro watched the world blur into slanting veils of gray, until even the rain vanished behind waterfalls streaming from the House's eaves. Everything coursed to wakefulness with the force of the storm: Ceramic roof tiles rang out a muted pattering; distant chimes clanged discordantly with the howling of the wind. The world smelled of moisture and freshly tilled earth. And the prince imagined the Mists rolling in now, pouring over the Palace and its luminous nightly flames like a great and silent thunder, until nothing remained except an endless oblivion of choking white.

"I never thought the Qu'su could infiltrate our House." Obajen-mahoe's voice blended with the rain. "Not so close. Not so cruel." He glanced at the vial of Kenwu's poison, resting atop a ceremonial salt box. The pale liquid glinted ominously in the storm light. "The Valley has gone mad."

Soh'shoro shook his head. "Kenwu turned traitor long ago. He aided my abduction. Even planned my killing of the courtier, I think." But he recalled his attendant's gifted ri'shou'an, when Kenwu had smuggled him inside the Gi'en shrine. Then he thought of his choked smile as he died. "Do you think the Qu'su took him unwillingly?" he asked, almost to himself.

"I know of no other way," Obajen-mahoe replied.

Dawn peeked through the paper walls.

"The courts are in chaos, Soh'shoro. The nobility whispers, and the priests hunt. I've sealed our House for now. But I can only buy us so much time." He scratched at his bandaged wrist.

"Do they know what I am?"

"I am at the limits of what can be concealed. This was a tactic. The Qu'su know by being so blatant, they cause your ruin." Obajen-mahoe ran trembling fingers through his silver hair. "Already the courts fear you, and now there is too much evidence. What you did as a child. Your time among the monks. Your brother's killing and now this murder." Tears streamed down Obajen-mahoe's face. "One trial by the Voice, and your true nature will be plain. Then all will demand your sacrifice to the Qu'su."

"Even if the monks are the true cause of this madness?"

"Will they seem so? When you are the Death they guarded against all along?"

Soh'shoro tried to take Obajen-mahoe's quaking hands, but he pulled away. The prince looked back in confusion.

"You need to leave our House," Obajen-mahoe stated flatly. "If you stay, you die."

Soh'shoro recoiled. "You'd cast out your own son?"

"What choice do I have?"

"To understand, Father," he replied simply. "I don't want this power. I never wanted to . . ."

"I understand enough," Obajen-mahoe interjected. "I love you, no matter what you are. But worse than living without you is living with your death." His voice trailed off. "Even you cannot tempt the Qu'su forever. We need to smuggle you out of the Palace, Soh'shoro."

"No." The prince stared down at his golden stains, bare upon his flesh. "As long as the Onan'ji thinks I'm alive, he will still hunt." Soh'shoro scratched at the markings, as if to somehow erase their vicious beauty. But the blemishes remained clear and lustrous on his skin as lilies beneath the sun. "We claim I died tonight."

"What?"

"Kenwu's poison. That drug is concentrated lily juice. He meant to knock me unconscious, I think. Steal me from the Palace. But if I were to drink it now . . ."

Obajen-mahoe considered this. "Lilies numb the mind. You'd slumber, terribly deeply."

"Deeply enough that I could be mistaken for a Rebirth?"

Now Obajen-mahoe understood the prince's plan, his regal face vacillating between guilt and hope. "If the dose were strong enough. But this is a terrible risk, Soh'shoro. We can't know for certain what is in that vial . . ."

"What other choice do we have?" The prince remembered the Onan'ji's embrace beside An-go'yi'ki's corpse, and his final, mysterious praise: *You were magnificent.* "I think the Onan'ji prefers to keep me alive, as long as I might prove useful."

Obajen-mahoe's eyes teared. "While you slumbered, the Traders could bear you out of the Palace as a corpse. Vanish you into the Valley. If we were careful, their silence might protect the truth."

Soh'shoro watched Obajen-mahoe's hands, toying with his bandaged wrist. The dark seepage beneath appeared to be blossoming into something far worse: pustulating and heavy.

"I will never see you again. I can never return."

"Eternity is a long time, Soh'shoro." Obajen-mahoe hesitated. "But one day, perhaps. One day in all the endlessness before us—when the courts settle, when the Qu'su no longer hunt—one day . . ."

Soh'shoro interrupted. "What about the princess?"

Obajen-mahoe's face darkened. "The burden of the Gi'en is too much for a single ritualist. The Houses cannot survive with only myself as their scion. There must be heirs, Soh'shoro."

The prince's stomach tightened with the implication. And in an instant, he made his choice.

"She comes with me."

"Impossible."

"She's still in her bridal chamber, isn't she? Secluded since the killing. We claim she died alongside her husband."

"She won't go. She won't agree."

But Soh'shoro knew the truth. "Ask. She will."

"This is madness. You cannot leave me alone to the Gi'en."

"We will make an heir. But in secret. Return the child as our own Rebirth. It is our best chance at restarting the Ang'soon line."

"And what does your bride know of life outside the Palace walls?" Obajen-mahoe shook his head. "It's not safe for her. Not with how she rots. Here rituals control it. But beyond the courts . . ." His voice trailed off. "She doesn't deserve that suffering."

But Soh'shoro craved his princess and her decaying beauty smothered beneath reams of silk. Her mask seemed so transparent then, as though Soh'shoro already knew what lay beneath it, as certain and immutable as a facade of stone.

"She is my bride, Father," Soh'shoro insisted.

Obajen-mahoe looked steadily into his eyes. "We risk everything, Soh'shoro. If this plan—"

"Ask," he repeated. "You will see."

The lord of the Quo'dai-ma nodded, relenting. "We waste no more time then." And he carefully pocketed Kenwu's poison vial before shuffling toward the princess's chambers.

Alone, Soh'shoro marveled a final time at the majesty of his stolen birthright: coruscating halls, smoking salt, iridized charms. But instead of opulence, Soh'shoro found himself focused on his mother's ri'shou'an, still sealed within its clay storage box for marriage. Even now the blade seemed to call to him, like a vow unfinished. And too soon he heard Obajen-mahoe's coughing again, echoing sharply through the House as he returned.

"You were right," he whispered, locking the sliding screen behind him. "She didn't even hesitate. But . . ."

"But what?"

"The priests are at our gates. We are out of time. She already took the poison."

Soh'shoro smiled thinly. "Then I must too."

Obajen-mahoe handed him Kenwu's half-emptied vial. "Are you certain?"

"It's too late for anything else."

Obajen-mahoe tousled Soh'shoro's hair gently, fighting back tears. "I just . . ." He fought down a cough. "I love you. No matter what you are. Or what you become."

"I love you too," Soh'shoro replied, drinking deeply.

Now his eyes glazed as the poison began its work. His mind swam with the Voice, as if the flower juice absorbed that ghostly essence from the Misty snowmelts on which they fed. Thoughts not his own expanded his consciousness. Soh'shoro tried to lie down, instead knocking over a low table and balling clumsily atop the reed floor.

"Easy," Obajen-mahoe begged, untangling the prince's numbing limbs. "Let me help."

But the Voice cried louder and louder, as though from beyond an unlocked door.

"I see her," Soh'shoro muttered. "She's trying to show me. To prove I'm not wrong."

Obajen-mahoe cried. But now Soh'shoro felt nothing, watching those tears as he might a snowfall. Each droplet blurred into the next, becoming part of a numbing chain of effortless passivity. Recollections poured incoherently, burning ever brighter, as the poison tightened its grip. His eyes settled again on his mother's ri'shou'an. And somehow that blade became the one in her memories.

But in these the sword had not yet broken, nor been recast with gold. Instead, its perfectly silvered edge reflected her sallow face, narrow and regal. Her pitch hair flowed long as a summer's day. Calico eyes, brilliant as fireworks, mirrored an eerily open sky.

This was the original Soh'shoro. His mother. He saw her so clearly he could only become her, the memory claiming him completely.

"You're certain it's buried here?" she asked. "Beneath the waves?"

"Yes," another speaker's voice hissed mechanically, as it was forced through its metal mask. "Thousands of fragments scatter these shores. But the Black only builds atop the grandest. Making ready for the rest of their fleet. We don't know how long we have."

Both sets of eyes narrowed: Soh'shoro's own and his mother's, their bodies blending in the shared remembrance. Before them spanned that vast infinity of water, too impossibly enormous to contemplate, stretching to the very stars. Atop its waves rocked a rafted city of banded iron and wind-worn wood, towering over the surf.

But his mother focused on something underneath the whitecapped currents. A metal monolith, sunken terribly deep beneath them, still pulsing thin light through its cold glass. A relic Soh'shoro knew.

A Qu'en Shard.

This isn't inside the Valley, Soh'shoro realized. *No place like this exists here*. And then came the terrible realization: *This memory is from Outside.*

But the lily drug burned impossibly bright. The next moments of his mother's memory fell away into a glorious blur of shared emotion. His mind glassed, then blotted.

And so Soh'shoro left his nobility behind.

He remembered little of what followed. Colors skewed to ash. Ribbons of memory flickered. His fingers flexed and unflexed, and Soh'shoro realized he was holding a hand. Hazy memories of the journey came: the Valley, the climb into its walls, the aching cold of the dark, the vanishing silhouettes of the Traders.

Soh'shoro opened his eyes to find his bride beside him. Her petal-white hand clasped his own. Her mask loomed vast and haunting, its melanized purple ever more stunning against her silent form. Outside, light crept through half-patched walls.

"Do you know why I am holding your hand?"

"No." Soh'shoro smiled weakly.

"Because I want you to know my affection. Just once. So every day after this that I deny it, it will hurt more. Until you understand exactly what you will never have." And she spat on Soh'shoro's face. In his delirium, her saliva tasted sweet with leaded lipstick. "I let myself be stolen. But I will not let myself forgive."

She dropped his hand, then left through the single door of the hut they now shared. Yet Soh'shoro wondered how much of the princess's cruelty was mere facade. After all, she was here with him now.

That first night, his old wounds ached terribly. Unable to sleep from the pain, Soh'shoro gazed up at the stars of the eastern Valley, watery and dilute through their shrouding Mists. He dreamed himself among them: a simple point of light, entirely separate, endlessly waiting, watching over a world creeping inexorably from paradise. He tried to imagine rising beyond them, breaking free from the boundaries of the earth. But that was only a dream.

This was all he had.

As Soh'shoro rested under the hut's rotting eaves, his mother's ri'shou'an waited beside him, a fresh bamboo hanging cord threaded through its ossuary. A final gift from Obajen-mahoe, he thought, to protect him. But staring at the smothered blade, he felt not safety but guilt. For he was still running, even here. He would never be free, so long as Yei'an's choked promise, An-go'yi'ki's last gasp, and Kenwu's fading smile haunted him.

But then he smelled the grass of the former princess's pillow, lingering with the damp and the cold.

The pair had planned to live in isolation, but it became clear they would never be completely alone, even high in the Valley's walls. Nearby farmers, tending ghost rice among the hills often blanketed by Mists, passed daily. Soon Soh'shoro found himself caught in their world. Most mornings, he planted gifted crops or foraged beside them for wild berries. In the afternoons, he learned to patch his meager hut, until it could withstand even the strongest storms. And with night he brewed barley tea and wandered as he had with the Onan'ji, venturing higher and higher toward the Mists. He would stare into the morass of those gray veils, searching for his mother beyond. But there was almost no Voice here. And Soh'shoro knew why.

He felt almost at peace.

"Why did you steal me?" the former princess asked one night, when Soh'shoro returned from the mountain peaks.

"Why did you agree to come?" he countered, throwing off his cloak and kneeling by the fire. "You hate me so. Why marry me?"

Her phage-stained eyes settled on him like curious crows behind her mask. Soh'shoro had still never seen her full face. Even here, in the mountains of the east, she kept her rituals of concealment.

"You knew when you asked. Because I am in pain."

Soh'shoro poured barley tea from the kettle, rolling the clay cup in his hands against the night's cold. "You hide it well."

"I have had Eternity to perfect my suffering." She folded and unfolded her long, reedy hands. "It fascinates you, doesn't it?"

"I understand it." The prince paused. "You're the only one in this Valley that shares something with me. A burden."

She softened. "Perhaps that much is true."

"Why do you rot?" Soh'shoro asked directly, just as he had when he was a child. "I thought there was no sickness in the Valley."

"It is not sickness." She smiled faintly.

"But there must be a cure." He shook his head thoughtlessly, misunderstanding. "Something in the Valley that could heal it."

"I have already endured an Eternity, Soh'shoro," the princess replied. "You think if there were something to ease my pain, I would not have already found it?"

"Then what about Outside?"

The magnitude of his suggestion saturated the patched hut like the heat of a newly kindled fire.

"You don't know of what you speak."

"Something is out there, princess." Soh'shoro hesitated. "Something calls me."

"You sound like your mother." She tightened her mask.

"Did she dream of Outside?"

"And more." The princess splayed her hands. "Obsessing over strange sciences, and the secrets of the Qu'su's eldest lore. If you hadn't . . ." Suddenly her whole form tightened, as a spasm passed through her like snowmelt swelling a river. "I can't." Tears ran black from the corners of her rotting eyes. "I need help."

Soh'shoro took her arm, guiding her to the small straw bed that they had never shared. She seemed scared by the need for his touch, but also accepting. He gently raised the thin grass blanket over her shivering form.

"What you did to my brother . . ." she began weakly, her breathing easing a little now. "I believe the monks twisted you. Hurt you. But I still think you had a choice."

"Maybe," Soh'shoro replied honestly. "I don't know if there could have been another way . . ." His voice trailed off. "I was told I was hunting a traitor who meant to harm the Valley. I didn't know the truth until it was too late." He swallowed. "I'm sorry."

"But you always have a choice," she insisted ominously. Still Soh'shoro's words comforted her. The princess smiled very slightly, stifling a cough. "I do see good in you sometimes. Kindness. But you also have another part." Yei'an flashed across her face, a ghost painted on another's flesh. "A horrible part, willing to hurt."

"You think I enjoy killing?"

"I think it is your nature." Her voice gentled. "And all things are true to their nature with time."

"You sound like the Onan'ji." Soh'shoro recoiled.

"No. I sound like *her*."

The real Soh'shoro. Rather than repel him, that sinister familiarity sparked strange comfort. The princess's rotting eyes, the soft contortions of her body beneath the tightened blankets, suddenly sped Soh'shoro's breathing. She fell into a shallow slumber. Her perfumed hair smelled of saffron and maple and grass.

Until her death, she would make her own perfume.

Many days passed in idle silence, until the next time her

illness struck. Now Soh'shoro found the princess lying on her back, drooling blood. Her chest arched and her hands shivered as if plucking invisible strings. Without thinking Soh'shoro dropped the firewood he carried and ran to hold her.

He forced her head back, pressing his own fingers into her mouth, shielding her tongue from each spasm. And he stroked her hair, again and again, through the horrors of the fit. But he never took off her mask, even when he thought it would help steady her breathing.

Afterward, she lay with her head in his lap, eyes swimming to consciousness.

"The rot grows worse outside the court," she whispered. "Inside my brain."

"There are lilies for the pain . . ."

"They make it worse. The phage feeds on them." Each half-whispered syllable slurred.

"Cold tea then," he whispered. "Wash away the blood."

"Not yet." She hesitated. "I need salt, Soh'shoro. The salt settles it."

But they had long ago run through the meager, gifted cubes of their Rebirthing bower.

So the next morning Soh'shoro risked traveling to the nearest hamlet. There, he traded what he could of his funeral finery for some of the villagers' bland, unrefined stocks. The grains were too rough to take alone, but bitterly soothing in brine tea. And with the dregs of each kettle, he made tinctures for his princess, which she massaged into the spreading roots of her affliction. The imitated comforts of the court eased her. For a time, she smiled.

Seasons changed. Soh'shoro returned frequently to the hamlet to barter more grains. Soon he found himself helping its peasants drain the rice terraces that snaked like a Trader's tattoos across the hills. Together they carved sluices from the rock walls, feeding waterfalls of raging white when the Valley fell to storm. Returning to his princess those nights, they would watch the cascades blur into the evening stars. Neither mentioned the sunken gardens they recalled beneath the Mausoleum.

"I should like to see them up close," she whispered.

So together they visited winter's first festival, and its floating lanterns and painted ice. The Ang'soon princess marveled at the sculptures, worked whole from the great faces of the loftiest cairns and carved with the skill of Eternity. She held his hand.

But that night proved too much. The rot crept deeper. Soh'shoro carried her all evening through the hills, until the morning grew heavy, and at last they reached their meager hut.

"You used to make me so unhappy," she whispered.

Soh'shoro could only smile. He helped her to bed, bound her in heavy blankets and old silks. Here the pair took brine tea together to ease her suffering, looking over the sweeping tranquility of dawn. Mists roiled. Thrushes sang. Snowflakes drifted. The whole world nested into the cold.

"It's getting worse," she said. "My phage."

"Tell me how to help."

"Just wait." She shivered. "Until there's nothing else. Until I know it is too late."

"Too late for what?"

But she held her silence.

"Do you want to die?" he asked directly. "Like you asked when I was a child? That's why you agreed to come, isn't it? So I might take your life, and you could find freedom from your pain?"

"Yes." She leaned forward, lips gleaming through the thin mouth slit of her mask with the last of her smuggled court dyes. "But that's why you took me, isn't it? To change my mind." Her lacquered visage slipped.

"It's not so terrible, being here with me, is it?"

"No."

And without hesitating, Soh'shoro pulled aside her mask.

In that moment, he gazed on the full ruin of her face. Pitted and rotten, the purpling strains streaking her eyes and gums, brilliant as fireworks. His thumb stroked them, fixated on their variegation. He wanted to lick his fingers.

"Careful," she whispered. "It's dangerous. If it gets in the blood . . ."

But still she leaned forward, kissing him. And Soh'shoro ran his hands across the strains of phage peeking from her sloping neck. He pulled away her upper robe, revealing veins deep and rich and blue as they scoured bare breasts, seeping into the hollows of her spine.

He held her so tightly then, it felt as if she might break. She grasped him back, kissing deeply. He pushed her down, carefully keeping the blankets beneath her. And they shuddered against each other. Through it all, Soh'shoro marveled at the black taint that scarred her body, like a vicious festival paint.

"I never let anyone see it."

He kissed her stomach, her breasts, her neck, following the corruption until he reached her shoulder blades, thick and refulgent. The stains called to him, a splinter of Death's true potential.

When it was done, they lay beside each other gently, breathing soft and shallow. He squeezed her hand.

"Ask," she teased softly.

"You already know my question," he replied gently. "You always do."

"And I will answer." Her pitted eyes darkened. "If you promise. When it hurts too much. When the change is ready. You will end it."

"We won't let that happen."

"But if it does . . ."

Soh'shoro nodded slowly. At that simple gesture, a terrible burden seemed to lift from the princess. Her body slackened. She nestled closer to his chest.

"I'll tell you exactly what your mother told me of the Valley," the princess began, blackened eyes refulgent in the dawn. "Or the nearest I can remember."

Soh'shoro remained quiet, torn between the comfort of her body and the anticipation of her words.

"There was a War," the princess continued. "One the Qu'en could not win because it was a War they must never fight. Because its time must never come . . ."

"I don't understand."

"Just listen. Much doesn't make sense to me either. But it's what she told me. And I don't remember more myself. Because my Rebirths are not like the rest."

Soh'shoro nodded, falling silent.

"The Qu'en's arts could shape the very forces of this world. They mastered mechanisms and manufactured relics, like the Emperor's Throne and the Valley's Shards. They rendered nature's abstractions concrete, and manacled them to their flesh. But their greatest art was of time itself. Contorting distances and abstracting relations." She swallowed. "It was not just Death they fought, Soh'shoro. But Death's grandsire. The creeping no-place at time's end, worshipped by the worst of their kind. So to escape it, they abandoned everything. Even themselves." Her voice darkened terribly. "Even us. We were students left behind. So we had no choice."

"No choice but what?"

She shuddered. "To live on the crumbs of their grandeur. To use what little was left: their secrets; their science; their bodies. Your mother claimed many sought to purge them. Because the

Qu'en were so alien no goodness could ever come from their arts. But here in the Valley, we ignored those warnings. We decided to endure." She coughed airily. "The priests pray for an Emperor that took pity on us. That sacrificed himself for our Eternity. But nothing could be further from the truth. We chained our Qu'en. To steal our sorcery from its flesh."

"You're talking about the Mists. The blood and the salt."

She nodded. "As long as some dim semblance of life flickers in the Emperor's Corpse, the Mausoleum's relic still functions. Not as it did in the grandeur of the Qu'en's kingdom. But as a fading shadow, powerful enough to shield some small pocket of our world. Our Valley."

"Why the Houses' blood?"

"This even I know. Because it matches. We make certain of that with breeding."

"And why salt? Why seal Outside if those grains are so valuable?"

"Because we were hunted, Soh'shoro. Outsiders sought to smother our dream. To wash away the Qu'en's legacy like rain against a pond." Her face darkened. "So we chained the Valley quickly and out of desperation. We did not fully understand the limits of our new world."

"And the rest of the Qu'en?" Soh'shoro asked. "The Emperor's Corpse is one. But you spoke of more?"

She laughed, high and haughty.

"Even your mother wouldn't tell me all she knew here." She clasped his hand, squeezing gently. "What little she divulged was this: Their kind was truly Eternal. Completely and apocalyptically enduring. And because of this they sought escape. Some beyond the seas. Some to the stars. Some even turning against time itself. And all, in their own way, failed." A quizzical look played across her pitch-scarred face. "The Valley's Qu'en is the last. We don't know what it wanted—or wants. Only that it found its answer—and its prison—in the Mists."

"There must be records of all this. Ways to understand."

"You sound so much like her." Her gaze swept the snowy morning. "But it's like we wanted to forget. It is all gone, Soh'shoro. Any record. Any writing. We burned it from not only memory but our very world. Because the things we did to the Qu'en were wrong," the princess finished forcefully. "Because we knew the burden of the Valley's birth must not follow us into Eternity."

Dawn's light streamed amber and gold. The thrushes' song deepened. Soh'shoro squeezed his princess tightly. Her breathing slowed. And though he wanted to ask more, her beauteous rot and waning warmth lulled him.

Together they slept.

But after that morning, her coughing grew worse and worse. Now even when Soh'shoro held her, as stars bled into midnight, the fits would not end. In those dark moments, he stared at her bloodstained mask with twisted fascination, hoping. They tried stronger tea, and brine baths, and even a makeshift brazier to mimic the salt smoke of the courts. But still her shoulder muscles fattened full and taut, her spine bending fishlike.

"This is the change," she whispered one night, looking at him from beneath her mask. "It's almost time."

"I love you," Soh'shoro whispered.

They had had so few seasons together, so few memories. All of Eternity had once yawned before them, but now they had only this long, and terribly too soon.

"I wish there was more." She forced a smile. "I am happy here, Soh'shoro. In a way." Tears brightened her phage-sick eyes. "You did change my mind."

The next morning brought fever, high enough that Soh'shoro

grew hot from her touch. He held his beauty beneath her blankets of grass, then stoked the fire as high as he dared. He started making desperate plans to return to the courts, and to seek the guidance of its epoxy priests. He packed what little belongings they had, dreaming of being anywhere but here. Where he knew what would happen.

There is no Death in the Valley.

But now her breathing softened to short rasps, like the sound of blossoms falling against water.

"Take the mask." Her words slurred so badly they could barely be understood. And she gripped its lacquer until it cracked, splitting from jaw to eye slit, like a vicious, severing scar. "Remember your promise. It's time."

He clasped her hand, stroking her blackened cheeks and neck. The phage worked like an animal building its den, burrowing deeper, bruising bone to its very marrow. Swelling her spine.

You are a stain, he thought guiltily. *A stain on everything that makes this Valley pure.*

"I can't," he whispered. "I love you."

"Fool," she teased, her voice recapturing some of its haughty, courtly nature. "I told you it would be harder if you cared for me."

Her eyes wandered to the ri'shou'an, its ossuary bright with leaping cranes.

"Do it."

Soh'shoro shook his head.

"Do it!" she commanded, her voice firm as when they first met. "Please, Soh'shoro. It's what I want. I'm ready now."

Elsewhere came the low creaking sound of wood beams; the sharp, rhythmic pattering of hail against thin walls; the sputtering of their sunken hearth. But Soh'shoro could only hear her gasp as the blade slid sharply across her throat. She cried out softly one final time, almost in surprise—

"It won't hurt anymore."

Blood painted her neck like firelight flickering over freshly fallen snow.

Then it was over. Once again, Soh'shoro held only a corpse in his arms.

Afterward, he lay beside her in the bed they had shared and cried, until even the spreading cold of her form seemed the greatest warmth he could clutch to his chest. She had asked for this. She had found her relief.

And still Soh'shoro could not forgive himself for what he had done.

The ghost of the princess haunted him. She would never again sip brine tea. Never again hold him close. Never again spit at him or loathe him, as she had done at first. Misery wormed its way through Soh'shoro's veins as surely as a Qu'su poison.

In that moment, he realized his power of Death meant more than murder. His very existence let oblivion seep in, spreading misery to all that he loved. The Houses could not possibly be the darkness, as the Onan'ji had warned.

He was.

"You were right," Soh'shoro confessed to her corpse. "I cannot deny my nature. I will always bring ruin to our world." His tears splashed across phage-scarred skin, running in rivulets of darkness. "But that is why I can also save it."

Calmly now, Soh'shoro's mind wandered to the City and its courts, to the Emperor and his Throne of Mists, and last of all to the Onan'ji. It was too late for his princess. And in a way, it was too late for Soh'shoro. The prince of the Quo'dai-ma was now lost, blurred away like ink left to storm. His innocence had been stolen with his childhood; his nobility had died beneath his blade. And his happiness had vanished into these hills.

He piled cedar wood against the hut walls, splitting logs

until his body ached with exertion. He set about cleaning, putting away one last time the daily things he'd shared with his bride—the teacups and the salt stocks, the homespun clothing and perfumed brushes. He smiled as he worked, eyes stinging from the tears that kept the world from focus.

Soh'shoro wrapped her in old silks, coarse and worn. He did not paint her face or bind her hands with lilies. Instead, he blanketed her with a simple veil of grass. Even in death, she seemed ethereally beautiful, merely another glimmering manifestation of her morbid perfection. He gently kissed her one last time.

"I will be Eternity's Blade," he promised.

He sent word down to the nearby hamlet. By evening a mendicant returned, asking of Rebirth. Soh'shoro lied until the man agreed to bear the princess's body to the Traders. He wanted to follow her corpse, but part of him could not bear to see those blue tattoos touch her.

So Soh'shoro merely watched his bride's pall vanish into the softness of the sleeting night. Still, she remained forever in the walls of their house, a lingering phantom of the life they had made.

"I'm going now," he whispered.

The flame caught the thin walls effortlessly, and soon the hut blazed into the snowy night. It burned like a shooting star, as though the heavens themselves sparked alight by kissing earth. Clutching the cracked mask of his rotted princess to his chest, Soh'shoro walked away without looking back.

And so Death descended upon the Valley at last.

CHAPTER TEN

HUSK

He made for the temple where the Qu'su had trained him. The trip was hard in winter. A terrible blizzard raged, as if the Valley itself mourned the death of his princess, leaving heavy snows and blocked trails. Lightning broke constantly, its winking fury dancing over Mists that roiled deep into the Valley. Their veils stretched so far now they sometimes kissed the basin itself, white on white, snowy lilies vanishing beneath. He had only too much time to think, trudging through lonely roads, as he crept ever higher toward the moldering demons of the hills.

The night he reached the Qu'su temple broke calm, the air crisp with the first hints of spring. Soh'shoro stood before the winding stairs that led to the prison of his childhood, remembering a life unmade. Now the stone steps were slick with ice, and the untended arches had been splintered by storm, littering the ascent with fragments of wood and shattered bells half buried in snow. Soh'shoro could not help but smile.

The main compound was all but abandoned. Most of the structures lay in complete disarray, and some had even collapsed under the weight of the seasons, snowflakes spilling in through torn walls and cracked eaves. Soh'shoro had known he would find as much before his journey began. Fearful of reprisal, the Qu'su had vanished after his escape, leaving only skeletons to hunt.

"Soon, Onan'ji," he whispered.

The main shrine appeared maintained, and thin firelight spilled through its papered walls. Nonetheless Soh'shoro approached without caution. Kicking open the door, he startled two junior Qu'su from prayer, their eyes wide and uncomprehending. These acolytes were all that remained of the mad monks who had trained him.

"Don't." Soh'shoro raised his hand in warning, but one had already moved for a ri'shou'an. "I am not here for violence."

"The assassin!" the other shouted. "The Onan'ji's shadow!"

The acolyte with the blade rushed him, slashing. Soh'shoro blurred with the Voice. And in one swift motion he disarmed the monk, forced his sword arm against the joint, and flipped him against the temple floor. Expertly, Soh'shoro reversed his blade.

"Don't," he warned again, pointing the ri'shou'an at the other monk. Neither moved. "I don't want to kill you," he continued. "But these floors will wash crimson if I leave unanswered."

Both acolytes remained silent.

"I have come for the Onan'ji," Soh'shoro sneered. "And you will tell me where he is."

"We don't know!" the disarmed monk protested. "Even if we did, he would . . ."

"What?" Soh'shoro snapped. "What could he do to you that I cannot? I bring Death. Does he?"

Still there was no reply. In calculated fury, Soh'shoro twisted the fallen monk's arm until he heard splintering bone.

"What do the Qu'su know?" he shouted over the monk's screaming. "Where is he?"

"We were only left to tend the shrine," the unwounded acolyte explained. "How would we . . ."

Soh'shoro twisted the arm the other way, and the small bones of the hand popped like heated rice. One broke the skin, flecking the floor with blood.

"I will ask one more time . . ."

"Please . . ." the wounded monk interrupted, choking out the word. "Please . . ."

Soh'shoro kneeled beside him. "Yes?" When he did not reply, Soh'shoro splintered the man's forearm until it fully broke flesh, the glistening marrow like dark pebbles seen through a stream.

"The priests!" the wounded monk screamed. "He met priests!"

After that the details came freely, though the acolytes knew little more than what they had overheard. The meeting Soh'shoro remembered between the Onan'ji and the Traders had expanded. The monk had even frequented the epoxy priests before shuttering this temple. To Soh'shoro, it made sense: The Traders reached Outside and into the Mausoleum. They would be the perfect ally to the Onan'ji's schemes.

"I don't care what you do now," Soh'shoro spat as he turned to leave. "But if you want to live, wait here until I kill the assassin outside."

The unwounded monk looked up from tending his fellow. "What are you talking about? What assassin?"

"The Onan'ji didn't tell you?" Soh'shoro smiled cruelly. "You were bait." And silently he slipped out into the cold.

In the seasons with his bride, Soh'shoro's dark talents had atrophied. Now his mother's ri'shou'an felt rough and unfamiliar against his palm. The thrill of coming violence made his heart beat too fast and his gait too eager. So Soh'shoro had no doubt that the assassin chosen by the Onan'ji to stalk this temple on the chance he returned could best him in the arts of Death.

But Soh'shoro knew too how he had changed. How the

Ang'soon princess's rotted eyes and leaded lips had burned away all but a terrible, hungry sorrow within him. For this reason alone, it would be the assassin's blood that stained the late snows beneath the waxing moon.

On the temple stairs, there came a thin whistling sound. But the Voice had warned Soh'shoro long before the throwing needle ever left the assassin's hand. Effortlessly he sidestepped, letting the shurishi bury itself in the arch behind him. Without looking he knew its tip was stained dark with poison. A second came, and Soh'shoro rolled away, five more striking the snow. Even before he finished tumbling, he coiled his legs to spring skyward. As the assassin leaped from frost-bowed branches, moonlight glinting off his open blade, Soh'shoro dashed up the arch, catching two steps against its split timbers before throwing his back behind him and vaulting his knee into the man's stomach. He felt the assassin's ribs break, the surging pain letting Soh'shoro lock his sword arm. As the pair smashed into the ice atop the temple stairs, Soh'shoro shifted his weight onto the joint and snapped the limb lifeless, rolling away. He had not even needed to use a blade.

"Is he in the City?" Soh'shoro threatened, looking down on the crippled assassin. "With the Traders? Tell me and I will let you live."

When the monk nodded in reply, Soh'shoro kicked in his throat and left the man to suffocate in the smothering cold of the night.

He reached the City, crossing the very bridge where the Onan'ji had stolen him all those years ago. Now its icy waters lay bare except for ghost rice cast by travelers seeking fortune. Already the spring's fresh crop of lilies blossomed, ready to choke the rivers, pure white and glorious. Atop distant hills, the Gi'en shrines descended for the coming festival.

And the Mists followed.

Soh'shoro rented a cheap room in the pleasure quarters for anonymity. That night he gazed across the vibrant colors of this world, tangerine and vermilion and cinnabar, smoldering with stitched silks. Over rice wine alone, he stared into the cracked mask of his princess. Twice he was approached by courtesans. And each time he turned away their leaded lips, he felt both kinship and sympathy. For their sad lives, too, were a part of the Valley.

With afternoon he departed for the Trading District. By now the roads were crowded with the final preparations for the Gi'en. Day laborers pulled overstuffed carts while merchants and craftsman bartered before shop fronts. A few wealthy courtiers, secreted beneath vermilion parasols, meandered in the pale-yellow silks of the Palace. Soh'shoro hid from their gaze beneath his own tattered shawl. Among the laborers and mendicants, at least, he belonged.

Ahead the City's bustle quieted. Its bright colors dulled to brasses and grays, and its wood and paper walls turned to bronzed brick and reed thatching. Soon the Trading District's great ceramic salt houses honeycombed the streets with dappled copper. And the massive, alabastrine rectory of the epoxy priests gleamed overhead. It would be here, Soh'shoro guessed, that he would recover the Onan'ji's trail.

He slipped between the rectory's beaten-copper gates, left ajar in ceremonial welcome. Dozens of bleached dormitories edged the inner courtyard, capped by bronze domes flaring in the daylight like magnificent, angry suns. Water sang from glass piping, taking on a distorted, sallow hue where it caught the refracted light. Traders bustled constantly, the tops of their sun-bleached robes half open, exposing their fierce circular and straight tattoos like wild eyes.

Soh'shoro strode for the main hall, its sequenced doors worn smooth and mirrorlike by years of passage. From beyond, the insectoid hum of epoxy dirges resonated, accompanied by wiry instruments of bur-reed. A small priest stood at attention, blocking Soh'shoro's entrance, eyes staring intensely from beneath his inky scars.

"Who? Only Traders here. Who?" he hissed. "Why have you come? Why?"

"I have been sent," Soh'shoro bluffed.

"Who? Who sent you?"

"You know."

"No. No."

"Call an elder if you must," Soh'shoro insisted.

The priest furrowed his brow, considering.

"Wait inside, yes?" The priest then stepped aside, letting Soh'shoro through the tan doors.

Within sprawled a massive circular chamber, strewn with great ivory columns and colorless hanging beads. Pallid reliefs curled on the walls, and bleached tableaux littered the floor. Other than the bronze dome above, there was no color save alabaster. Traders dotted the chamber, face down against the cold stone, praying silently before a marble likeness of the Emperor's twisted mechanical catafalque. The smell of incense, sweet and buttery, floated in the air.

Soh'shoro followed the priest to a tiny alcove, filled with dull cloth mats arrayed before a series of burnished copper bowls. Each was heaped with long-cold soups, dyed bright, unusual colors, like weedy crimson or deep ocher, the heavy scents of spice and honey wafting from them. Along the walls water ran in shallow depressions that reminded Soh'shoro of ant tunnels.

"Eat," his guide suggested. "Be pure. Our food makes pure while waiting. Yes?" He pointed ecstatically at the hospitality ritual, exclaiming, "Blessed, blessed!" Then he wandered out of the room without saying more.

Soh'shoro sipped at the soups in silence as he waited for the priest to return. The food, though frigid, tasted strangely complex. He was still eating when the music of the bur-reeds stopped, and his guide reappeared with an elder.

"Who sent you?" the new priest asked, his phrasing slightly more natural. "Why have you come? Be quick."

But Soh'shoro already glimpsed recognition in the elder's eyes. This was his chance. "Must I speak the name aloud?"

Silence.

"The Onan'ji."

Soh'shoro still hoped to be wrong—that the elder would shake his head in confusion, casting him from the rectory with dismissive courtesies. Instead, the man's tattooed eyes flashed.

"No message. He sent no . . ."

But Soh'shoro knew his mentor well. Without pausing, he stripped off his sleeve, displaying his veinless scars: the marks of a Qu'su.

"Do you still doubt my purpose?"

The elder shook his head with alarming fervor. "No. No." Then he quickly added, "We are almost ready. As commanded . . ."

Ready for what?

"You will show me your work, immediately."

The elder bowed meekly. "Of course." He turned to his compatriot, eyes narrowing strangely. "Leave us. And make sure none follow, understand?"

Returning to the domed chamber, the elder parted a silken shutter, revealing a narrow stairwell lit by candlelight. A sweetly pungent scent, like earth after rain, rose from below.

"Deep place now. Yes? Very deep," the elder muttered, leading him into the darkness. "No one comes. Because of the husks."

Their steps fell away in muted paces. In narrow alcoves lining their descent, hidden by thin curtains, Soh'shoro heard shallow breathing and airy mutterings. Once or twice motion flittered behind the shades, lethargic and broken. *This is where the priests keep those whose minds are eaten by the Mists.*

The Voice stirred to their catatonic mumblings. Soh'shoro's steps quickened with fear. He smelled burning flesh.

"Here," his guide cautioned. "Watch step. Here."

Ahead the stairs terminated in a towering double door. The priest unlocked it fearfully, spilling alkali-soured air as the portal's iron hinges grated slowly open.

Beyond loomed a vast natural cave. A peculiar variety of lily, rooted to the ceiling and faintly bioluminescent, created a hanging jungle of cerulean stars. Bathed by their radiance, shrunken shapes toiled mindlessly at inscrutable tasks, weaving strange wires or joining scraps of steel. Their bare hands had been charred black by the heat of blue-burning welding fires, or scraped raw by the endless repetitions of their fugue-like labors.

"These are husks?" Soh'shoro asked.

The priest nodded. "Good for something. Their minds are so swollen by the Mists that, with enough lilies, they slip into the deep past." He paused. "They remember the machine."

Soh'shoro flinched at the Old Word, even as he intuited its meaning.

"You mean the Emperor's Throne? That's what they're making, isn't it?"

For the husks appeared to be building a bulbous ball of steel and silver, suspended by narrow wires amid the distant gloom. Soh'shoro had glimpsed its form before in the Mausoleum: the pulsating dome above the Emperor. The priest's artifact appeared to be its missing portion, designed to repair the Throne's damage. Already the orb reflected the hanging lilies' light with terrible potency, humming deeply and hideously, as if singing to its silent servants.

"He's rebuilding it, isn't he?" Soh'shoro asked. "The Onan'ji is fixing the Emperor's Throne."

"Of course." The elder arched an eyebrow at Soh'shoro's ignorance.

For a brief moment, the prince wondered if his mentor had not lied. If the Onan'ji truly was trying to save the Valley.

But why strike at its Houses? Why cause such Death?

"Where do these fragments come from?" Soh'shoro asked.

Once more the priest looked askance, now deeply skeptical. "Outside. Traders smuggle them in their own flesh."

Soh'shoro remembered the Traders arriving at the Qu'su temple. Now the horrific harvest he had watched the Onan'ji reap from tattooed flesh made sense. How many years had the broken fragments of this artifact passed into the Valley, sliver by sliver? Safe beneath skin.

But why?

"How long before the Throne is repaired?"

"Soon." The elder priest beamed. "The Corpse will die at this very Gi'en festival. When its blooding does not come." He paused. "We must all be ready then. For the Onan'ji's ascension."

Soh'shoro barely stifled a gasp. *The monk plans to usurp the Valley. To install himself as its new Emperor, atop a reforged Throne.* To what end, the prince could not guess.

But it did not matter. He must stop him.

When its blooding does not come. The priest's words echoed fearfully through Soh'shoro's mind. For only one ritualist remained to feed the Emperor's Corpse. *My father,* Soh'shoro realized. *He is in danger. I have to warn him.*

Without so much as another word to the priest, Soh'shoro raced to the cavern stair. The elder called after him. But the prince sprinted heedlessly now, bursting through the alabaster hall, the bronzed courtyard, the copper gates; out into the fading sun of the Traders' stony streets.

He knew only panic and fear.

He was almost out of time.

For the City resounded with fanfare and raucous shouting. Already drums beat out their metered welcome, beckoning the shrines toward the Palace's salted glory. The Gi'en festival blossomed once more.

And within that beauty lurked the Onan'ji's long-planned darkness.

CHAPTER ELEVEN

VENGEANCE

The Qu'su watched.

As soon as Soh'shoro fled the Trading District, he caught their twin shadows following. *Did the Onan'ji plan this too?* Had the priests' openness merely been another baited trap, like the acolytes left at the Qu'su temple? Buying time for the Traders to warn the monks?

Soh'shoro made quickly for more crowded streets, trying to vanish amid their costumed chaos. He weaved between ethereal rainbows and tinted awnings, even cutting directly through a parade of half-clothed dancers. Still the ghosts persisted, hunting.

Violence remained his only choice.

Soh'shoro took a lonely detour down a disused alley, pretending to drink from its public font. In moments he caught shadows in the sunset, atop nearby eaves. The Voice sparked.

Two steps up the wall Soh'shoro mantled onto the roof, bringing his legs round in a wide sweep, tripping the first Qu'su. The man was quick, pivoting his weight midair and shoulder rolling away. Soh'shoro caught him as he rose, locking his blade at the hilt with one hand while the other struck him hard in the face. As the assassin staggered back, Soh'shoro drew the man's ri'shou'an against his flesh, splitting his side wide open. Blood raced off the eaves, pouring into the fading dusk.

The second assassin towered over Soh'shoro, using his greater reach to lunge deceptively. But the prince spun his ri'shou'an to the Voice's keening, catching the slash and throwing all his weight against it, knocking his opponent's blade wide. The Qu'su leaped soundlessly away, hurling three shurishi to create space, but Soh'shoro dodged the needles with quick tilts of his head. He hurled his blade in response, its razored edge reflecting the sunset.

Perhaps the Qu'su might have dodged in time. But he seemed to hesitate for a precious instant—as if he wanted to be struck—allowing Soh'shoro's blade to bury itself into his throat. The assassin tumbled flat to the eaves, gasping.

"I would never lead your kind to my father," Soh'shoro menaced, as he silenced the assassin's helpless breaths. "Never."

And leaving the bodies where they lay, Soh'shoro left to find Obajen-mahoe.

He joined the Gi'en procession with nightfall, just outside the Imperial gates. The deepest crowds choked these streets, furious and seething, casting gifts of ghost rice and folded lilies. Shrines danced atop the Traders as they slithered through the morass, their jangling bells and lacquered finery floating over the revelers like lily petals on a current. Above, a thin moon hung coldly luminous, peeking through the sky's Mists. The chants and the shouts; the streams of many-hued ribbons; the snap of fireworks being tested for their midnight displays—never before had the City seemed so vibrant, coming alive with impossible alacrity and terrible eagerness.

Soon the Palace gates swung open, revealing the half-remembered world of silks and incense beyond. One by one, the Gi'en shrines began processing inside, toward inner courtyards of silvery brilliance, leaving their swarming celebrants behind. Soh'shoro tried to follow, but an honor guard blocked him, shaking his head coldly.

"No commoners in the Palace. Your festival is outside."

"You don't recognize me?" Soh'shoro threw back his shawl. "I am the prince of the Quo'dai-ma. Soh'shoro."

And the guard laughed heartily, offering a swig of his rice wine in recognition of the joke.

"The lost prince himself! A taste to your honor!"

But Soh'shoro merely turned away, slinking back into the crowds. He no longer belonged to that world.

And it was then he caught the face, veinless and haunting.

The Onan'ji.

Soh'shoro lost the monk a moment later to swarming revelers. His hand fell to his mother's blade, and every sense lit up as he stalked the crowd, searching. A silver slash flashed by him in a rush of ringing bells. Sharpness flicked his flesh with trailing ribbons. Someone struck him hard in accidental revelry. Everywhere Soh'shoro glimpsed Death as he hunted the Onan'ji.

At last he caught sight of him again, his darkness looming atop the Palace's massive outer walls, clear and black against the skyline. The figure paused for a second, as if checking the passage of the shrines, hands flaring like polished stones. Then the Onan'ji leaped into the Palace beyond.

Soh'shoro knew he had to follow.

Tonight, he would confront the Onan'ji at last. He would protect both his House and Obajen-mahoe. He would reveal the Qu'su's full treachery.

There was no other choice.

The Palace's walls loomed impossibly high, their heartwood inlay and baked plaster too smooth to climb. So Soh'shoro turned to the shrines. The anchors of their single-file procession still danced before the Imperial gates. Their cavernous bulks loomed like mountains, soaring above the bruised backs of their mute carriers.

And Soh'shoro saw his chance.

As an enormous shrine drifted close to the walls, he vaulted from the crowd, snatching the monument's lip and mantling atop its wooden gables. Two steps later, he flew free again, briefly silhouetted against the midnight sweep of stars. Then his feet slammed against baked clay, scrabbling upward until his hands snatched ceramic eaves. Soh'shoro flipped atop the Imperial wall, vanishing from the gasps of disbelieving revelers below.

The Palace sprawled before Soh'shoro in three gated rings: first the epoxy temples, second the courtly compounds broken by expansive gardens, and last the soaring glamour of the House pagodas and the Emperor's Mausoleum itself. The shrines wormed their way through it all, in an endlessly winding procession, making for that final heart. There Obajen-mahoe would perform his ritual. There Soh'shoro must follow.

The prince sprinted low and lithe, his peasant sandals catching awkwardly against the wall's decorative slats as he leaped into the outer courtyard. His hands snatched cherrywood, swinging him atop the nearest roof. And so he vaulted again and again, crossing eaves like a great bird soaring on the winds. Beneath, the chants of epoxy priests rose, sickly as the cloying scents of their boiling sealants and baking salts. A light rain began to fall.

A gatehouse drew near, and Soh'shoro chanced leaping. The jump was wider than a mountain river, so he barely caught its sloping latticework with a single outstretched hand. Soh'shoro swung into the shadows, just as a guard turned toward the sound of his landing. He fell icily still, holding his breath, until the sentry moved on. Then Soh'shoro rolled down the gatehouse incline, dropping into the Palace's second ring and its courtly compounds.

Here manicured gardens divided every building, elaborate and beaming in the rainbow haze of festival light. Courtiers lined the covered walkways to watch the coming fireworks, packed so closely they looked like unfurled bolts of brocade. Others lounged atop thick blankets in the gardens, their attendants struggling to raise canvas tents against the intensifying rain.

Soh'shoro slithered invisibly through the paulownia boughs, making his way through the gardens. But the sculpted greenery grew thin and naked, and only rarely could he vanish into old growth. In the glaring light of the colored lanterns, everything cast shadows, but nothing lay in darkness. He moved mainly by timing and instinct, winding his way through open spaces with practiced rapidity and calculated abandon. Once he passed within a hand's breadth of two guards swapping stories against a stone idol. If either had turned, Soh'shoro did not know what he would have done.

He drew close to the courtly dormitories now, rising in sweeps of dark wood and mesh screens. Beneath their covered walks, Soh'shoro noticed an unlit lantern. He made toward its welcoming gloom.

A paper screen slid wide.

But the Voice had already warned him, quickening his instincts. As the guard turned, Soh'shoro took two steps up a roofing pillar, jackknifing his body into the walkway's upper ribbing. Spidered overhead, he watched the sentry pass directly beneath him. The man paused before the dead lantern, struggling to spark tinder in the rain. Eventually he gave up trying, muttering in frustration before continuing his rounds. Soh'shoro slithered back down onto the walk. It took him only moments to find the unlatched door the guard had come from and slip inside. His last view of the courtyard came from the corner of his eye: terns seeking shelter beneath a rain-soaked miniature maple.

In a way, this was a coming-of-age. From his childhood, Soh'shoro knew the internal windings of the court dormitories, their tangled corridors and half-lit antechambers drowning in silks and beads. Now among them again, he plied the very talents for which he had been stolen. For anyone else, the maze of paper walls and reed partitions would be impossibly confusing. But Soh'shoro had learned so much among the Qu'su, and now his craft consumed him with the unbridled joy of a power set free, of a wolf among lambs.

Soh'shoro blurred between shadows and drapes, timing his motions with the snapping of the first fireworks. One by one the passageways fell away, buried in miasmas of salt leaking from endless braziers overstocked for the Gi'en. Even the pleasures of his youth had turned against him now, and Soh'shoro's eyes grew irritated and raw at the stench. He moved through the gossamer labyrinth, deeper and deeper, alien to his lost nobility.

Soh'shoro's sharp ears caught copper bells and jangling chimes. The Gi'en procession was close. He clambered out a nearby window, joining the jittering shrines before the final gatehouse. As they processed beneath its barbican, Soh'shoro raced above, suspended and invisible atop the great strings of lanterns lighting the way to the Emperor's tomb.

Inside the Palace's final ring, the metallic riot of the Mausoleum soared with lustrous gold and nacre in the moonlight. Here too rose the House pagodas, spanning their waiting salt vats in sweeps of shimmering pulchritude. This was the home of Man, simultaneously perilous and sad. Its glory was chained by form: bound to shaped stone and worked steel, enfleshed by sculpted wood and tempered leafing. Nothing could free it beyond flame; nothing could equal it save its lily-garden reflection and the strange pods of the icy waterfalls beneath.

Soh'shoro leaped from the lantern string, vanishing into

the upper boughs of a sculpted pine. From here, he scanned the abandoned Ang'soon pagoda and its pitch-black balconies. Gormless attendants wandered that darkness in pantomimed service to dead scions. Turning, Soh'shoro found his own House's spire still bright and blaring. A figure stirred behind a bier screen at its peak.

With an unsteady hand, what must be Obajen-mahoe cast a welcoming fistful of ceremonial lilies into the pouring night. But something was terribly wrong. His fingers were pocked and bloodied, their joints heavy and swollen like oversoaked rice. He could discern little more, for the rest of Obajen-mahoe lay secreted behind carefully placed silken screens. Still, Soh'shoro noticed horrific, trembling coughs racking his silhouette.

Even at this distance, Soh'shoro recognized the sickness. *The princess's rot.* His mind thrummed with guilt. *Our ritual infected him when we blooded the Emperor together.*

The shrines danced furiously, clanging copper bells and osmium charms. Each wooden frame shivered and swooped, grinding cruel weight against its bearer's flesh. Saline fumes fanned the ruddy lantern light. All the world seemed oblivious to Obajen-mahoe's suffering.

"Please," Soh'shoro begged. "Hold on. I am coming."

The bronze drumming intensified. The shrines danced with disharmonic fury. And Soh'shoro leaped from his perch, skipping across two more sweeping branches of sculpted greenery before scrabbling onto the lowest eaves of the Quo'dai-ma pagoda. As he rolled flat against its roof, the downpour turned furious.

He climbed toward the pagoda's peak. It was slow, dangerous work. To ascend, he had to kick off a lower wall, reverse his hands, and catch the lip of the story above him. His fingers constantly clawed for purchase in the deluge. Often, he would freeze in shadow, as attendants ghosted past shades still open to the storm. Beneath, the Mausoleum's ponds glimmered sapphire and crimson in the festival light.

Then, as he leaped for the highest story, his hands slipped against the wet tiles. He gasped, a terrible stifled sound, free-falling back into the night. But the Voice held him fast, quickening his purpose, stoking him to motion like fire in his veins. Soh'shoro's ri'shou'an sang out, biting deeply into ceramic and wood. His weapon shuddered hard as the full force of his fall caught against it, wedging in the timber. But the blade did not pull free. Soh'shoro hung still, listening. Between the beating of the drums and the snap of the fireworks, he doubted anyone had heard his fall.

Leaving his ri'shou'an speared into the wall, he balanced his feet atop it before catching the eaves overhead. Then he pulled his blade free with his other hand, mantling up. Here he caught his breath against the drive of the rain. Then he clambered through an open window, into the Quo'dai-ma sanctum beyond.

And the Voice screamed with unbridled fury, as before him loomed the Onan'ji.

CHAPTER TWELVE

DEATH

The monk lurked on the other side of a heavy screen, his spectral outline unmistakably angular and lithe. One hand extended above the shade's edge, veinless fingers brandishing a naked blade. The Onan'ji prepared to strike something distended and alien beneath him, a bloated figure of hissing darkness. Soh'shoro knew he had mere seconds to act, before either the monk noticed him or his strike fell.

And the prince didn't hesitate then. All the hate he felt for the monster who had stolen, tortured, and twisted him sped his draw, blind vengeance quickening steel like lightning from storm. His blade cleaved through the screen in a bright arc of justice, its golden seams singing out the joyous fury of ending his mentor's evil so easily.

But only now did Soh'shoro realize why the Voice still cried. It was not to speed his stroke but to warn him.

For the Onan'ji had merely been waiting.

The monk moved now, in an effortless blur of streaking shadows, his silhouette shrinking beyond the screen too late for Soh'shoro to reverse his strike. The prince's golden blade bit soft flesh, then softer bone. The shade sheared apart moments later, cleaved in two. And Soh'shoro looked down on the distended figure he had cut.

Obajen-mahoe lay sprawled atop plush matting, blood spewing from his split neck. Black spores leaked alongside the gore, pooling into fatty rivulets of hungry phage. His dying body was riven with rot, swelling his shuddering rib cage, crusting his quivering skin, choking his last breaths. One hand dangled over a windowsill, still clutching lilies for the Gi'en's blessing. Its phage-stained fingers shuddered open now, casting those final petals pathetically over the revelry below.

"Father!" Soh'shoro dashed toward him, for one instant forgetting the danger of the Onan'ji. Obajen-mahoe's fading eyes brightened at the sight of him. Then they flashed in warning to the waiting shadows, and the danger lurking there.

Again, the Voice screamed. It shrieked like never before, until Soh'shoro's vision swam black, and his eyes teared with pain. It burned his skull, choked his ears, drowned his thoughts. Its pleas, cold and miasmic, bled past everything until the world shuddered beneath its inchoate misery. He had no choice but to listen. He moved just in time.

And the Onan'ji's shurishi buried itself in the wooden window frame with a hideous, swelling thud.

"I trained you well." The monk smiled, slipping from the shadows. "I thought this would have ended simply. But the Voice truly quickens you."

"You led me here. You tricked me into killing him." Guilt racked Soh'shoro, his gaze darting back to Obajen-mahoe's dying form. It shuddered a final time, eyes dimming until lifeless, black blood still spurting from its severed neck. One last word escaped the lord of the Quo'dai-ma's lips:

"Run."

But the prince merely raised his blade.

"If it gives you any solace, the rot would have claimed him eventually." The Onan'ji smiled. "The spores on the Corpse are fetid with Death. You ended his suffering. Like you ended your princess's."

Soh'shoro's blood ran cold, even as tears for Obajen-mahoe streamed down his face.

"I always knew where you cowered in the eastern hills. I let you escape. I even watched those final nights as you spooned brine tea to your sick bride." The Onan'ji's voice hovered on each word, as if licking them.

"You could not have known," Soh'shoro gasped in disbelief. "You would have come for me then . . ."

"Why?" The question hung for a moment. "Why, when I knew what would happen when you took your frail bride far from the safety of her courts? When your pity finally bested your love? You are of Death, Soh'shoro. I need only wait for your purposes to become my own."

The Onan'ji's dispassion cut more deeply than a sword.

"How could you? I loved her."

"Just like you loved this corpse?" The Onan'ji gestured cruelly to Obajen-mahoe's broken form. "I have loved too. But still I must teach." His veinless fingers danced against each other like light on water. "Demonstrate that desire itself is a trap. You would not obey the Qu'su by choice. Nor by force. So I found another way. There are always other ways." The edges of the Onan'ji's mouth rose impossibly high, as if his very jaw unhinged with joy. "I chose to command the murder of An-go'yi'ki. But for your bride, I selected love. And for Obajen-mahoe, the blindness of vengeance."

"Why?" Soh'shoro sneered. "Why end the Emperor and the Houses? Why are they so terrible?"

"I've told you so many times, if you'd only listen." The

Onan'ji laughed, like water crashing over rocks. "They are jailers, prince. Nothing more. Jailers of our true Eternity."

"This is madness." Soh'shoro shook his head in disbelief. "All I see is Death, and the lives you have taken."

"Have I taken them?" the Onan'ji questioned. "The Qu'su are bound by the Valley as surely as any man. Except you." The Onan'ji's grin grew wider still, until even his veinless eyes vanished beneath folds of grimacing skin. "You killed them all, Soh'shoro. You are the final stain. For all your choices, you have only been led. You are a puppet, nothing more, just as much as anyone in this Valley."

The cracked mask of his bride felt terribly heavy against Soh'shoro, begging to be put down.

"Not if I kill you," Soh'shoro threatened. "Not if I end this here."

The Onan'ji advanced, awful efficiency in his gait, robes flaring in the candlelight like fish scales beneath stars. "You couldn't." The Onan'ji laughed again. "You are barely stronger than when I trained you. You know anger and fury. But such emotions are mere distractions. A real killer is hollow, Soh'shoro. Empty like me, to everything except his purpose."

The Onan'ji's smile somehow widened further, seeming to split his whole head with vicious appetency. But tears joined it, streaming down his face in voiceless sorrow. "You are the last of the Houses. When you die, no blood remains to sustain our Emperor. The priests care not what flesh fuels his Throne. Only that it feeds." His voice fell to barely more than a whisper. "Soon I will feast."

They stood separated by little more than a sword's length.

"Your death gives all the others meaning, Soh'shoro. Even your mother's."

Did he kill her?

"I will avenge them."

Soh'shoro stepped forward, drawing himself into a wide stance, one hand clasping his ri'shou'an's ringed hilt, the other balancing its cold, blunt spine. He gazed steadily into the perseverative calm of his mentor's veinless eyes.

And the Onan'ji's voice was ice. "Show me."

In the instant it took for Soh'shoro to strike, the monk had already closed the distance between them. The Qu'su's motions were like dry foliage catching flame in the summer heat, sparking to life from nothingness, full of sudden and insatiable hunger. Shadows scattered beneath the blade's reflected light, as the Onan'ji flickered beneath the cut. The Voice called. Soh'shoro quickened. But still the monk's elbow caught Soh'shoro in the stomach, cracking two ribs and slamming him back. The prince staggered over a calligraphy table, but the Qu'su kept pressing. Again he listened to the Voice. And again the Onan'ji weaved past his counterslash, driving a palm into Soh'shoro's face, stepping his knee into his stomach, then sweeping him cleanly to the ground. As Soh'shoro fell, the dense iron weight of the Onan'ji's adiabatic touch ached through his expertly fractured bones.

What is wrong with the Voice? Why isn't it working against him?

Soh'shoro rolled as he hit the floor, but the Onan'ji ghosted with him. He kicked Soh'shoro in the face as he rose, snapping his jaw and scattering blood against the paper screens. Soh'shoro slashed again, this time reversing the blade at the last instant. And the Onan'ji's own ri'shou'an answered, flaring from its sheath with such practiced fury the cut seemed one unbroken arc. The swords sparked against each other. Then Soh'shoro slammed his free hand against the blunt edge of his blade, throwing the Onan'ji's guard wide. But the Qu'su let himself be disarmed, weaving close even as his ri'shou'an spiraled across the chamber to clatter beside Obajen-mahoe's distended corpse. Overbalanced, Soh'shoro could not counter before the Onan'ji caught the hilt of his own blade and forced it aside, slamming his free hand into Soh'shoro's face. In three quick motions the Onan'ji disarmed Soh'shoro, snapped his wrist, and drove his own fingers, tensed like darts, deep between Soh'shoro's ribs. As the prince collapsed backward, the Onan'ji flew after him. The monk's right hand twisted into a talon, dripping crimson where it had torn into his flesh. With his left hand, he grasped Soh'shoro's blade, which glistened beside his veinless skin like a stream-borne minnow. And the Qu'su drove the golden ri'shou'an toward Soh'shoro's chest.

Again the Voice cried.

Again Soh'shoro listened, sidestepping. But the monk merely turned the lunge into a shoulder, pushing the prince off balance. Suddenly the Onan'ji leaped, his knee driving into Soh'shoro's chin, his free hand smashing into the side of his neck, using the force of his jump to twist him off balance and hurl him sideways against the chamber's wall. Soh'shoro smashed against the hardwood, cracking a support beam and snapping its rich latticework before collapsing to the ground.

The Voice is useless against him, Soh'shoro realized at last. For the monk had truly mastered the arts of the Qu'su. He could anticipate its very cries. *He can't hear it speak to me. But he predicts its warnings nonetheless.*

There was no space between the attacks. In the next instant, the Onan'ji flipped Soh'shoro's ancestral blade and hurled it like a spear, chasing headlong after it. Unable to roll away, in desperation Soh'shoro at last ignored the Voice, throwing his forearm up instead to block the cutting edge of the sword. The ri'shou'an sliced through his arm, dividing the flesh like a stone sinking into water. But somehow Soh'shoro knocked the weapon away. And in the last instant he snatched its hilt, catching the ri'shou'an reversed and slashing out defensively.

The Onan'ji had not anticipated this swiftness. He stumbled for a second, caught by the very tip of Soh'shoro's sword. A thin stream of blood sprayed. The prince saw his chance. Through the pain he lunged, lancing the sword with both hands to support his shattered wrist. But the Qu'su had already mastered himself, his motions blurring too fluid and erratic for Soh'shoro to follow. A backstep from the Onan'ji became a dash, and suddenly he rolled toward Obajen-mahoe's fetid corpse. Now the monk snatched up his own fallen ri'shou'an, spiraling back toward Soh'shoro in a wild skein of flaying blades.

Through reflex alone he parried, a single crisp note resounding in the candlelight. In the same motion the Onan'ji locked their swords, surging like a flood, twisting both guards wide. Soh'shoro stepped back just in time, as the Onan'ji's cut scratched a razor's line against his neck.

He stumbled into the wall, snapping a calligraphy brush in two and spilling ink across the reed matting. With no ground to give now, the Onan'ji was inside his guard in moments, lunging. For one terrible instant their blades clashed, spitting sparks into the dimness of the candlelight, knife-edge metal shrieking into the silence. But expertly the Onan'ji leaned into the block, overextending Soh'shoro's elbow, then driving palm backward into bone. Soh'shoro's arm snapped like a pine bough beneath winter snow.

In the next instant the Qu'su drove his ri'shou'an through Soh'shoro's chest. The weapon slicked past collarbone and sinew, burying itself up to the hilt in flesh. The force threw Soh'shoro off his feet, cracking his body against the weakened wall. Warmth unfurled inside him like a blossoming lily. And as the Onan'ji surged his full weight forward, Soh'shoro burst through the chamber and onto the rain-soaked eaves outside.

The fireworks echoed brilliantly against the hastening dark. Even with the downpour they still exploded, amethyst and ruby, emerald and lazuli, against the uncountable stars gleaming behind Mist and storm. It was like the whole night sky of the Valley had come alive with a thousand new possibilities, frantic and fantastic, more radiant and stunning than any earthly luminosity. Beneath their rolling thunder, the wash of the City, still glowing and majestic, heedlessly watched the heavens for its joy.

And Soh'shoro smashed onto the ceramic eaves, skidding against the roof's edge. He vomited blood, coughing again and again as a bright heat filled his lungs. His vision swam between reality and emptiness, as if the Mists closed about him. When his eyes focused through the pain, he saw the cracked mask of his princess beneath him, its lacquer now crimson with blood washing clean in the rain.

"Get up."

The Onan'ji came slowly through the broken wall, like a spider on the strands of its web. Instinct made Soh'shoro try to move, but his wounds were too deep and only shivers greeted his efforts at motion.

"Get up," the Onan'ji repeated. He advanced, calmly and leisurely, flicking his blade like a cat's tail.

Soh'shoro breathed through the pain. Slowly, his hand reached down for the mask. But all he managed was to dash more blood against the hardness of its lacquer.

"I'm sorry," he slurred.

"Get up," the Onan'ji repeated one last time. "I will not kill my apprentice without paying him his final lesson."

Soh'shoro heard the Voice again, through the fireworks, like a prisoner crying through walls of stone. It was as if the whole of the Valley shouted with its terror. And Soh'shoro rose one final time, using his ri'shou'an as a crutch.

"Let's end it." Blood dribbled from his mouth with the words.

"You don't understand," the Onan'ji marveled. "There is no end, Soh'shoro. Not here. Not in the Valley." Sorrow crept into the corners of the Qu'su's mouth and eyes. "That is the price; the secret prison of Eternity. For Death is a kind of escape, Soh'shoro, from our memories, from our desires and our regrets. Death alone absolves us of our past. And there is no Death here."

"What is this madness?" Soh'shoro choked out.

The Onan'ji raised his blade in answer.

The pair circled. Tiles threatened to shear loose in the storm, and with each step they fought for balance. Soh'shoro feigned tripping, baiting the Onan'ji to lunge, then whipped his blade from behind him in a cunning trap. But pain and injury slowed his slash. Effortlessly, the Onan'ji slid underneath the cut.

Both blades snapped back, striking dull sparks into the hush of the rain. Soh'shoro's splintered bones slid against sinew, his muscles giving out. Unable to parry, he lost ground before the Qu'su's slash, feet slipping precariously at the roof's edge. Foolishly and reflexively, he let the Voice steady his balance. And Soh'shoro threw himself beneath the Onan'ji's next strike, cross-stepping into a final slash.

But the Onan'ji was waiting. Expertly the monk's palm slapped the flat of the prince's blade, guiding it harmlessly away. With Soh'shoro's side completely exposed, the Qu'su's ri'shou'an tore through his torso, spilling blood into the festival rains. For an instant, Soh'shoro felt only washing heat, bursting like steam from an overheated kettle. Then he collapsed onto the roof, beside the mask of his bride.

"I'm sorry," he gasped again, his fingers scratching anemically against the lacquer wood.

The Onan'ji looked on in disgust.

"Do you understand? What the Qu'en always knew? That time's truth is what I must teach?" The Onan'ji then bent beside the dying prince. "We can live forever, Soh'shoro, but we are never free from ourselves. True Eternity is tainted with regret. Because true Eternity must not be endured alone. All I do is seek to change that. For myself. And for you."

With all his strength, Soh'shoro looked into the eyes of his former master. The Onan'ji's veinless orbs glared back, burning with hideous sadness.

And Soh'shoro smiled, because he noticed the deep gash running down the Qu'su's face, streaming milky blood from a clouding eye. One of his cuts had severed cleanly through the Onan'ji's orb. The Qu'su was half blind.

"Almost," Soh'shoro choked.

"I know. I told you that you were magnificent."

Gently, the Onan'ji closed his hand over Soh'shoro's face, raising him high over the edge of the Palace eaves. Nobles and onlookers shouted through the fireworks now, gesturing up from the courtyard at their duel's climactic end.

"A clean cut, I think, is easiest for the priests to stitch," the Onan'ji snarled. "And when they find your body here, they will know it as the traitor who murdered the Houses. It will be the Qu'su who protected the Valley from your madness. And then I will be all that is left in this world to trust. Soon, Soh'shoro. Soon I will taste the purest lily of all."

More voices, more shouts, but the prince's dying mind blurred all sound together. Then one last time the Onan'ji pulled his disciple close, speaking for only him to hear.

"We'll meet again soon," he whispered reverently.

With one clean stroke the monk slit Soh'shoro's throat. The prince felt those final moments almost forever, suspended in free fall, choking blood, staring back into the monk's single, sorrowful eye. Then Soh'shoro's corpse thudded wetly against the eaves, completely still.

Above, the fireworks continued, furious and beautiful, blotting out the stars.

PART III

THE OCEAN OF THE CLOUD

CHAPTER THIRTEEN

AWAKENING

"Dry the hollow," someone said. "The powder has to take."

"Wet or not, it will work," another voice replied. "The old ones always do."

"Not in rain," warned the first. "Even Old-Make struggles to spark in rain."

Soh'shoro felt droplets against his face, body numb except for the dull cold of the storm.

"Water," he choked at last. "I need water."

There was shuffling near him. Then the feeling of a figure close. A bowl pressed against his lips, and a thin trickle ran past the taste of iron and lilies that clotted his mouth. In the back of Soh'shoro's throat, blood clots flaked away, exposing angry rawness beneath.

"He's waking," the first voice called. "I may need extra hands." Then drawing close, speaking only to him now: "Not too much. It will start to hurt soon."

As if on cue, Soh'shoro started coughing. It was like wet snow pressed into his lungs, leaking out a slow, teasing ache. Hands worked steadily in answer, unwinding lily cloth from around his neck and chest to let muscles stretch. His eyes rolled open, straining to focus, but only pale washes of color answered.

"I know your voice," he forced out. But mucus loosened, and he vomited. The rich taste of dried blood gummed his senses.

"Easy," soothed the familiar voice, rolling him sideways. "Waking is always painful, and you did not die peacefully." He felt the speaker's hands tremor slightly as they wiped his lips. "I died the same way."

"What do you mean?" Panic crept at the edges of his mind. But he spoke too quickly, and another coughing fit seized him.

From a distance another voice called back:

"We don't have much time."

"We can't move him now," the familiar voice replied.

"Just get him up, Yei'an."

He knew the name. And with it he smelled winter bur and honey.

"Is it you, Yei'an?" He asked the question slowly, making each syllable clear. "From the temple?"

"Yes."

And suddenly everything came back: the Valley; his House; his betrayals. And the Onan'ji's blade, snicking through his throat.

Soh'shoro jerked away from the remembered cut, but his weakened muscles only spasmed in response. In moments he twisted himself against his funeral bindings, starting to choke.

"Be still!" Yei'an shouted.

Still Soh'shoro fought his bandages. He could feel the ri'shou'an slicing through his neck, all thought overcome by a primal need to escape its inevitable cold. But tangled by bindings, he merely thrashed until his chest heaved mightily for air.

"He'll kill me!" he forced out, voice like shale loosening. "He'll kill me!"

With a final surge of strength his hand broke free, tearing bandages as it groped for the flesh of his neck. But the Onan'ji's blade was gone, replaced by the roughness of epoxy and fresh, angry scar tissue.

"Easy. It happened. But it's over now."

And Soh'shoro gasped disbelief into the muddy damp.

Yei'an worked with the confidence of routine. After freeing the last of his funeral wraps, letting ice-sharp air kiss his skin, she massaged his arms and thighs, forcing thickness from flesh and blood to move once more. Soh'shoro's eyes focused at last, adjusting to the twilight of the rainstorm.

Framed by a black willow cloak pulled tight against the downpour, Yei'an's bronze face loomed above him like a mouse peeking from its hollow. Her soft nose and full cheeks, her wide eyes and thin mouth; she was all the same monk Soh'shoro had loved and killed in the Qu'su temple, another life ago.

"I'm sorry."

"We all panic when waking," replied Yei'an, misunderstanding. "But there is danger, Soh'shoro. We need to run."

He dug his hands into the tar beside his funeral bower, struggling upright. "Why? Where are we?"

But he already knew. Somehow Soh'shoro felt it with a certainty beyond anything before:

Outside.

"In a mountain pass," Yei'an whispered reverently. "Beyond the Valley. Beyond the Mists."

Soh'shoro craned his head, looking up now at their cloying veils, cinereal and hungry. They churned crueler than they had in the Valley, gray and perilous, blotting the snowy slopes above.

"I need to go back," Soh'shoro declared. "I have to stop the Onan'ji."

"How, prince?" Yei'an asked. "We passed through the Mists with Death, but that is a one-way journey. There is no return. Trust me, others have tried." Soh'shoro recalled the charred courtier before the Emperor's Corpse. "We have only Outside now. Look."

Yei'an pointed down the mountain. And for the first time, Soh'shoro stared across his new world:

Past the rocky descent, great sweeps of amaranthine sand ran almost as far as the eye could see. Yellow-leafed glades and pale, opalescent rivers pocked these dunes to verdant life. Occasionally fires illuminated shadowy walls, sparking ginger and violet in the rain. *Villages,* Soh'shoro realized. *People live Outside.* And judging from the frequency of the lights, far more than in the Valley.

The largest settlement lay beyond the sands, atop what Soh'shoro thought must be a great pond. But those dark waters stretched forever, vanishing into the horizon. Great silver waves sparkled across its surface like earthly stars. *From my mother's memories.*

"That city is called the Haven," Yei'an explained. "And the waters beyond it are the Ocean. Stunning, isn't it? I remember my first time seeing all this too." She smiled. "And look further! Look up!"

And he did. But no Mists darkened the skies over Outside. Instead, no matter where Soh'shoro stared, naked heavens unfurled miraculously free, virginal and burning with the ruddy cut of the tempestuous dawn. The most brilliant clouds swam through that ether, storm cast and slate cored overhead, silvered and honey bright in the distance, tangling into countless mutable, morphing shapes. Their billowing majesty stretched to the limitless horizon, converging with the waves into a single kiss of rainbowed brilliance.

"It's beautiful," Soh'shoro gasped.

"And dangerous," Yei'an replied, suddenly darkening. "Outside is not like the Valley, Soh'shoro. Violence comes from here."

Her eyes darted past Soh'shoro's funeral bower, to the edges of its trail. Bloody corpses lay haphazardly scattered beside it, azure tattoos glistening in the stilling rain.

"Those are Traders. They died . . . ?" Soh'shoro asked in confusion. "How?"

"My men defeated them. Both the Traders and the Cultists escorting them." She swallowed. "Everyone can kill here. Death belongs Outside."

Soh'shoro's eyes swept farther down the trail. The men who had shouted at Yei'an massed there, all wearing the same onyx cloaks. But unlike the monk, their skin matched the tarry earth: a rich, dark tone like ghost rice seared for festival cakes. Scars and small cuts storied their cheeks and hands. One had lost an arm; another's face was swathed by bandages. And still Soh'shoro saw subtler marks of violence, in the way the Outsiders' guilty eyes mirrored his own.

They are like me, Soh'shoro realized, as if waking from a dream. *The Outsiders share my stain*. And he felt terrible revulsion at his own abhorrence cast over an entire world.

"We have to get him up!" one of the men snapped. "The Cult of the Lily-Eaters just crossed the lower ridge. They'll flank us if we don't move now."

Farther down the mountain, dozens of ill-defined shapes picked their way unsteadily up the slope. Each wore saffron robes, recalling a poorly spun imitation of courtiers' cloth. Most carried strange pouches overstuffed with flowers. At first Soh'shoro doubted the contents. But even at this distance, the pale, acerbic white of lily petals could not be mistaken.

"By the Black!" Yei'an snapped, now shouting to her men. "We'll take them as they climb. Form firing lines!"

She helped Soh'shoro limp to cover, into the shadows of a rocky ridge. A heavy rod, wrapped in cloth and slung across her back, kept jarring his side as they walked.

"Where did you get this?" he asked, struggling to remember the Old Word. He had seen this tool before. It was identical to the foreign weapon brought into the Mausoleum, beside the burned courtier. "This is for War."

"This *is* War," Yei'an stressed, laying Soh'shoro on the bare stones. "And you're a part of it."

Deftly she uncovered the device's metal length. Then she pulled a paper roll free from a pouch by her waist, biting it open and rolling its small metal ball into the hollow at the tool's end. A dark powder remained in the packaging, which she tapped carefully into the rod's dented pan, taking great pains to shield it from the rain.

"Black Cloaks, rifles ready!" she commanded. Then, to Soh'shoro: "Wait here."

Yei'an strode toward her men, as each aimed their weapon. Billowing in the rain, their willow cloaks looked like the sails of rare boats plying the Valley's ponds for lilies.

"Hold!" Yei'an shouted. "Hold your fire!" Then—"Powder free!"

Suddenly the rifles exploded with smoke and noise, like nothing Soh'shoro had ever experienced before. The cliff face echoed thunderously, rocks sheared loose, and the battalion vanished beneath plumes of white smog. Dust blossomed in a wide pan across the lower ridge. The saffron shapes jerked backward in clouds of red mist, their distorted screams blending with the fading cannonade.

"Those weapons . . ." Soh'shoro gasped. *Accurate as throwing needles. Deadlier than swords.*

"Cover!" Yei'an shouted. "Take cover . . . !"

Cultist shots replied, blasting back at the Black Cloaks. Pelting sounds hissed like angry hornets. Dust pocked and blood fountained. Outsiders tumbled flat, missing whole chunks of limbs. Soh'shoro had never seen such violence. He fought the urge to vomit at the sheer barbarity of these killings.

"Reload!" Yei'an commanded. "They're charging! Fire, then brace for melee!"

The Black Cloaks finished a final salvo, muzzles flashing silver. The trail disappeared once more beneath billowing smoke and its acrid scent of sawdust. Lily-Eaters burst from the smog, swinging clay swords or firing small, hand-sized rifles point-blank.

Fear and confusion quickened Soh'shoro's lethargic body. *Should I help them?* But he did not understand why the men fought, or what purpose these killings served. He looked for Yei'an, but she had vanished into the smoke.

Then he glimpsed it. A flash of lacquered memory, amid the now-trampled wreckage of his funerary bower. The carving called to him like a siren's song. Without thinking, Soh'shoro stumbled toward it and into the melee. He moved low and animal-like, partly to remain hidden and partly because his spine ached with leaching cold. Still his Qu'su instincts held, timing his motions with the drifting smog. He reached his litter unnoticed. And kneeling amid its crumpled silks, he grasped at the icelike lacquer.

The mask of his bride.

"You're alive," he whispered breathlessly. "You will all be alive."

For if Soh'shoro had awoken from Death to this place, why not his wife? Why not An-go'yi'ki? Even Obajen-mahoe? They too might have crossed those same Mists, just as he and Yei'an did. *They could live again*. The world fell away in the face of sudden, unbelievable possibility: that a rotting princess might still hold him; that a murdered brother might still forgive; that a suffering father might call his name once more. That all the horrors of the Valley might be undone beyond their veils of Mist. That Outside, Soh'shoro might find himself redeemed.

"I'll find you," Soh'shoro repeated, clutching her mask to his chest. "I'll find you."

But it was already too late.

In the Valley, the Voice always accompanied violence. So Soh'shoro's instincts had habituated to its warnings, anticipating danger only alongside its keening rush. But now, no such cries called. So the gunstock caught him completely off guard, smashing open his face. Soh'shoro spilled to the ground, tangling in the wreckage of his funeral bower. His back jarred against something flat and heavy, brightened by dancing cranes. *My ri'shou'an.* The Lily-Eater stepped over him, raising his clay sword for its killing stroke. But instead, a strange smile widened the man's glassy eyes, stopping him.

"Found him!" the hulking Cultist slurred. "I've found our last. The prophet he wants!"

Soh'shoro's heart thundered icily, as he tried to draw his ancestral blade. But his muscles, atrophied by Death, struggled pathetically. Funeral bindings held its ossuary firmly shut, and his sword never left its sheath. The Cultist sneered derisively, pinning Soh'shoro to the ground.

"I'll crush the fight out of you . . ."

Lily stench poured from his mouth as the Cultist reared back. But the prince waited for the Voice to time his dodge. So the strike caught him full force in the face. The world spun. His grip on his ri'shou'an slackened.

The Voice! Soh'shoro panicked. *Where is the Voice?*

Once more the Cultist struck. And again, Soh'shoro listened for his mother's haunted warnings. Still there came only silence. The blow shivered his ribs, and he spat blood. *I can't hear her anymore.*

Only now Soh'shoro accepted the truth:

Beyond the Valley, no supernatural force existed to protest life's brutality. *There is no Voice Outside.*

Now as the Lily-Eater hit him again, Soh'shoro trusted only his own reflexes. But mere personal instinct felt stilted and labored. He managed a weak block. Then his counter arced far too slowly. Another exchange, and only now did Soh'shoro manage to catch the Cultist's wrist, exposing his neck for a killing blow.

But he hesitated. *Where will this man go when he dies without the Voice, without the Valley?*

So Soh'shoro merely drove his knee into the Cultist's ribs, setting his hips into the motion as hands seized shoulders. The Lily-Eater flipped overhead, thrown into the gun smoke.

"Retreat!" Yei'an shouted over the chaos. "There's too many! Fall back!"

Soh'shoro gasped for breath, fury and fear refusing to quiet. And lifting both blade and mask, he ran toward her voice.

"Yei'an! I'm here!"

"Soh'shoro!" She lurched from the smog beside him. "We've got to run! I gave orders to explode the hillside. To cover our retreat."

Yei'an snatched his hand. The pair weaved through the melee, toward a final formation of Black Cloaks, firing in staggered rows. Behind the line, a small group packed heavy powder satchels into a mountain fissure.

"Hold fire!" Yei'an called, gesturing desperately to her fellows. "By the Black, hold fire! It's us! It's the prince of the Valley!"

But her cries drew the attention of another rifle.

Soh'shoro wheeled just as the Cultist aimed; the same man Soh'shoro had thrown from the bower. He imagined Yei'an's heart's blood, fountaining over mountain moss, as the gunshot echoed. And he shouldered her wide, knocking them both flat to the ground.

The bullet sailed overhead, hissing through the rain. Saltpeter sparked as its errant arc struck the powder satchels. Then a brilliant flash caught skin like sunlight. Compressing air rattled bones as black smoke mushroomed skyward. The entire trail shuddered.

"Avalanche!"

Yei'an scrambled upright, hauling Soh'shoro beneath the nearest ridge, just as the landslide started. Scree pounded overhead, building in intensity, until the world stormed stone. Rock dust billowed. Dead-falling trees and earthy tides smashed flesh to pulp. Everywhere men screamed.

"Hold on to me!" she hissed. "Don't let go! If we . . ."

But the prince could hear nothing else over the thunder, as the trail beneath them sheared away.

CHAPTER FOURTEEN

REMEDY

Instinct saved them.

Ossuary bindings snapped. Golden webbing flared through quaking dust. Metal sparked. And Soh'shoro's ancestral sword speared into the mountainside, catching just as it had atop his House pagoda. One hand grasped the weighted ring guard, the other Yei'an's arm. And he held her close like that, as the avalanche churned overhead.

He did not know how long the world shuddered. Each moment both stretched and aborted, terror and exertion quickening time even as they numbed perception. Soh'shoro heard only the pounding of stones and the miserable rush of earth, as hideous rivers of rock reverberated around them. Scree split his forearm, exposed beside his ri'shou'an. Gravel pelted his shoulder, bruising bone. But the worst of the avalanche deflected against the ridgeline, tumbling past its overhang and thundering deeper into the lower hills.

Eventually Yei'an's breathing, panicked and animalistic, grew audible over the slowing stones. Still they clung to each other, hanging by the blade, until the landslide's last tremors faded. Lily petals floated alongside dust motes, framing the collapse and its crumpled corpses.

Such strength. The powder could destroy anything. A strange thought came to Soh'shoro then: *even the Mausoleum.*

"The mountain's settling," Yei'an interrupted, letting go of Soh'shoro hesitantly. Nimbly she slid down the avalanche's track, perching on a level rock. Soh'shoro wrenched his blade free, slipping after her.

"You're hurt," she gasped, staring at the prince's bloodied sword arm. Angry gashes, where scree had scraped free flesh, streaked the limb. Each laceration blended with the veinless stains of the Qu'su, as if extending them toward Soh'shoro's heart.

"Nothing is broken. I'll manage."

"We got lucky then," Yei'an replied. "Between the overhang and your blade." But a bone-deep gash brightened the monk's brow. Testing it, she flinched tenderly. "I doubt anyone else made it. But we check for survivors all the same."

Together the pair picked their way down the avalanche, past disjointed limbs and half-buried corpses. Close by, a Lily-Eater retched with pain.

"I watched you fight this man," Yei'an began, "beside your litter. You could have finished him." She kicked the Cultist's gun away before drawing her own narrow dagger. "Why didn't you?"

"What's the point"—Soh'shoro swept his hands across the massacre—"of all this killing?"

"To live," Yei'an answered, slitting the Lily-Eater's throat. And without even glancing back, she continued down the collapse, to check if the next body breathed.

But Soh'shoro did not follow. "Why are you fighting these men?" he called. "What is going on?"

Yei'an turned. "You hate the Onan'ji, like I do?"

He nodded.

"They're his, Soh'shoro. The Cult worships the Valley as paradise, and the Qu'su as its guardian angels."

Still Soh'shoro hesitated. Everywhere was splattered blood and broken limbs, painting a prophetic tableau of limitless suffering. *Is this all my power brings when it is shared?* And for the first time he wondered—for all its static misery, for all its rotting secrets—*Was the Valley not better than this?*

Yet he followed her.

Ahead Yei'an bent over a wounded Black Cloak, pressing his upper chest with both hands, counting strangely between each compression. "Please," she kept muttering. "Please." Tears streamed from her eyes. "He is a friend."

Soh'shoro kneeled beside her. "Let me help."

"Press here." She clasped his hands with hers, teaching him to pump the Outsider's chest. Despite the horror and exhaustion, Soh'shoro still shivered at her touch.

"Keep steady," she instructed. "This is a science. The chirurgeons taught me that."

"And who are they?" he asked between rhythmic pushes.

"The leaders of the Black Cloaks and of Outside, before the Cult conquered their Haven." Soh'shoro recalled the city's floating lights atop the Ocean. "I've got to take you to them."

"Why?"

"Because the Valley has changed," Yei'an replied ominously. "And what you remember from before you died might tell us why. Explain how we can stop the Mists."

Soh'shoro froze. "Stop them?"

"Look."

He glanced up at their gray veils. Already the upper trail, where he had awoken, lay smothered by shifting plumes of silver. As if the Mists leached farther and farther into Outside.

"They're spreading?"

"It began recently," Yei'an explained. "Slowly at first. But every day since, they've quickened." She swallowed. "The Cult claims the Mists will soon swallow the entire world. Purging the unbelievers and welcoming the faithful back into the Valley."

Is this the Onan'ji's madness?

But before Soh'shoro could ask more, the Black Cloak coughed to life. Spittle and blood dribbled from his mouth, as his eyes rolled with small seizures.

"Easy," Yei'an soothed, probing his torso gently, speaking now to the wounded man. "You're breathing again, but your ribs are broken." She pulled bandages from her pouch, cinching the Outsider's stomach. "Just hold on. We'll get you to Remedy soon." She looked up at Soh'shoro. "That's the settlement where the chirurgeons retreated." She swallowed hesitantly. "And where I took your father, after I found him."

"He's alive?" Soh'shoro's eyes widened.

Yei'an nodded, unwrapping her onyx cloak. Carefully, she rolled the Outsider atop it, creating a makeshift litter. "He told the chirurgeons what happened in the Palace. That's why we searched for you. Because he thought the Onan'ji would . . ." Her voice trailed off.

But Soh'shoro completed the thought: *He thought the Onan'ji would kill you*. Was the Qu'su so obviously his better? Even if Soh'shoro could return to the Valley, how could he hope to defeat such an opponent? After all, he had already failed to do so.

"Were there others with my father?" Soh'shoro pressed. "From the Valley?"

Yei'an flinched as if struck. "You're asking about her, aren't you? The Ang'soon princess?" She sneered the name.

"Yes."

She shook her head suspiciously. "I don't know. The Traders took many corpses to the Cultists at the Haven. Before the chirurgeons realized what was happening."

"Then I need to go there." Soh'shoro instinctively reached

for the lacquer mask, where it lay nestled between his robes and chest.

"That's suicide. The Cult would kill you on sight." But Soh'shoro remembered the Lily-Eater's strange shout from the bower: *I've found him. The prophet he wants.* "Besides, I can't carry the wounded by myself. And you must see your father, before it's too late."

"What do you mean?" *The rot.* "Is he sick?"

"I can't describe it." Pain creased her face. "And I don't want to try. We just need to hurry. For all of our sakes." She lifted her corner of the cloak, signaling for Soh'shoro to do the same. "Come on."

Together they finished searching the avalanche's terminus. Only one more Outsider still breathed, but when Yei'an rolled her over and saw only half a face, she slit the woman's throat just like the Lily-Eater's before her. Then she opened the corpse's powder case, scavenging it to refill her own, before moving on.

Eventually their descent led back to the beaten tar of the mountain road. But Yei'an remained wary of Cult reinforcements. Twice they heard shouts somewhere down the trail. Soon they fled the track entirely, forging across scrublands before vanishing into an overgrown ravine. The monk kept rubbing at her head wound, as if trying to relieve pressure beneath its swelling skin.

As night fell, they reached Outside's amaranthine sands. Strange centipedes, sparkling cinnamon in the starlight, skittered curiously close. Yei'an sparked a small fire beneath a rocky bluff to mask its light. The wounded Black Cloak slept the miserable sleep of pain. And Soh'shoro watched the Mists. Always they continued their inexorable creep, as ice seeps across a winter pond, gradually swallowing more and more of the world.

"Let me see your arm." Yei'an dangled needle and thread in the firelight.

Soh'shoro kneeled beside her. The scent of winter bur and honey filled him once more.

"We can't risk infection," she explained, swabbing each gash with clear liquid from a narrow bottle. Then the needle darted. Soh'shoro's heart quickened with both pain and closeness. For a time neither spoke.

"What's wrong?" he asked, as Yei'an's eyes sparkled silver with small tears.

"You know." She licked the needle distractedly, smearing blood across her lips. "We both know." Her luminous face beamed up at his, like the sun through a storm. "I lost you, Soh'shoro. And now you're here."

The fire crackled sharply.

"I never meant to hurt you."

"Then don't. Not again." She dropped the thread, stroking his cheek.

"Yei'an. I can't."

"Yes, you can." She smeared blood across his lip as she kissed him.

"Yei'an . . . Stop . . ."

But her mouth ran over his throat, then his chest, and she stripped back his shirt to scrape fingernails over old scar tissue. She traced the Qu'su's veinless staining, pinching slightly. And without speaking, she pulled him down atop the rough sand.

"This is what I learned Outside," she whispered fiercely. "Nothing matters in the end. But it does matter now." She licked his neck with feral eagerness. Her heat filled him. "This isn't like the Valley. There isn't more. There's just this."

Her body danced brightly over his. Her luminous eyes swallowed the world, like a lake drinking in its drowning. The suture needle caught beneath him, lancing his ribs. The cracked mask of the princess watched from where it lay beside his mother's blade.

Afterward she rested against him. But as he stroked her hair, she flinched each time his fingers brushed the gash on her forehead.

"It's getting worse, isn't it? Your wound?"

"The chirurgeons will know what to do."

Though they tried to sleep, both pain and anticipation prevented it. So they set off into the sands well before sunrise.

Here great drifts of orange silt piled against scraggly shoots of hollyhock and elderberry, punctuated by sparse weeds and weakly flowering shrubs. Overhead, the clouds blazed brilliant calico streamers. Soh'shoro traced their ribbons through the dawn, beyond and above the sparkling sea. On and on into that limitless forever.

"Does the Ocean end?" he asked. For the sea's ceaseless span seemed too incredible, compared to the Valley's finite frontier.

"Not as far as I know," Yei'an replied. "But there must be other lands, beyond those waters. That's where the Black Ships came from, in the beginning."

Soh'shoro wanted to ask more. But it clearly pained Yei'an to speak. So instead, he shouldered the Outsider's full weight, tying the wounded man to his back like a traveling satchel.

"We can't keep going like this."

"There are farms ahead, beside the rivers. We'll find help there."

Soh'shoro scanned the horizon for the willowy green of rice plants. But though several broad tributaries cut inland from the Ocean, only stone houses and wooden partitions dotted their banks. Silhouettes of men raked clumpy whiteness from their currents.

Is that salt? he wondered, tasting sour familiarity on the wind.

They limped closer. With afternoon they reached the nearest farm, shouting for help. Soon Soh'shoro found himself eating a gifted meal of soup, strangely reminiscent of the Traders' food, but full of thick chunks of chewy rawness. A low, grinding wheel spun outside the stone cottage. Its bucketed ruts churned with the river's current, rotating a central axle that hissed with rust.

"Does Outside have more relics like this?" he asked Yei'an. She lay beside him, a wet towel soothing her brow.

"Of course," she forced out through increasingly shallow breaths. "Outside makes things to survive. This world pushes us, unlike the Valley."

But the prince could not understand how a turning wheel helped men to live. Between mouthfuls of soup, he watched her nervously.

"I'll be all right," she replied to his unanswered question. "You'll see. Whatever's wrong, the chirurgeons can fix anything."

Just before evening, the farmers loaded the Black Cloak and Yei'an into a wheeled cart. The group marched through the night, past tawny shrubs and brambly wisterias, following a winding waterway. The men bantered for most of their journey, while Soh'shoro marveled at their unusual accents—the vowels too soft, the consonants cropped. But otherwise the Outsiders' speech sounded strangely similar to the farmers he had known in the Valley. *That is where we came from. In the beginning.* Soh'shoro recalled the Onan'ji's words. *Outside.*

By dawn they reached Remedy. The town encircled a broad lake, its waters plied by black-sailed ships, its foaming banks stripped of trees and striped with open ore pits. Spear palisades barricaded ring after ring of long houses, their tar-stained chimneys foul with fire and fog. An ancient tower dominated the settlement, its old stone completely blackened with ash, its peak split centuries ago, its shadow cradling the fort like wings of a bird about its young.

Yei'an smiled, drawing in a deep, smog-filled breath.

"Their surgery is close."

Winding through the sooty streets, Soh'shoro peered inside the strange stone buildings. In many massive fires blazed, churning tinctures of molten metal that fed great iron molds. Workers tended these forges; their skin welting with the heat and pocked by burn scars.

Could we do this in the Valley? Soh'shoro wondered. *Would the Voice allow such danger?*

In another house, he smelled caked blood. Beyond its narrow window, he glimpsed animals chained to walls, and a young couple slitting a brown creature's throat with a wicked, curving knife. The beast barked pitifully and painfully as it died.

"They killed that animal!" Soh'shoro gasped.

"For food," a farmer replied. "It's called a butcher's."

Soh'shoro thought of the spiced soup he had eaten and the strange chunks floating within.

Now the tower loomed ahead. Even stained by smog, its stonework marveled. Corbels and ramparts swept beside bartizan cupula and parapet walks. Thousands of small, angular idols decorated the close-cut grasses of its outer courtyard, in row after row of grave-like symmetry. Soh'shoro strode past these relics' fading paint, ascending the mossy threshold beyond. Then he pounded the tower's heavy oaken doors for entry.

"Tell the chirurgeons who I am," Yei'an insisted, eyes foggy with delirium. "Tell them who you are."

But Soh'shoro's mind swam with doubt and fear.

Who am I?

Prince of the Quo'dai-ma? Assassin of the Qu'su? A corpse Reborn Outside? What did it matter? What was this world? His purpose in it?

And the doors shuddered wide, billowing the stench of sickness from beyond.

CHAPTER FIFTEEN

SURGERY

Dozens of alien figures warmed themselves beside boiling fires. Others rested in ornate chairs or blended chemicals atop limpet-shaped refectory tables. Glass ovals covered their eyes, and elongated metal beaks protected their mouths. Stylized animal fur completed the masks, giving each the impression of a bearded, mechanical bird.

"Chirurgeons," Soh'shoro guessed.

"And what are you?" a tall figure replied, blocking the doorway. Despite her monstrous visage, the woman's voice sounded strangely kind. "Why have you sought us?"

"For help." Soh'shoro pointed to the farmer's cart, and the monk and Black Cloak resting in it. "You know the woman, Yei'an. You sent her searching for me, I think."

The tall chirurgeon glanced at the wounded before turning her gaze hungrily on Soh'shoro. "Could it be?" She took a step closer. "Are you her lost prince? Soh'shoro of the Quo 'dai-ma?"

When he nodded in reply, the chirurgeon paced still nearer. "No matter how many times I meet your kind, Valley-born always surprise." She smiled, an expression visible only by her cheeks curving against their avian mask. "I am First Surgeon An'na, and we have much to discuss." She faced her fellows. "Reward these men for bringing our prince, then take the wounded into surgery. I'll treat the monk myself."

Chirurgeons swarmed, voices eerily dissonant through their filtered masks, as they gifted small disks of metal to the farmers. Next their thin, gloved hands seized Yei'an and the Black Cloak before carefully carrying them inside. Soh'shoro tried to follow, but An'na cocked her head in warning. "Best wait until my kind's work is done."

"I'm not leaving her."

An'na frowned. "If I let you follow, you must trust me. Valley-born have a way of"—her voice trailed curiously—"misunderstanding our arts."

Soh'shoro nodded.

"Wash yourself." She gestured to an opalescent font, warming beside one of the boiling fires. "Thoroughly."

The prince laved his face and hands, scraping away grime and dried blood. The font smelled strangely like rice wine, and its water stung his wounded arm like snagging brambles. After he patted dry, the tall chirurgeon quickly wrapped his cuts with a thick, honey-scented mesh.

"Now follow."

Beyond the entry room lay a corridor of narrow cells, each containing a metal bed and a wiry table. Soh'shoro glimpsed the Black Cloak inside one, just before its painted door slid shut on polished bearings. An'na entered the next chamber, where Yei'an now rested.

"How long has she been like this?" the chirurgeon asked.

"Two days. At first, she seemed fine. But the pain grew worse and . . ."

"Something blunt did this?"

Soh'shoro nodded. "An avalanche. We were its only survivors."

"A high price to save a prince." An'na frowned underneath her mask, the gesture revealed by her prickling cheeks. "I hope you prove worth it." She drew out a clear bottle, tapping it carefully. A narrow shurishi glimmered in her hand, deftly lancing inside. Soh'shoro had seen its like before. *The needles of the Emperor's Throne.*

"Sleep now," An'na cooed, pricking Yei'an's arm. In moments, her breathing quieted, and her eyes rolled back. Only then did the chirurgeon swab her brow, testing bone.

"What's wrong with her?"

"A brain bleed. Blood clots beneath the skull, creating pressure. I must relieve it."

The chirurgeon took a narrow blade from the side table. The knife looked like a miniature ri'shou'an, without its ringed hilt. Gently she shaved Yei'an's hair with it, revealing an angry split in the bone beneath. An'na nodded thoughtfully, tapping at the fracture. Yei'an did not even flinch. Whatever drug the surgeon had given her was potent.

"She needs trepanning," the chirurgeon continued. "Can I trust you to hold her still?" She placed Soh'shoro's hands on either side of Yei'an's head. "Firmly," she insisted. "Like this."

Then, with frightening alacrity, she whittled the exposed bone. Yei'an shivered.

Soh'shoro gasped. "You're hurting her."

"She doesn't feel through the drug. Not really. It's just reflex." But Yei'an kicked violently, sending Soh'shoro lurching over her for leverage.

"I said firmly!" the chirurgeon snapped. "The scalpel can't slip too deep."

Soh'shoro watched in disbelief as the miniature ri'shou'an

bored farther and farther. Yei'an's jaw clenched white. An'na glanced up at him with steely confidence.

"You must understand. Violence does not have to hurt. Sometimes cruelty cures. That's the secret of surgery. The art of all chirurgeons."

Now the knife vanished beneath the bone, still carving. Slowly, a steady trickle of blood ran from the whittled hole, sparkling in the candlelight.

"Good," An'na purred. "The pressure is draining away." She took up a square sheet of silk, placing it over the ravaged bone. For a moment, Soh'shoro glimpsed something rich and pinkish gray beneath, covered hastily. "Must be careful now. Contamination would be fatal." The surgeon gently stitched, until fabric sealed the wound. "Careful," she kept muttering. "Careful."

At last, she leaned back on her heels, surveying her work. Then she cinched the suture shut with a confident snap. Only now did she remove her beaked mask. Even stained by perspiration, the dark face beneath glittered with surprising, slender beauty. A single, piercing eye turned to Soh'shoro. The other was finely worked glass, resembling a blue iris.

"Thank you," Soh'shoro whispered in amazement. Already Yei'an's breathing grew less labored, and the tension in her jaw eased.

"You will do more than thank me in return." An'na licked her lips eagerly. "Best let her rest now. My disciples will tend her. You must follow."

The pair left the cell, crossing the sterile corridor and entering a spiral staircase. They climbed in silence, Soh'shoro's head still spinning with what he had seen: *Violence that heals.*

On the tower's second floor, a library glimmered gloriously in candlelight. Ancient casings clung to the ashlar walls, beside aumbries of black-and-golden brocade. Endless shelves spilled gilded manuscripts onto half-rolled carpet, beside gateleg tables strewn with pendulums, sextants, Old-Make aeolipiles. These words the chirurgeon spoke reverently as she pointed to each, the sounds as foreign as the objects.

"All left by the Black Ships. All secrets of their world, to teach of surgery and science. To make great things: gears and rifles and even grander cannons. All part of their bargain."

Soh'shoro scanned the endless books. If he only had time to explore these truths, what wonders might he learn of the Outside?

"Before they disappeared to distant seas, the Black Ships tasked us with watching the Valley," An'na continued. "In case it ever tried to escape. Like I believe it is doing now."

"Are you talking about the Mists?"

"The Qu'en." The chirurgeon's good eye narrowed fiercely.

"How do you know about that demon?"

"We know much of your Valley," An'na replied cooly. "We even permit its salt trade, to help contain the rot." She passed a gilded table, with a great map spread across it. Black blots marred most of its masses, with cryptic lines and eerie crosses spanning what little land remained. *Is this all of Outside? Even worlds beyond the sea?*

"And the Qu'en is not a demon," An'na continued. "Despite what the Valley might believe. Their kind knows neither good nor evil but is beyond mere morality. And thus far worse." Her rich lips pursed themselves into a terse line. "Your Valley must think itself so clever to have bound it. But many believe the Qu'en wanted to be caught. To cultivate its vessels." She hesitated. "What your father risks becoming."

Soh'shoro startled. "He's here, isn't he?"

"I'm taking you to him now," the chirurgeon replied, winding deeper into the library, past lumps of flesh floating in amber tubes. "We tried everything to treat him. But his rot is different from others we've studied. It's more cancerous and fetid. So it spread"—she considered her next word carefully—"unchecked. Already it grows far too dangerous. The next step must be his last: euthanasia."

Soh'shoro did not know the Old Word. But he intuited its meaning, from the distasteful way the chirurgeon's lips curved over each syllable.

"I won't let you hurt him," he snapped.

"I give the orders here," An'na countered indignantly. "Do not think you are still a prince Outside."

"He is my father!"

"Not anymore." The chirurgeon stopped at the foot of the next staircase. "You'll see. We've locked him in the solarium, just atop the stairs." Her next words were gentle. "I am not trying to be cruel. Eventually you will understand why my kind fights: with surgery for sickness, and munitions for monsters. We have much to speak of after, Soh'shoro. But for now"—her good eye darted to a rifle resting inside the stairwell—"I've already loaded the gun."

Soh'shoro balked. "I don't need a weapon to see my father."

"A chirurgeon's warning is never idle," An'na demurred. "Take it. And shout at the first sign of danger. Otherwise, this reunion is your own."

Soh'shoro hefted the weapon, considering its strange weight. Then he began the final ascent alone. In that winding darkness, his heart pounded so loudly he could barely think. He vacillated between fear and disbelief. The narrow world of the Valley he had known seemed to expand limitlessly with each new revelation.

But Soh'shoro had no time to wonder. Now came his first chance at redemption. *My father needs me. I can still help him.*

The stairs were slick with dirty moisture, like the drainage from porous stones. Motion stretched lethargically, as if space itself distended slightly. A familiar coughing sounded, guttural and hungry. He reached a sealed door, triple bolted from outside. One by one, he slid the latches free.

And Soh'shoro's eyes squinted into the solarium's radiance, its massive windows refulgent with disorienting brilliance. Telescopes and stranger lenses cast long, slender shadows against the glare. And in the center of the chamber, slumped atop an inner dais of latticed wood, loomed Obajen-mahoe.

White medicinal robes swathed him, bleached a shocking silver by the buttery light. His body strained against their fabric with the hideous lumpiness of ill-mixed clay. He had bloated to three times his size in the Valley, distended and savage and somehow leaking.

"Father."

There was no response.

Soh'shoro drew closer, climbing atop the dais, resting his hand on Obajen-mahoe's shoulder. The skin swelled against his touch, nakedly soft. Pale, listless eyes, as though carved from soapstone, stared back from beneath their bubbling pits of blackening rot.

"Is it the boy?" Obajen-mahoe gurgled.

Soh'shoro beamed with hope. Even sickly and suffering, Obajen-mahoe still lived.

"It is." And the prince hugged his dripping flesh. "I'm here."

Obajen-mahoe shivered strangely beneath his touch. This close, Soh'shoro saw how terribly the sickness had progressed. This phage far outstripped the princess's, sporing ever more viciously and randomly. *Cocooning him. Like a chrysalis.*

Soh'shoro peered at the crystalline pus caking Obajen-mahoe's back. Great lumps of fatty flesh unfurled from his shoulders, the pinions distending pathetically to the ground. Even now their masses writhed, steaming with strange heat.

"You're changing?" Soh'shoro gasped, remembering the wings of the Emperor's Corpse, tangled in its catafalque of steel.

"Poorly." The lump coughed.

"I don't understand," Soh'shoro begged.

"My rot is of the Corpse, and not the dolls," the creature blubbered, blood dribbling from its mouth. "So it mutates strangely, after feeding on such Death. I doubt it will serve."

"You sound insane."

"No, I was mad before," the lump whispered. "I know now the lie of our Houses. We were mere jailers, Soh'shoro, when we might have become judges."

"Whatever you are becoming," Soh'shoro protested, "it must be stopped. Look at yourself. The rot is killing you."

"Like you killed me?" The mass's milky eyes rolled fiercely. "You think I love you now? After what you did? After my murder?"

"How can you say such a thing?" Tears streamed down Soh'shoro's face. "I never meant to hurt you."

"Yet here we are! Because of your true nature!" The mass trembled. The fleshy wings tensed. "You think me the monster? When it is your kind that wakes Death itself."

The prince stepped back, as if struck.

"Can you even deny it? Where is the Ang'soon princess? Is she safe in the Valley, as you promised?"

Soh'shoro could not reply.

"Where is the heir? The last hope of the Houses? The reason I sent you to secrecy?" Rotted blood pitted blackened lips. "Where, Soh'shoro, where are all your promises now?"

"Gone," he replied at last, voice barely more than a whisper. "I failed."

"Because your kind sows only suffering. Reaps only ruin."

Now Soh'shoro could not contain his anger.

"Because of your lies!" he spat. "You hid everything from me: the Emperor, his rot, even Outside!" His voice quivered. "How can I control what I became, when you lied to me about everything I am?"

The creature chortled in answer. A contortion of muscles shot through its body, as if the fleshy protrusions fed on Soh'shoro's fury. A tendril spurted, cracking the wooden dais, bleeding fatty blood.

"That has always been your power's true purpose. To end everything. Even itself!"

"No!"

"You deserve to die! You are no son of mine!"

But at these words, at last Soh'shoro realized the truth. He remembered Obajen-mahoe's rainbow-stitched brocade and the loving sternness of his touch. The salted seasons of their togetherness were heavy with ritual and silence. But also love.

The chirurgeon had been right. The thing before him was not Obajen-mahoe. Not anymore. The rot had claimed both his body and his mind.

"What are you?"

The fleshy lump laughed. Another knot of malformed pinions ruptured from its spine, thumping to the ground and expanding with inhuman speed, cracking the solarium's glass, leaching through gaps and chinks in the stonework, flowing and folding through the detritus of the chamber, drinking in splintered wood and rotted machicolations. As if the body itself absorbed the world.

"Free." The milky eyes rolled to hold Soh'shoro enraptured. Time slipped and space slid. The prince tremored uncontrollably beneath the creature's sightless, chortling gaze. And behind it, beyond the solarium's windows, pulsed the Mists. They had already overtaken the mountains to stretch into Outside's sands. But now a single tendril led the roil. A handlike plume, far ahead of all other drifts. Reaching toward the tower.

Toward Obajen-mahoe.

Soh'shoro raised the rifle. "Give my father back!"

"Soon." The lump laughed, the sound blending into guttural coughing.

Then it was as if Obajen-mahoe melted away, his skin and bone pouring toward Soh'shoro and threatening to drown him. The prince kicked away from the leaking mass, rolling across the wooden scaffolding. Boils of skin lurched from the stump of what was once Obajen-mahoe's face, seeping after him. Another shiver, and suddenly the lump's entire rib cage ruptured, propelled outward in an explosive tendril of thumping fat and marrow. Without the Voice, Soh'shoro moved far too slowly. The swelling mass speared him against the solarium's wall. His head dashed against stone. Air rocketed from his lungs.

Soh'shoro tried to shout for help, but podding flesh swam over his neck and throat, suffocating him. He wedged his elbow against the stone wall, wriggling one arm loose, clutching the rifle. In moments pseudopods swelled around it, swallowing it whole.

One shot. The weapon is loaded.

He pushed with all his might, setting the gunstock against the chamber's wall, then levering its barrel against the swelling flesh. His other arm lay completely buried now, so he could not pull the trigger. But he did not have to. Instead he kept the weapon braced, aiming where the lump of Obajen-mahoe's face had vanished. Then came another swell, crawling over his fingers, depressing steel. The muzzle flashed.

Black smoke swallowed the chamber. The bullet burrowed

into the hulking growth with a moist, muted thud. A small trickle of dark gore rocketed free. Next came a sound like bird wings beating against their cage. The fleshy mound strained, then distorted. And in one sudden burst the creature that had been Obajen-mahoe fountained open, deflating like a paper lantern. It spasmed a final time, angry and malevolent and unthinking. Then only a pool of silent skin remained, riven wide in a jarring puncture of wing-speared rot.

CHAPTER SIXTEEN

BURIAL

"What is Outside?"

Dusk stained the silver-tinted windows of the refectory an angry red. Beside its raging hearth fires, chirurgeons stroked their bearded masks, and Black Cloaks fingered distinguished necklaces of heavy gold. Servants offered orange liquors from smelted cups. The room smelled of sweat and anticipation.

And the beautiful chirurgeon rose from her seat of honor: a grand chair of stuffed animal skins that smothered her like a deep snow.

"Broken." She took a sharp drink from her amber glass. "We Salt-born lost touch long ago with the lands beyond the sea. Whether because they abandoned us to our task, or for some darker purpose. So for centuries we contained the Valley alone, holding back its seepages. But at last it escapes. Now we too must fail, or finish our work."

"And what is your work?" Soh'shoro asked.

"The same thing you want, I think." An'na took another deep drink, grimacing at the liquor's burn. A servant immediately approached, refilling her glass with fearful diligence. "To destroy the Valley."

In the silence that followed, Soh'shoro tried again and again to reply. For he hated much of what lay behind the Mists: from the Onan'ji to the Corpse's bloody stasis. But another part of him loved his home. Found beauty in its Eternity. Treasured its composure and constancy, despite its rituals and repetitions. Must it all burn away, because of its dark heart? What did it mean to obliterate an entire way of life and its infinite lifetimes?

"But now we are out of time," An'na continued. "We must act, before the Mists claim us all." She gestured through the refectory's windows, at the coming roils of oblivion, swarming ever closer across Outside's sands. "So tell us, prince of the Quo'dai-ma. What happened in the Valley? Why does our world drown?"

Soh'shoro rose slowly from his upholstered seat.

"The Onan'ji," he began hesitantly. "He causes this catastrophe."

"Yei'an warned of this Qu'su," the chirurgeon confirmed. "You can assume we know all about him and his Order. As we know much of the Valley from centuries of study. What we do not understand is how this monk gained the power to free the Mists."

"He didn't," Soh'shoro replied coldly. "He had help. He used me to break the Valley's bonds."

At those words, the chamber erupted with terrible anger and chaotic shouts. One Black Cloak lifted a chalice, as if to hurl it at Soh'shoro. But An'na merely raised her hand, like sunlight splitting storm clouds. Stilling all into silence.

"There will be no judgment here," she pronounced, after the room had settled. "And I doubt you would be helping us now if the monk's aims were your own." Her gaze swept the assemblage imperiously, an animal pacing its den. "Speak freely. Tell us what has been done."

And Soh'shoro felt the princess's mask tug against his chest, as if begging to be put down.

"I was born unlike others in the Valley. An anathema. A child who could kill."

More whispers coursed through the assemblage.

"But instead of purging me, the Onan'ji stole me from my father. Trained me as his assassin. Tricked me into killing my family. Noble by noble, House by House. Ever against my will. And when it was done"—his voice cracked at the remembered terror of the blade opening his throat—"he murdered me too. All so the Emperor would starve without blood. So the Onan'ji could claim his Throne."

"You mean the Valley's machine?" An'na pressed. "The device that makes the Mists?"

"Whatever you call it, he repairs it. He has for decades, I think. Smuggling shards of it into the Valley, hidden inside the Traders' flesh."

Another murmur passed through the room. One man spat openly in disgust.

"The Cult of the Lily." An'na frowned. "We've known for centuries they scavenged artifacts from the sea. Fragments from when your Mausoleum first fell to earth." She swallowed. "But we thought these mere objects of worship. Broken idols."

"They are not idols," Soh'shoro pressed. "They are parts."

"But why?" An'na stroked her full lips curiously, as if caressing a beloved pet. "What purpose does repairing the Emperor's Throne serve? And why would he then seek to sit upon it, when the machine consumes its scion so? The Onan'ji already has immortality." She paused. "What more could he want, Soh'shoro?"

The prince's mind swam, as he remembered the monk's dark tutelage. The endless riddles and inscrutable promises. The mysterious Mist walks and their inexplicable sorrows. And then at last, the Onan'ji's mysterious admission: *True paradise must be shared.*

"I can only guess," Soh'shoro began.

"Then do so."

"The Onan'ji once told me the Valley was incomplete. That its paradise was imperfect because it preserved so few. Perhaps that is why he spreads the Mists. To share the Valley." And suddenly the full depths of the monk's darkness yawned before him. "To gift Eternity to the entire world."

"And kill us all in the process?!" a Black Cloak blurted out. "The Mists blot out everything they touch!"

"The Onan'ji will not see it that way." Soh'shoro's voice grew firm. "To him, your lives—the lives of everyone Outside—mean nothing. Because they are impermanent. Your deaths can't matter against Eternity's stretch. Not when you would die anyway."

Once more the room shivered into whispers. But again the lead chirurgeon held her hand up for silence.

"Then to survive, our path is clear. There will be no barter or reasoning with this monk. Nor does his kind yield to mercy or regret." An'na smiled viciously. "We must either kill the Onan'ji or destroy his machine. There is no other way to stop the Mists."

"But both are inside the Valley," Soh'shoro replied. "We would need some way to cross."

Now the room exploded in riotous terror:

"Impossible!"

"No one survives the Mists!"

"All who tried have failed!"

But somehow the certainty of those shouts set Soh'shoro's mind churning. His thoughts returned once again to those terrible seasons of tutelage beneath the Onan'ji. Because he remembered more than mere cruelty. The monk's touch had been strangely loving, his violence often delivered with alien affection.

Even now, Soh'shoro believed the monk cared for him, in his horrid way. So why let him wake Outside at all, if only to drown?

And the monk's final riddle resounded: *We'll meet again soon.*

"Silence!" Anarchy swallowed Soh'shoro's calls. "Silence!"

"The prince needs silence!" An'na commanded. At her words, the hall hushed almost instantly. Still the chirurgeon waited for even its smallest whispers to die away before continuing. "What do you know, Soh'shoro? What have you realized?"

"First tell me: Why send Yei'an to rescue me?"

"What does that have to do with this?"

"Why?" Soh'shoro insisted.

An'na frowned at his impudence. "Because the Cult reveres the Valley's dead. They sought to steal you to the Haven for worship."

"The city that floats atop the Ocean? The one the Lily-Eaters captured?"

"Yes," An'na replied. "But why does this matter, prince?"

"Because the Onan'ji could have kept my corpse in the Valley. But he let me wake Outside for a reason."

The chirurgeon's glass eye sparkled curiously. "And why would he do that?"

"Because he cares for me," Soh'shoro replied. "Like a son, I think. He wouldn't send me Outside to merely die again. If he thought the Cult would take me to the Haven, then that city must be special. There must be something there that might protect it from the Mists."

An'na considered this carefully. "The Haven is built atop ruins. Ancient things, sunk deep beneath the waves. The Black Ships used them as a foundation when they first raised its pillars."

Soh'shoro remembered his mother's memory, from the night he drank the lily poison, of a great Shard sparkling beneath whitecapped waves.

"In the Valley, there are artifacts that keep back the Mists. Qu'en Shards."

The chirurgeon nodded. "We know."

"What if one of them is buried there? Underneath the Haven." And Soh'shoro's voice rose, as he realized the magnitude of what must come next. "That relic would ward the city, like a bubble in a pond. Keep it safe while the Mists passed over it."

An'na smiled curiously. "It is possible."

"No, I think it is certain. I've seen such a Shard. In memories gifted me by the Valley's Voice." Soh'shoro tightened with conviction. "We must return to the Haven. Recapture it from the Cult. It's the only place Outside that will survive."

But the grin faded from An'na's slender face, replaced by freshly settling fear. "A bold plan, prince. But with one flaw." She licked her lips cautiously. "We have yet to retake the Haven for a reason. We need rifles and guns to do so, of which we have precious few. Our Vault was in that city, Soh'shoro. Our great steel storehouse of powder and rifles. We might reforge those weapons, yes, but that takes seasons. If we attack the Haven poorly armed, we will be slaughtered."

"Is there another choice?" Soh'shoro demanded, voice trembling. "Or would you merely wait for Death in the Mists? When we might do more than survive, but snatch victory from ruin?" He gripped the gilded fabric of his chair. "Think of it. The Onan'ji's mercy is his weakness. After the Mists pass, the whole Valley will lie exposed. Unprotected and unknown to violence, with only the Qu'su to defend the Emperor's Throne." Soh'shoro leaned forward eagerly, imagining his conquest as a hunter stalking his quarry. "Beneath the fury of Outside's powder, even the Mausoleum might fall. We could destroy the Valley's darkness once and for all."

War. But Soh'shoro felt no revulsion at his woken horror,

merely certainty. *War will save my home.* And if there was any contradiction in such triumph, he could not see it.

More shouts erupted, both nervous and eager for the coming violence. Black Cloaks shoved and cajoled. And the beautiful chirurgeon merely stared at Soh'shoro, considering. Their gazes met once more.

Then An'na tapped her glass eye curiously, as if signaling approval.

After midnight, Soh'shoro returned to the tower's courtyard. Amid the rows of metallic markers lining its close-cut grasses, a new relic speared the soft earth. The idol's freshly painted gold glittered in the starlight, like tears reflecting a candle's flame.

"I knew I'd find you here." An'na glided beside him.

"This is where you buried him?" Soh'shoro asked. "My father?"

"Symbolically." The chirurgeon frowned. "We burned the rot. But still made the grave."

Night blanketed the pair, cool but pleasant. Winds howled.

"Do you think they wake up somewhere else?" Soh'shoro asked. "Like I woke from the Valley?"

"Who knows?" the chirurgeon answered cryptically. "But there is little magic Outside. No Mists and no Voice." She swallowed. "I don't think so."

Kneeling, the chirurgeon cast a handful of dirt across the grave. Soh'shoro hesitated, then bent to do the same. The clump made a heavy, pleasant thud as it struck the burial marker. He wanted to cry. But he had no more tears.

"You said you tried to treat my father's rot."

"Yes."

"Does that mean there's a cure?"

The surgeon licked her lips thoughtfully. "Not a cure. But our drugs and tinctures are powerful. If such sickness were caught early enough, before its growths advanced as far as Obajen-mahoe's, we could keep it in stasis, I think. With surgeries, cutting out the mutations as they formed. It would be a lifetime of suffering. But a lifetime nonetheless." She reached out, taking Soh'shoro's hand. The gesture was not romantic, merely compassionate. "But your father is dead, prince. What do you care now for a cure?"

"Because there is another. One who is sick like him."

The chirurgeon's glass eye sparkled. "The Ang'soon princess."

"You know of her? Where is she?"

"We know of all the Houses. But the Ang'soon brother and sister are beyond us. Stolen to the Haven."

Soh'shoro let the chirurgeon's hand fall away. "Yei'an told me she didn't know for certain . . ."

"Are you blind?" The chirurgeon laughed. "Even I can see that woman loves you. I knew as soon as she volunteered for your rescue from the Mists." Her voice softened with understanding. "Do you really think Yei'an would have told the truth, given what you might have done?"

Soh'shoro's heart thundered. He kept glimpsing the princess choking on the lily-sweet breath of Cultists or drowning beneath the Haven's waves. Then he took up another handful of earth to cast over Obajen-mahoe's grave.

Never again. His lips twisted into a ferocious grin. *I must save her.*

"What are you planning?" the chirurgeon asked. "I glimpsed it earlier. After I spoke of the Vault."

"Promise me first." Soh'shoro's gaze met her good eye, holding it steadily. "Promise that if I somehow rescue her, you will treat the princess. No matter how cruel or desperate the surgeries, you will fight her rot. You will protect her from my father's fate."

An'na did not reply. Instead she reached into her pouch, withdrawing a narrow pipe of smooth lead. Carefully she sparked its end, puffing deeply. Spiced smoke filled the air. "She is dangerous, Soh'shoro. She too might change."

"Not if your arts intervene early enough. You said as much yourself," he insisted. "Please."

An'na inhaled again, long and slow, her good eye glassing. A lazy smoke ring rose heavenward, vanishing into the night's clouds.

"The risk is too great."

"I am not asking you, then." Soh'shoro's voice hardened. "I am warning you. When we defeat the Onan'ji, the Valley will look for leadership. And I will be its rightful ruler. So if you seek peace with my people—instead of endless revenge—you will save their princess. Do you understand?"

An'na took another deep taste of the pipe, her lone eye watering. "I see." She tapped away the loose ash curiously. "Then I promise to use all my arts to keep your bride safe. I can't guarantee success. But I will try."

"Thank you."

"Your plan, then."

Soh'shoro stood, turning away from Obajen-mahoe's grave.

"The Vault full of guns and powder you spoke of. I will steal into the Haven and detonate it myself. Then it will be an even fight between Cultist and Black Cloak."

"You can't possibly," An'na sneered. "You are one man."

"You don't know what I truly am. What the Qu'su made me. What I made myself."

As a prince and a son. As a husband and an assassin. He was ready.

"And what are you?" the chirurgeon hissed. "I first asked when you arrived at my surgery. Do you have a better answer now?"

Inside the tower, he visited Yei'an's sallow figure one last time. She lay wrapped warmly in thick cloth blankets, her brow bruising a brilliant purple above one eye, almost like rot. The orb beneath had shriveled. But her breathing came steadily.

He wished he wanted to stay with her. That he might live a life beside her, loving and happy despite its finality. That her brightness might be shared, and one day blend completely with his own.

But instead he craved the princess. Not because of her pain, but because even now he believed only he could save her from it. That only he understood her suffering, and what it meant to live apart from and against the world.

So he kissed Yei'an goodbye, drinking her warm lips one last time.

"I'm going now."

Behind Soh'shoro, Remedy's lights blurred into the stars, as though the heavens themselves kissed the earth. Clutching the cracked mask of his princess against his mother's blade, Soh'shoro walked away without looking back.

And so Eternity's Blade descended upon the Haven at last.

CHAPTER SEVENTEEN

HAVEN

Soh'shoro spent days crossing the beach. As he traveled, summer came in earnest to Outside. Blossoms took the acacia trees, growing willowy and overbright. The wind gentled, soothing tides along comber-lined coves. Clouds brightened with thawing, fustic sunlight.

And the Mists crept closer, swallowing the world. At night Soh'shoro slept facing into their lingering veils, almost as if he camped again beside the Onan'ji. With morning he woke to find the haze hungry, reaching for him in fetid tendrils like broken fingers, threatening to vanish all of Outside beneath their slithering roils.

With the Mists spread War. For trailing up the coastline, Soh'shoro caught the dark sails of Black Cloak ships. Whether An'na trusted him enough to command this conflict, or the Outsiders simply had no other choice, he could not guess. Either way, the Haven would soon be under siege.

Soh'shoro reached the floating city just in time.

A massive stone bridge, arcing over the waves, spanned shore to settlement. Once, Soh'shoro guessed, its painted tiles had bustled with commerce. Now the crossing swarmed with refugees, driven before the roiling Mists. Desperate tides of sunburned flesh pounded on the shuttered gates of the bridge's barbican. Light spilled from its inner fortification, as Cultists patrolled rifle-slit windows. Occasionally gunshots sounded, driving back the frantic crowds.

Soh'shoro used the mob as a distraction, weaving through its throng to reach the gatehouse. With the next reckless surge of pleading faces, he pretended to be pushed, tumbling toward the sea. But he merely caught the bridge's barnacled trestles, swinging underneath. Now he lurked invisible in the arches above the waves. And monkeying hand over hand, he climbed his way past frothing whitecaps and into the Haven beyond.

Passing the bridgehead, he clambered up a floating strut and onto the city's streets. But he did not find the Haven gripped by fear, as he expected, but festival. Everywhere fluttered tangerine pennons and polished bone charms, brightening the pier-lined avenues like trinkets in a courtesan's hair. Floating platforms and inner canals bristled with brine-soaked celebrants banging seashell drums. Buildings gleamed beneath fresh washes of nacre and matte clay. A faint haze of lily smoke lingered over everything, saturated into the city's very stones.

And to Soh'shoro's horror, he noticed Traders among the merrymakers. Worse, they bore atop their backs the very Gi'en shrines of his home. Outsiders jostled and cajoled alongside them, pantomiming with their own miniature temples. *Imitating the Valley's rituals.* Already, Soh'shoro guessed at what might wait at the parade's end. So he followed its celebrants, as they danced to water drums and insectoid flutes, flowing into a stone amphitheater, lofted above the waves.

"Prophet!" the crowds chanted. "Hear the prophet!"

Great braziers dominated the distant stage, fountaining sparks skyward. Cultist guards flanked the fires, eagerly fingering rifles. More and more merrymakers packed the amphitheater, so even standing, Soh'shoro struggled to breathe. Still he threaded the crowds, drawing close to the podium.

Soon a lone figure strode between the stage's pyres, swathed in indigo robes, face hidden by a pale bone mask. Its eye slits squinted fiercely and its mouth hole narrowed wickedly. Silver charms tangled from the carved scalp, jangling beside brass bells. And the crowds screamed—

"Prophet! We listen!"

"Salvation!"

Through the bone mask, an eerily familiar voice whistled in reply: "Bring forth our final harvest!"

Now the Gi'en shrines gained the stage, streaming lilies from their gilded innards. Bulk crates and overpacked jars, bound by reams of twine twice as thick as a man's arm, burst beneath Cultists' hammers. Men shoveled the petals in great clumps like snow, fueling the braziers. The perfumed smoke rose faintly at first, the cloying oils slow to vaporize. But soon heavy plumes drifted across the crowds. The amphitheater fell into silence, as smog obscured swaying bodies and silent stone.

"Gi'en!" the onlookers muttered. "The last Gi'en!"

Soh'shoro breathed the fumes too. And for the first time Outside, he heard the Voice. It came in fractured whispers, like tiny shards of minds entombed, all glimpses and thoughts and broken impressions. He grasped his temples, shivering. This cacophony sounded nothing like the quickening instincts of the Valley. Instead this Voice cried with the madness of a caged animal, struggling to break free.

"Breathe deep the scent of paradise!" cried the prophet's familiar voice. "Its visions of our coming Eternity!" His skeletal visage slipped slightly.

Now Soh'shoro was certain. He knew the masked man.

An-go'yi'ki! What happened to you?

"This will be our final festival! Our greatest Gi'en before battle!" his brother preached. "We need only defend our Haven against the coming Black Cloak ships! One last War! Using their own storehouse of rifles and powder against them!" He gestured toward a cavernous structure of steel, its rusted eaves towering beyond the amphitheater's walls like the wings of a great bird.

The Vault, Soh'shoro intuited.

"War for Eternity! Death to end Death!" An-go'yi'ki continued, his melanized robes swirling through the fog. "Our time is at hand! The Mists draw close! Soon they will swarm our city. And then—when they part—the Valley will open before us! Our promised paradise will welcome us at last!"

The multitudes screamed lupine howls, as they descended deeper into the Voice's haunting malaise. And Soh'shoro took a terrible risk.

Because he still trusted his brother.

Fighting the swaying bodies, he forced himself to the very front of the crowds. As he advanced, he raised his hand high, straight and purposeful as a tern's dive. Despite the festival's chaos, he knew he would be noticed. For in his palm, the cracked mask of the princess gleamed aloft.

Almost instantly, the prophet's gaze swung to it. Then it settled on Soh'shoro's face, studying. Beneath its bony visage burst a smile of pure joy.

"That faithful!" An-go'yi'ki commanded. "That one there! Bring him here! Now!"

Cultists descended from the stage, surrounding Soh'shoro. They raised him overhead, parading him like a Gi'en shrine through the stupefied merrymakers, before lowering him atop the podium. The Voice cried its disjointed, alien shrieks.

And the prophet hugged his brother terribly close.

"You came!" he whispered. "I thought they'd stolen you. Doomed you to the Mists." He held the prince at arm's length, still beaming. "You came!"

Again An-go'yi'ki turned to the crowds. "The last prophet! This is the last prophet! Arriving at our time of salvation! Just as the Onan'ji foretold!"

Screams shook the amphitheater so madly they shuddered even the waves. The Voice itself echoed the refrain, hissing and gurgling with bestial eagerness.

"Paradise at last! For the faithful! For the deserving! For us all!"

And An-go'yi'ki led Soh'shoro from the stage.

The brothers entered a complex of sloping wood, freshly painted purple and pearl. Beyond its bronze gates rose water-lofted row houses and seashell-pressed monuments, encircling a massive pagoda. The spire had clearly been erected recently, in mimicry of the Valley's own.

Inside, An-go'yi'ki and his Cultists led Soh'shoro across a wide hall, hazy with lily smoke. The prophet opened a gated screen at its end, revealing a sumptuous suite fanned by salt breezes. Divans and silk pillows molded in the sea air, their odors congealing beside lilied brine and preserving wax.

"Now leave us!" An-go'yi'ki commanded the guards.

But his Cult escort hesitated. "If this is Prince Soh'shoro, the Black Cloaks stole him first. We don't know what lies they plied him with. You need protection . . ."

"And what help would you be, drunk on lilies?" An-go'yi'ki snarled. "Besides, I have other defenders far more reliable than you." He raised his hand. "I said leave us. You will do so."

The Cultists relented, shutting the screen. Now the brothers stood alone, surrounded by only opulence and lily smoke.

"A blockade," An-go'yi'ki snarled, pointing out a seaward window to the black sails circling the whitecapped horizon. "But why do the chirurgeons hesitate to strike? Despicable. Desperate . . ."

"Brother," Soh'shoro interrupted. "It is you, isn't it? Really you?" His voice faltered. "What is going on?"

At last An-go'yi'ki unclasped his bone mask, fully revealing the warm smile and pale skin Soh'shoro remembered. But now, deep lines of worry creased his cheeks, like lily roots worming through soft soil.

"Isn't it obvious?" the Ang'soon prince replied. "I'm dying, Soh'shoro. We are all dying. Outside is cursed with mortality." His eyes, dilated by lilies, grew wide with sudden fear.

"I'm so sorry," Soh'shoro pleaded. "I never meant . . ."

". . . to kill me?" An-go'yi'ki finished, trembling with the memory. "I know the Qu'su tricked you, Soh'shoro. That much is forgiven." He shook his head mournfully. "Besides, your blade helped me understand. For after my death, there was nothing. No future nor past. Just a snap; the brevity of oblivion." He grimaced. "I will not let that be my fate."

"It can't be true. Are you really helping the Cult?"

"Of course I detest it." An-go'yi'ki shook his head disdainfully. "But what choice do I have? They are the only way back to the Valley."

"You mean the Onan'ji is the only way back," Soh'shoro corrected.

"I don't deny it."

"How can you serve him?" The prince's voice trembled. "After everything he did to us, to our Houses? To you?"

"I am pathetic, I know." An-go'yi'ki fanned his hands, as if considering choices. "The monk is cruel, Soh'shoro. Even mad. I wish his schemes had never fallen upon our world." The prophet's auburn eyes glittered with fearful passion. "But he is selfless, in his own way. He means to save us. To gift the Mists beyond the Valley, stretching Eternity over the entire world."

So it is true. He plans to make all pure and perpetual. Soh'shoro's thoughts darkened. *But also sedated and static.*

"We can't let him," the prince pressed. "The Valley isn't paradise. It is enduring, yes. But it is also unchanging. A prison, with evil at its heart."

"You think as I once did." The Ang'soon drew close. "You see darkness in the rigid repetitions of Rebirth. But that is a small price to pay against Death. Who are you to cast a graveyard sentence across the entire world? If anything, the Valley did not dare enough, and that is the Onan'ji's true dream."

Feast. Soh'shoro did not know why he suddenly recalled the word, licked from the monk's lips, as he took the prince's life.

"Listen," Soh'shoro begged. "There must be another way. The Black Cloaks already know the Haven is a sanctuary against the Mists. We could invite them in. After the veils break, we'd have an army to end the Onan'ji's schemes."

The lingering Voice of the lily smoke quickened with his words.

"You think the Cult would allow that? Even were I to command it so?" An-go'yi'ki arched an eyebrow. "They are faithful, not fools." He shook his head. "Besides, this is the only way to save my sister."

"What do you mean, *save* her?" Soh'shoro shivered with anticipation. "Where is she?"

"I'll show you," An-go'yi'ki said sadly. "Come."

He led the prince deeper into the suite, onto a balcony overlooking the pagoda's interior. Now Soh'shoro realized this spire was erected not as a palace but as an excavation site. The tower's core rose hollow, open to the sky and encircling a great stretch of Ocean. Gargantuan augurs and dredging hooks groaned over the enclosed waters, their work recently complete. For a great metallic salvage hung overhead, suspended by thick cords and counterweights.

The Qu'en Shard.

Its angular geometries sparked brightly in the newly fallen dusk. Its fustic fragments hummed with Ocean breezes. But something black and bloated stirred behind its fogging glass.

"Is it her?" Soh'shoro stepped closer in disbelief.

"Of course."

For ensepulchered within the Shard slept the Ang'soon princess: her rot refulgent and her elegiac eyes static as a doll's. Soh'shoro gasped in both revulsion and recognition. Because he had seen such a sight before. In those silent simulacra sleeping within the cells of the waterfall gardens.

"Why do this to her?"

"To slow the rot. Just as I learned from the pods underneath the Mausoleum. To keep her in stasis. In slumber." An-go'yi'ki flinched with revulsion. "It was the only choice. To buy time until we returned to the Valley. To her rituals and her salt baths and . . ."

". . . her suffering?" Soh'shoro balked in disgust. "Would the Valley really save her? Or merely torture her?"

An-go'yi'ki softened. "You really do love her, don't you?" He clapped Soh'shoro's shoulder affectionately. "I see it plainly on your face, even now. Even at the end of the world. Still you don't understand."

"Then tell me."

"This is her kind's purpose." An-go'yi'ki gripped the balcony railing, knuckles whitening. "When the Emperor wastes away, when even our blood no longer quickens his Corpse, he must be made anew, Reborn inside fresh rot." His eyes glistened with coming tears. "It is for this we keep the princess, Soh'shoro. It is always her. Always her flesh ensepulchered on that horrid Throne. Imagine her pain. Pumping poisonously to stave back ruin. Absolute and interminable agony, moment by moment, on and on, into forever." He placed both hands on Soh'shoro's shoulders, partly in appeal, partly for comfort. "That is why I help the Onan'ji. He offers to take that burden from her, to bear the rot himself. To become the next Qu'en."

Feast. Soh'shoro stepped away in disgust. "Madness."

"Salvation, Soh'shoro."

"Listen to yourself, brother. I don't know what the Valley truly is. What the Qu'en are. Or why their world broke. But to give the Onan'ji such power?" Then came the terrible insight, as he remembered the monk's mysterious words: *The power of its hand is invisible.* "The Qu'en craves freedom from the Valley's prison. I think all this might merely be its escape. The monk nothing more than its puppet."

"You offer riddles." The Ang'soon's face hardened. "Whereas I speak simple truth. We can return to Eternity and spare my sister her darkest fate."

"Never. The Onan'ji must be stopped. Alongside whatever evil he seeks."

"No." The Ang'soon's eyes darted dangerously beneath their lily fugue. "I think not."

"You care only about yourself!" Soh'shoro snarled. "You'd sacrifice the world to live forever?!"

"Of course!" An-go'yi'ki shrieked. "I will not die again! Nor will my sister!"

The two stood barely a pace apart now, eyes locked, bodies menacing.

"I will not serve the Cult. And I will *never* serve him."

"And what if I make you?" An-go'yi'ki sneered. "After all, you will have Eternity to forgive me."

Neither moved.

"Call your Cultists."

"Soh'shoro, please . . ."

"You can't, can you?" Soh'shoro smiled viciously. "You still care that much."

An-go'yi'ki's lips tremored. But he remained silent.

"I will be back for her," Soh'shoro continued, "for you both, when the Black Cloaks come."

"If you so much as touch my sister . . ."

But Soh'shoro vaulted atop the balcony's railing before An-go'yi'ki could finish. Then he leaped again, catching a hanging rope, swinging against its counterweighted pulley, arcing atop the pagoda's open eaves. Below him, An-go'yi'ki shouted a desperate, final warning.

"Please! I don't know what they'll do if you leave! They'd relish your death, as payment for theirs."

But the prince didn't understand.

"Goodbye, brother."

Soh'shoro ghosted over the excavation's walls, vanishing into the coming night. He did not know how long he had before An-go'yi'ki's sympathy faltered, or his brother guessed his plan.

He had to act now.

So Soh'shoro stole through the Haven like a phantom, vaulting its rooftops, dancing its ropeways, leaping canals and creaking columns. Atop the distant seas, the ships of the Black Cloaks circled, their dark masts blotting out the early stars. Along the shores, the Mists churned dangerously close, their tumescent veils choking away the world. Ahead the metallic wings of the Vault glimmered, argent and ethereal beneath the newly brightening moon.

But the structure was offset from the city streets by defensive bridges, each patrolled by Cultist rifleman. Soh'shoro dared not approach directly. So he clambered underneath the city itself, into its inner lattices of load-bearing pylons. Whitecaps churned handholds terribly slick, salt gummed senses, and the scent of gunpowder piqued the wind. Soh'shoro advanced mainly by forcing his fingertips into gaps in the trestle ribbing. He doubled back often, finding the way forward impassable where rusted iron gave way to furious sea. Moonlight filtered through cracks in the flooring above, tiger-striping the waves beneath.

Halfway across one of the Vault's outer bridges, a Cultist patrolled too closely overhead. In desperation Soh'shoro let himself fall, bracing each leg against a different sea pillar, split like a birthing charm. The deeper shadows, closer to the waves, shielded him from the guards' torchlight. The Lily-Eater passed overhead. Still Soh'shoro waited until his legs cramped with the pressure of the hold, making certain. Then he ghosted on, as if through forest boughs.

Now he clambered beneath the Vault itself. Here the footfalls of guards echoed ceaselessly as they circuited its outer terraces. Soh'shoro stumbled across a latrine, open to the Ocean but slick with urine. Pride died before necessity. Swallowing, he scuttled up its fetid walls.

Inside the outhouse, he listened to make certain no one approached. Then he moved like lightning, dashing onto the outer walkway. He had only moments before the next patrol. And Soh'shoro leaped, taking two steps up the Vault's banded iron wall, kicking upward, then arching his body back. Parallel to the ground, his fingers snatched the sloping steel cornices swinging overhead. He rolled atop the Vault's eaves, smiling at his own talents.

Then his world exploded in pain.

CHAPTER EIGHTEEN

WAR

The roundhouse kick caught him completely unaware, nearly snapping his neck. He spilled across the roof tiles, scudding against their banded metal. Only the Ocean slickness saved him, as two shurishi buried themselves beside his sliding form.

Qu'su. Soh'shoro spat blood from his mouth. *Of course they would wake Outside too.*

He kipped up just as the three assassins closed. A ri'shou'an arced overhead, searing across his back as he dove away. On instinct, Soh'shoro reversed his momentum, shouldering the monk. But a second darted to attack, drawing his weapon in a long, low slash. Soh'shoro tumbled over it, spiraling against the roof tiles to sweep the man's legs. The assassin spilled sideways. But another shurishi sang through the starlight, warding Soh'shoro away from his killing blow. Now he turned, gazing at the slipping shadows encircling him.

And Soh'shoro drew his mother's blade, flashing electric blue in the watery glow of the moon.

"I killed you in the Valley," he threatened the closest Qu'su, remembering how he had sliced his ribs atop the City's eaves. "I can't wait to do so again."

But one assassin towered above the rest. His stance was easy and confident, his footfalls eerily silent as he prowled closer. There was no doubt in Soh'shoro's mind: This was a master Qu'su, trained far beyond his brothers. *When I defeated him before*, Soh'shoro realized, *he wanted to die. To serve the Onan'ji Outside . . .*

And the elder assassin tapped his ear, smiling luridly. Moments later, Soh'shoro realized the guards below had heard their battle.

The first of the Cultists' cries broke: "On the roof!"

Then: "Something's above us."

"Fire to kill!" called the master Qu'su. "This abomination does not belong in our Eternity!"

And suddenly, in the brilliant sweep of the night, only violence remained.

The first weapon cocked beneath him, and instinct blurred with training as Soh'shoro moved. The roof's tiling exploded in a gout of flame where he had stood moments ago. The two novice assassins lunged for him, flanking and cutting with terrible eagerness. Soh'shoro worked flat between their blades, reversing mid-step to elbow one in the soft part of his neck. Leaning into the blow, he weaved beneath the other's cut, trying to finish the counter.

But without the Voice, he moved too slowly. The master Qu'su intervened, sliding from the night, catching Soh'shoro's wrist, and twisting. He rolled with the joint lock, backhanding another slash away as he kicked the elder assassin. But the Qu'su stepped into Soh'shoro's blow, torquing his knee cruelly and hurling him flat to the roof's edge.

And all three monks descended upon him, like vultures for the feast.

Soh'shoro rolled sideways as another gunshot disintegrated the eaves behind him in a cloud of needling shrapnel. He half cartwheeled over a slash, trying to stand. But the master assassin's cut caught him off balance, spitting blood into the night as he slit Soh'shoro's arm wide. He fell with the blow, tumbling from the roof. Reflexively, Soh'shoro's hands snatched rafters to swing him onto the Vault's latticed walkway. A Cultist stood right beneath him, caught completely unaware. Soh'shoro kicked him so hard his skull cracked open against the powder house's ribbing. Another Lily-Eater rounded the corner, and Soh'shoro snapped his gun loose, catching the stock and firing through the man's chest.

Blood hissed over his face and hands as the Qu'su leaped from the roof above.

Soh'shoro dove away from the first shurishi, catching the second on pure instinct and hurling it back at the master assassin. The elder Qu'su twisted midair to avoid the weapon, landing off balance on the brine-slick walks, suddenly separated from his companions. Soh'shoro saw his chance. *There is no Voice here. You must trust yourself.* And in the next instant he slid between the other two monks, tripping one and rounding with the blow, throwing three lashing kicks that worked up the other's body: cracking his knee, then his ribs, then his neck. The man crumpled like a doll, even as Soh'shoro cut the other Qu'su in two.

Only the master assassin remained.

Soh'shoro tumbled reflexively as a blast of gunfire broke from the walkways behind him. Shouts were everywhere now, as Cultists descended upon the Vault like an army of ravenous shades. Glancing back, Soh'shoro caught two more Lily-Eaters sighting their rifles. He desperately sprinted full tilt for the elder assassin, hoping the Cultists would not risk shooting their own. Closing, he slashed early with his golden ri'shou'an, anticipating the Qu'su's counter and weaving beneath the blow.

A burst of gunpowder broke from behind Soh'shoro.

He dove sideways as bullets rippled past his leg. The flooring between himself and the master Qu'su crackled with the errant shot, then split wide. Suddenly Soh'shoro and the assassin tumbled through the collapse into the latticework pillaring beneath the Vault.

Free-falling, for one instant the elder Qu'su gained the advantage. The monk's legs caught an Ocean post, levering his body overhead to stab for Soh'shoro's stomach. But midair, Soh'shoro parried the blow, kneeing the assassin and flipping him beneath. The Qu'su turned his blade, slashing again, but Soh'shoro snatched a support beam, his other hand locking both ri'shou'ans dangerously close to flesh. Momentum did the rest. The master Qu'su fell along the length of Soh'shoro's sword, spilling warm blood into the night. Moments later, the man's limp body splashed into the Ocean depths, floating serenely to the surface amid a smattering of sea foam and lily scum.

"Fire!" a Cultist cried.

Soh'shoro glanced up in panic, finding Lily-Eaters blasting at the Qu'su's floating corpse, mistaking it for his own. Each bullet spat blood and splintered bone into the restless waves.

Soh'shoro climbed beneath the walkway, drawing close to its collapsed flooring. As Cultists reloaded, he leaped among them, sword flaring. Soh'shoro slew four helpless men clumped together in the space of a single breath. The last two died moments later, fountaining crimson screams into the salt-stained air.

Look what I've become. Soh'shoro fought down fury, surveying the butchered corpses. *Only I did this.* For he had killed these men without any whispered guidance from the Voice. Talent and training alone had gifted Death. Nothing more.

Could I be ready? Could I face him again?

Elsewhere in the night, gunpowder retorted, shattering his reverie. Already more Lily-Eaters rushed to protect the Vault.

Soh'shoro had to act now. Snatching a rifle from a fallen Cultist, he scrambled back atop the powder house eaves.

He ran to where gunfire had cracked the roof's iron banding. Soh'shoro kicked at the remaining tiles. Their slats gave way easily, creating a hole just wide enough to shimmy through. Then he half fell, half stumbled into the innards of the Vault.

He landed atop elevated scaffolding before scanning the bulky dark below. Only a thin crescent of light spilled through the cavernous powder house. Its halls stretched on and on, like a shrouded tomb, in metallurgical litanies of ancient weaponry. Quickly he identified the largest store of saltpeter, freighted alongside massive rifles, twice the size of men and made entirely of iron. *Cannons*, the chirurgeon had called them. *One shot and this whole place will take flame.* The massive guns slept monstrously on their carriages, beside crates of wadding and fire starter. Soh'shoro clambered down to their graveyard of steel.

In moments he smashed open the closest cannon case, scattering fistfuls of primer. Then he tore free iron lids and slashed leather tarpaulins, exposing everything he could to open air. Last he kicked into the powder kegs, their splintered wood leaking stinking yellow filament across the bare floor.

Now he climbed, madcap and desperate, back atop the Vault scaffolds, then onto the roof. Here he turned, sighting his stolen rifle through the narrow gap. Without hesitating, he pulled the trigger. And the powder store exploded skyward.

Soh'shoro never heard the full detonation; his ears already rang dead from the muzzle flash. Instead he felt it: rippling across his skin like water, singeing his flesh with vicious heat. The Ocean itself illuminated, reflecting vermilion fury like a shattered sunset. Then the blast broke Soh'shoro, snapping his vision black and buffeting him into the cold of the waves.

Time jumped.

He jolted to panicked consciousness in the frigid depths. When he gasped on reflex, water scorched his lungs. He began to drown. Desperately he kicked for the surface, before spotting sheets of flame blistering its waves. Soh'shoro fought every instinct in his body, forcing himself to swim underwater to escape the fire-scoured sea. He stroked until his senses bled, until his mind thrummed with stains like melting glass, until even the heat of the tides lapped dead against his skin. Then at last he had no choice but to breathe. The last fiery comber washed overhead instants before he burst through the Ocean's calid break. And Soh'shoro choked watery gasps again and again, the taste of their salt blending with blood and sick in his mouth.

For a long time after, he floated atop the waves, letting his heaving quiet. Half aware, he watched the Vault-born fire spread on wings of smoke, leaking from its skeleton wreckage and fanning across the Haven, staining even the stars a gory cerise. A corpse drifted past, charred to the bone. Elsewhere screams blended with the sea's evaporating hiss. At last, Soh'shoro forced himself to move, the pain of the explosion numbed by the sea's frigid burn.

He swam toward the nearest sea walk, clambering up to look across a city fully aflame. Soh'shoro's explosion had caught the Haven's bright nacre, and the summer winds spread that conflagration easily. The silhouettes of Cultists flickered erratically, shouting as they tried to tame the insatiable inferno. Still, more and more structures sparked a brilliant burgundy into the night.

It was too late to stop now. The whole Haven would burn.

Then he heard it: cannon fire, echoing from the sea.

Soh'shoro climbed split tiles and sparked timber, gaining vantage to look out across the deep sea. There the Black Cloaks' ships shelled fiercely, as they descended upon the Haven's weakness. The same winds fanning the blaze protected their ships.

Already long yawls disembarked, rowing infantry toward the city's ports.

War.

There is no time.

Soh'shoro knew he was badly hurt. That he was mad to try to rescue his princess. But he could risk nothing else. Blood flowed from his calves and forearms; burns protested the damp fabric of his charred robes. And always the blaze's heat drifted over him, billowing ash and lily-scented smog.

I promise.

And Soh'shoro sprinted into the inferno. He lost track of everything then, except the chaos of the streets and the pounding desperation of his run.

Approaching the Cult's pagoda, Lily-Eaters scrambled futilely to douse fires. Beyond its bronze gate, Soh'shoro stumbled blindly into an entire battalion. They should have shot him dead. But instead they rushed past, focused only on the flames. Not one of them noticed the prince; he was just another panicked survivor of the firestorm.

He slipped deeper inside. Now the terrific beating of warning gongs, pathetically late, blended with the cacophonic snap of blaze-buckling timbers. He glimpsed a smearing of rot atop an upper staircase. And then, squinting through the smoke, he made out the princess. She still lay encased in the Qu'en Shard, its weight carried by countless Cultists straining beneath mighty plinths. An-go'yi'ki stepped into view moments later, shielding the relic from falling sparks, shouting commands.

"The docks!" he ordered. "To the inner docks!"

Soh'shoro tried to follow. But a sudden bombardment of cannon fire rocketed through the pagoda. Streaking shrapnel shattered its grandeur, shivering bodies into maimed mists. A roof support cracked, collapsing rafters in an inferno of nacre-fueled heat. Soh'shoro had to turn back, sprinting from the ruin as the spire disintegrated into flames.

In the courtyard outside, he caught the Shard's silhouette again, on the opposite side of the collapse, crossing a wooden walk onto windswept jetties. In the canal beyond, Black Cloak yawls docked hastily, disembarking their first battalions onto the Haven's streets.

They could kill her by mistake while fighting the Cult.

Heedlessly, he chased after the princess. Ahead a bridge smoldered to tinder, and Soh'shoro flew across its blackened beams like a sparrow alighting on twigs, leaping spar to spar to cut the canal. But his route was circuitous, and he reached the docks only as An-go'yi'ki's procession boarded a waiting ship. The galley's sails were already unfurled; its mooring lines swung half free. The Shard hung at its lee side as pulleys wrenched it atop the deck.

Suddenly gunshots pocked the ship's ribbing, splitting timbers and bone. He turned to see the Black Cloaks reloading after their opening volley, even as more and more rowboats settled into the canal berths, disembarking waves of riflemen. Soh'shoro found himself pinned by cross fire as the Lily-Eaters aboard An-go'yi'ki's ship blasted back. Dark shapes surrounded him. Pyre light spilled across an approaching face.

Soh'shoro gasped.

"Yei'an."

"Hold!" she screamed, moving her body to shield Soh'shoro. Black Cloaks flanked them, guns raised.

"I said hold!" Yei'an cried again. "He's our friend!"

Thick cloth bandages wrapped Yei'an's brow, and a strange, dark patch covered her right eye. *Complications of surgery.*

"You're here?" Soh'shoro asked, disbelieving.

"I couldn't leave you." Yei'an smiled brightly. "Not yet."

The pair crouched behind dock crates as the Cultists' counterfire pocked the jetty.

"My family is on that ship." Soh'shoro jerked his head toward the galley. "The Ang'soon and—"

"We know. We followed the Shard here. We can't let them escape with it." She shook her head. "But they're pinning us on purpose. Buying time to set sail."

Soh'shoro smiled savagely into the ruddy flames. "Cover me."

Yei'an's single eye creased with fearful anticipation. But instead of protesting, she merely pressed her hand over his, resting both atop the ringed pommel of Soh'shoro's ri'shou'an. "I know you care for her." She smiled sadly. "But come back to me."

The Qu'en Shard thundered onto the galley's deck, churning the waves white with the impact of its massive, settling weight.

"Fire!" Yei'an screamed. "Now! Now!"

The wharf vanished beneath gun smoke. Aboard the ship, Cultists ducked for cover, giving Soh'shoro one precious instant. And he vaulted the dock crates, unthinking as he dashed toward his bride. Already her vessel rocked free, its mooring lines floating lazily. And Soh'shoro took one final step atop the jetty, leaping after it.

Everything happened at once. The Cultists returned fire, their rifles fountaining smoke. Soh'shoro's shadow danced above the sea, like a swooping heron. The galley drifted into open water. The Haven burned brilliantly, its blazes perfectly mirrored in the pyre light of the clouds.

Soh'shoro took two full steps atop the waves before slamming against the warship's lee side. His hands snatched one of the Shard's loose pulleys, swinging round the keel as Cultists fired down at him. The depths drank each bullet, before Soh'shoro mantled atop the sloop. His ancestral ri'shou'an glinted ginger beneath the inferno's light as it flew from his side.

I promise.

He moved like chain lightning made flesh. Sliding beneath rifle fire, he slashed into the first Cultist, catching his flintlock in the same motion and striking the muzzle wide. Its shot echoed fatally into another man as Soh'shoro wheeled behind masting, bullets ricocheting off the spar like driving sleet. Rolling free now, he slashed a third Lily-Eater from sternum to neck, rounding with the cut to shoulder another into gunfire. He skipped flat across the prow, weaving low between rifle arcs and closing on a group of men reloading. They died before powder ever touched their hollows, the last blocking with a gun barrel that split like dry reed. In the same motion Soh'shoro hurled his blade, spearing a distant Lily-Eater and knocking his shot wide. He then vanished into clouds of gun smoke, emerging at the other end of the deck, killing three men unarmed before reclaiming his ancestral blade. A lone Cultist remained, dodging Soh'shoro's first slash and palming a dagger. He caught the man's counterstrike before kneeing him into the rigging and cleaving him in two.

In the moments after, Soh'shoro gasped again and again into the crimson night, alone among the dead. His muscles quivered in stilling fury, mind numb with ardor and hate. At last he wiped blood from his eyes, blinking up at the clouds. The ship's masting gouted flame. Either gunshots or fiery breezes had sparked its sails. Already the sloop listed with the wind, rudderless and drifting toward the shoreline. It wouldn't be long before the winds drove the vessel into the beach, to crash and burn.

The Qu'en Shard.

It loomed before him, anchored tightly to the deck with heavy ropes. But its glass had been folded back; the chamber inside was now as hollow as new bamboo. She must have fled belowdecks. Soh'shoro descended after her.

At the base of the hold's stair, two more Cultists lay in ambush. Soh'shoro killed both before they even sighted their rifles. Just ahead, the freight compartment door stood barred. But with two solid kicks Soh'shoro splintered its lock-beam. He stalked into the cargo cabin beyond.

Everything swelled with lantern light. Packing crates and half-chained shipments littered the floor, their contents spilling with the rolling waves. Amid the freight An-go'yi'ki stood, indigo robes swirling like an exotic flower. In one hand, he held a narrow pistol, small and cruel looking, its center bored into a rotating cylinder unlike any of the Black Cloaks' rifles. Beneath his other hand shivered the broken misery of the Ang'soon princess.

Soh'shoro lowered his blade, gazing at his beloved. She hung ravaged by rot, her once-thin form swelling with the weight of coming wings. Congealed blood dribbled from her mouth, staining her throat like charcoal cast into water. Even now An-go'yi'ki forced his fingers down her throat to stop her biting her tongue, spattering his pale skin with gore and saliva. He held the princess like a paralyzed doll, all the more perfected for the terror in her eyes.

"Soh'shoro," An-go'yi'ki menaced. "I warned you not to come for her."

The princess screamed through her brother's twisted fingers, her cry reverberating through the cavernous hull, catching against its bridging pillars and leaking through its sealant walls.

"Let me take her," Soh'shoro begged. "I don't need to hurt you."

An-go'yi'ki shook his head. Tears spilled from his eyes. "You don't know anything!" he yelled. "I was so close. So close to the Valley."

"Let her go, An-go'yi'ki."

"You've ended Eternity. The Cult was our only chance. He

was our only chance." His eyes shone wildly. "I won't die! I will never die!" But the life in his words sputtered, like a spent candle. "This is your fault, Soh'shoro. You murdered me! You condemned my sister to rot in this horrid world! You brought fire and Black Cloaks to our Haven!" And An-go'yi'ki raised his pistol menacingly. "He can still feast. I can still take her to him. We can rejoin the Valley and . . ."

Soh'shoro had heard enough. He advanced across the hold as overhead flames scorched the ceiling timbers.

"You won't shoot me," he gambled, measuring each pace. "I am your brother. You can't."

"I will," An-go'yi'ki swore. "You were never my blood. You were always his!"

They were terribly close now. When Soh'shoro reached for his princess, An-go'yi'ki aimed his gun. But in that instant, Soh'shoro snaked between brother and sister, driving his elbow into An-go'yi'ki's stomach. The Ang'soon prince jerked like a tightened prayer strip, slamming into the ship's bearing wall.

"You never stood a chance."

The princess fell against Soh'shoro, blood dribbling from her mouth. He smelled lilies on her skin like poison. And Soh'shoro gazed again into her guileless eyes. But there was no monster there, merely a hideous void of black.

"I came for you," he whispered. Then he took her hand, leading her limping from the burning hull of the ship.

"Demon!" An-go'yi'ki called. The Ang'soon prince stood once more, pistol shaking. "I can't let you take her." His weapon cocked into the flames. "She'll suffer, do you understand? She'll change into one of them!"

And in horror Soh'shoro realized the pistol wasn't aimed at him.

He didn't think. Instead, he leaped in front of the princess, knocking her to safety even as she snatched for bright lacquer. And then An-go'yi'ki's shell struck Soh'shoro full force in the face.

The world cracked in a warm burst of blood and wood. His head snapped with the impact, the vexing spiral of the gun flash vanishing into the princess's cry. The hum of the world went dead. Soh'shoro slammed against the ship's flooring, gasping into concussive silence.

But he was still alive.

He blinked senselessly, trying to understand. When he raised his hand, it came away with bloodied slabs of lacquer. Fragments of her cracked mask. Soh'shoro had carried it here but never fitted it atop his own face. There was only one other who could have.

Turning his head, he saw it was the princess who had saved him. Even now she clasped a thin shard in her trembling hand, splinters scarring her palm bright and bloody. Her wooden visage had shielded him, breaking beneath the bullet instead of his own skull.

And Soh'shoro rose, unbelieving.

"How could you?"

"I won't let her suffer. If she's going to change . . ."

He flew toward An-go'yi'ki like a demon. When his brother fired, he dashed askance, falling low as the next bullet hummed overhead. Again and again, he weaved past the shots, anticipating each jerking motion of the pistol's barrel. For one instant the brothers seemed to mirror each other, a perfect dance of reflexive violence. Then Soh'shoro's blade sang free, splitting a bullet in two even as it gashed his brother wide. The pair spun past each other in arcs of crimson, back-to-back for one instant as An-go'yi'ki thrust his gun behind for his final shot. The needle-sharp sound of blade catching metal rang as Soh'shoro locked the muzzle away, driving his sword, reversed, through An-go'yi'ki's stomach.

And the Ang'soon prince slumped against him, head leaning into Soh'shoro's shoulder as his muscles fell slack.

"I'm sorry," An-go'yi'ki slurred. He fell forward, pulling free of the sword and collapsing to his knees in gushing wetness, painting the floor with his majesty. "I just wanted . . ." He choked on his own blood. "I just wanted not to end." He coughed one last time.

"But we must," Soh'shoro promised.

Then An-go'yi'ki, prince of the Ang'soon House, died for the second time by his brother's hand.

PART IV

THE END OF ETERNITY

CHAPTER NINETEEN

DEMON

He blinked as if awaking from a trance. His muscles ached. His body protested burns and cuts. She helped him stumble, step by step, from the dark of the hull.

Soon.

The burning sloop drifted ashore, listing awkwardly. Somehow Soh'shoro climbed down to the beach, even as fire disintegrated the ship. But the brilliant metal of the Qu'en Shard remained, lancing heavenward like a grasping hand as it settled into the shallows. The Haven burned beyond. Dawn brightened the horizon's black sails with a chimeric, ruby riot.

"Thank you. For saving me."

"I saved myself," the princess replied forcefully. "I couldn't let him take me."

"Why? What did your brother mean? When he said the Onan'ji would feast?"

The princess stayed silent.

"Is that why you tried to bite your tongue?"

Still nothing.

"You've known all along, haven't you? Ever since we first met?"

"Some." She looked away. "Some I learned Outside.

Or remembered, as I changed." Her eyes ran the depths of the sea.

Soh'shoro leaned against her. She held him, gently raising her hand to where the exploding lacquer of her mask had scarred his bloodstained cheek. She traced those gashes down his chest and into the veinless staining of the Qu'su, as if connecting them.

"We all suffer. But some of us were made to. That's my purpose."

"What purpose? I need to hear it from you."

When she next spoke, her words came carefully measured, each syllable metered and calculated. "To hook into the machine."

He trembled.

"I've told you so many times, Soh'shoro. But you never listened. I am a backup. A copy. Hiding in plain sight."

"No, you are the Ang'soon princess."

"Why can't you see?" She laughed bitterly. "I don't even have a name. Just like you only stole your mother's."

He froze.

"The rot is not a disease, Soh'shoro. It is a sequence telling the body how to change." She enunciated each word harshly and gutturally. "My kind are contingencies. Bred to incubate the essence of the Qu'en. So its Eternity can be ever enfleshed."

"That's what he meant by feasting, isn't it? The Onan'ji will consume your rot to change."

"To shape Eternity to his will." The words shivered in her flesh, as if waking something alien within. "His original schemes were for the Corpse, I think. But through your father, he will have learned the rot must be fresh, from my kind before we change." She swallowed. "There are so many of us, underneath the Mausoleum. I doubt he knows how to wake those copies without ruining them. While I'm alive, perhaps he can't." She smiled faintly. "But I don't think that will matter. To him, we are just components. Waiting to be consumed."

The feast.

"Who knows how far along the Onan'ji's transformation is? Who knows what else he might dare, once he discovers his Cult has failed?" Her blackened eyes met his. "We must stop him now. No matter what."

Shouts came from farther up the beach, as Black Cloaks rowed out of the storm. They had been found.

"How long do you have?"

She hesitated. "What do you mean?"

"Before you change too."

In answer she lowered her robes. The rot spread, deeper and deeper, down her breasts and back, into the small of her stomach. Spiraling and lacing, in gorgeous arcs like whirlpools in a pond. Beneath her paling flesh, bones poked through, thin and hollow, fragile as a bird's. The bulging swept worst across her neck and shoulders, with the rising pressure of a pinion mass straining beneath.

"My brother tried to delay it. With the Shard. But it's already too late."

"Not for surgery," Soh'shoro insisted. "I saw with my own eyes what the chirurgeons can do."

"I don't want that." She pulled her robes tight, hiding the darkness.

"And I don't want to lose you."

"But you must." She turned forcefully. "It's what *I* want, Soh'shoro. The end of all their kind. For the Qu'en to die with me." The princess smiled brightly. "Promise me. Like you did before."

But Soh'shoro did not reply.

Instead, exhaustion and pain took their toll, and he lay

down on the damp sands, breathing heavily. And the princess merely waited patiently beside him, statuesque and sorrowful as a broken doll.

The Black Cloaks dragged the Shard back across the shore, crossing the Haven's bridge just as the Mists reached the Ocean's edge. Refugees, once barred by the barbican's gates, streamed inside beside it. All just in time. Soon the last suggestions of the amaranthine plains vanished, alongside the waterlogged tresses connecting city to sand.

Until only the Mist and the sea remained.

The Black Cloaks carted the Shard to the amphitheater, as if mimicking the procession of the Gi'en shrines. There Outsiders gathered in speechless rows and huddled clusters, spreading blankets and tents across the fire-blackened stones. The Mists swarmed tighter, roiling now over the charred platforms of the Haven. All held their breath, fearing the magic of the Qu'en's relic spent.

But suddenly the Shard sparked with alien colors: electric greens and putrescent blues. The Mists cleaved apart, as surely as waves breaking against stones. The amphitheater, and its nearby districts, endured inviolate. All else was blotted away, except a narrow sliver of sky. Then this, too, vanished.

During that longest night, the Outsiders watched in horror as something monstrous circled their sanctuary. As the Mists drifted past, an alien specter stalked within them. It was more wraith than wing; more force than flesh. A horrid, mouthless face kept pressing the edges of its prison. Yet somehow it cried with the Voice, again and again, repeating the same word with absolute, cosmic indifference:

Soon.

Then it was gone.

With dawn, the Mists drifted into the outer seas, the once-blue horizon vanishing beneath their argent bands. And any lingering pall from the horror's presence faded as moonlight behind clouds. The Outside, or what little remained of it, had survived.

Soh'shoro watched all this barely conscious, through the haze of the lead chirurgeon's leaden tinctures, as An'na treated his burns and cuts. He had been hurt terribly: in his battle with the Qu'su, in the Vault's explosion, and then in his final duel against An-go'yi'ki. He could do little else but endure. And day after day passed like that, into that dim awareness of recovery.

The Ang'soon princess never visited. But Yei'an was with him always. Ever smiling warmly, gently squeezing his hand, just below the stains of the Qu'su.

"We can see clearly to the mountains," she told him the morning she left. "To the Valley itself. The Black Cloaks make ready to march on the City. To finish the Onan'ji and his Qu'su once and for all."

Soh'shoro leaned against her, testing his legs. And Yei'an helped him pace the narrow infirmary, as had become their routine, patiently encouraging his muscles to heal.

"I need to go with them," Soh'shoro declared at last.

"You're still hurt." Yei'an shook her head. "You need to rest."

"I need to see him," Soh'shoro insisted. "I need to be there when the Onan'ji loses everything. When his broken dream burns." He trembled in terrible anticipation of that moment. "Besides, I am still the prince of the Valley. I should lead the army's march upon my home."

"But you don't have to," Yei'an protested. "This War will be won with or without your blade. The Black Cloaks bring powder and cannon. In numbers far beyond the Qu'su. Even the Onan'ji cannot defeat such a force."

"Nonetheless," Soh'shoro replied, "he will still fight. I must go."

Yei'an nodded slowly. "We can start with the walk to the War camp at least." She forced a smile. "The fresh air might do you good."

Together they shuffled outside the infirmary, into the Haven's streets. But the stench of Death lay heavier on the breeze than even sea salt. Cultist corpses, strung up like butchered animals, baked in the afternoon sun. Gulls picked at their soft flesh, cawing cruelly.

"How many died?"

"So many," Yei'an replied. "The chirurgeons saved what they could. But the Cult killed more. And the Mists took almost everything else."

On and on they paced the desolate streets, leaning against each other. Soh'shoro savored Yei'an's rich scent, her easy touch, her winking eyes. Being beside her, even among such Death, made his heart quicken.

But he never rethought his choice.

The Black Cloak encampment marshaled at the Haven's bridgehead. Here riflemen stocked powder into tented carts, as others drilled formation to heavy drums. Chirurgeons clustered among grand bowers of blackened iron and knotted heartwood. Soh'shoro noticed An'na among them. She gestured warmly, inviting him to join her.

But instead of approaching, he stopped stock-still, then turned to Yei'an. Her luminous eyes gazed back at him with nothing except care.

"I need to tell you something."

"Anything," she replied, her breath like sweet melon.

"Most of the Houses are dead. Soon too the Onan'ji and

his monks. All that will be left to govern the Valley is myself"—he hesitated—"and the Ang'soon princess."

Yei'an nodded slowly. Her good eye welled, ever so slightly, in a way Soh'shoro had not seen since the very first night they met, amid the sorrowful shadows of the Qu'su temple.

"After we reclaim our home, it will need a new dynasty. Tradition will matter more because of what is lost."

"I know you married her," Yei'an replied coolly, lips trembling. "We never spoke of it, but I know."

"Then you know what I must do."

"No, I don't." She seemed suddenly small, like a cornered animal. "Everything has changed, Soh'shoro. Why not this?"

He tried to hold her gaze. But her single eye kept slipping away like a carp through broken netting.

"I care for you. Maybe more than her. But . . ."

"You're lying." She smiled sorrowfully. "You see yourself in her, I know. The same suffering. The same pain."

"Yei'an . . ."

"But there is another part of you, Soh'shoro. A better part. You can be more than your darkness. You do not have to choose Death." She swallowed. "*Please*. Choose me."

He wanted to. So badly. For a moment he imagined again the other life that might be: of biting kisses and confident smiles. Of caring and being cared for, not out of need but out of gentle trust. Of wanting nothing else, because only she remained.

And still Soh'shoro shook his head.

"She's a demon! Look at her. She needs to die! She asks for it herself!"

"She is not thinking clearly. The rot reaches her brain," he insisted wildly, as if trying to convince himself. "The chirurgeons can cure her."

"Listen to yourself!" she shouted. "Is this what you want to become? When you might be anything at all?"

He darkened. "Yes."

"I will not watch you force surgery—" She swallowed the words, looking away in disgust. "You do it. You order them to torture your bride! You risk your life alone for a War that no longer needs you! I want no part in your madness and your misery anymore. If this is what you choose, you choose it without me."

He glimpsed the cracked mask, its broken shards somehow still worming their way into his skull.

"Don't leave," he begged. But his words were hollow, the appeal halfhearted.

"I'm not the one leaving." Yei'an stood terribly straight, every muscle in her body tensing with anger and sorrow. Tears streamed down her face, even more beautiful for her betrayal. She forced a final smile, swollen like a house grafted onto thin frames. "I still love you." And she vanished toward the sea.

Now Soh'shoro stood alone, struggling without her aid, still smelling her winter bur and honey. He willed himself not to care, as he clenched and unclenched his hands, grasping for her ghost.

"You came," An'na called, approaching tentatively. "But the monk . . ."

"She's gone," Soh'shoro said flatly. "We won't speak of it."

The chirurgeon nodded, her glass eye sparkling with the noonday sun. Now she took Soh'shoro's weight, helping him limp toward the chirurgeon's bowers.

"You are to join the War, I take it?"

Soh'shoro nodded.

"I can treat you as we travel, then. It's still many days to the City. You'll have time to heal and . . ."

"You will stay," Soh'shoro ordered. "To supervise the princess's treatment."

"Oh." As if in answer, An'na tapped the surgical pouch at her waist in thought. "I have already tried many techniques. Her rot is terribly advanced."

"Try more."

"Soh'shoro, what I would do next . . ." An'na gazed at him steadily. "It would be too painful. There can be no anesthesia. No . . ."

"Do it."

"She wants to die, Soh'shoro," the chirurgeon begged. "She asks for it."

"I don't care. She is my wife."

"You know she is more than that." The surgeon's breath misted sweetly. "Let her end. Please."

"That is not what you promised." His next words twisted terribly. "Or do you not remember my threat? As lord of the Valley, I command you to honor your word and save its princess. Do you understand?"

That evening, Soh'shoro set off with the first regiment of Black Cloaks. And though they cleared much of the beach before nightfall, as he bedded down amid the baking heat of the sands, he was certain he could hear the chirurgeon's answer:

The princess's screams echoing, dry and reedy, beneath the clotting stars.

They passed too much misery as they marched on the Valley: settlements husked by the Mists; mindless forms wandering broken roads; corpses, baked by the blasting sun, pitted by rain and worms; and endless stretches of ghostly sands, broken only by silt drifts and fustic winds. The Onan'ji's veils had scoured so much there seemed little left of Outside to save. But that only strengthened Soh'shoro's resolve. The less that endured, the more protecting it mattered. The more the extent of the monk's madness made itself manifest.

Days passed. The Black Cloak army reached the mountains, shivering with the blistering winds of unfamiliar altitudes. Campfires smoldered like falling stars, fighting back the cold alongside amber wines. One night, Soh'shoro slept within sight of the Old Road where he had first awoken Outside. But after the avalanche, little more than tarry talus wormed that mountainside. He thought of Yei'an then. But still he did not doubt his choice.

Soon after, the Black Cloak army summited the peaks, and Soh'shoro stared down at his stolen home. He smiled bitterly, fighting back tears of joy and rage. For the limber pine and black spruce still grew thick and heavy. The grasses and lilies unfurled just as beautifully, in impossible runs of emerald waves and pearlescent petals. As always, the City glimmered gloriously, even as the pale spire of its Mausoleum vomited the Mists to choke away the sky.

The army descended into Eternity, its Outsiders marveling at this new realm's majesty. Just as in turn, the Valley-born watched their sunburned invaders from behind cracked doors and veiled windows with equal wonder. Days of marching passed into trepidatious acceptance, as both peoples took the other's measure. Bent on battle, the Black Cloaks interacted rarely with the Valley-born. But Soh'shoro glimpsed occasional moments of connection: gifts of wrapped rice; offerings of Outside's wine; a few words exchanged, here or there, during chance meetings beside ascetic shrines or roadside wells. In that hesitant curiosity, Soh'shoro imagined the realm that might be, of sea and sand unified with slope and vale, of a world healing itself.

But still the City loomed, luminous and luxuriant, fountaining the Mists. They approached it now: the final fortress of the Onan'ji and his legion of Qu'su. Now came the last battle to decide the fate of all.

"We'll bar the City's bridges first," a Black Cloak commander declared. "Make our siege camp just beyond the river. Ready the powder and unlimber the cannons there"—he pointed to a grassy hillock overlooking the Trading District—"where sight lines are strongest. We might even bring the Mausoleum down just by shelling. Without ever setting foot inside the City." He smiled eagerly. "But just in case . . ."

The Black Cloak commander handed Soh'shoro a leather satchel, cinched fiercely by black bands and smelling terribly of saltpeter.

"The chirurgeons offer you the honors."

"What is this?" Soh'shoro asked.

"Concentrated powder. Enough to even blow apart one of the Black Ships' legendary castles, I'd wager." Soh'shoro didn't recognize the Old Word. "All yours to spark. When we reach the Mausoleum." The commander smacked Soh'shoro's back warmly. "Congratulations."

The prince tested the powder bag's weight, as if setting it upon scales for judgment. Then he slung the pouch across his chest, gazing once more over his splendorous City. For the first time in its existence, his home would be ravaged by War. Exploded by powder and cannon. Broken by rifles and swords. Born of Death, Soh'shoro had awoken it in the Valley at last.

And only then, as he mourned his marvelous paradise, did he realize it was already too late.

Because he heard the Voice, for the first time since his return to the Valley. His mother's whispers again quickened his flesh, in what should have been a joyous moment of ghostly reunion. But her cries called beyond fearful, warning of a darkness already descending.

"Of course," Soh'shoro whispered in horror. "He controls the Mists."

The gray veils above the Mausoleum suddenly surged. Plummeting from the heavens, waterfalling like whitecaps on a frothing sea. Before Soh'shoro's eyes they choked away the irises and reeds, fogging the City's bridges and rivers, walling away the sanctuary behind an impenetrable dome of gray. In literal moments the luminous metropolis, and the dark Mausoleum at its heart, completely vanished.

"How?" the Black Cloak gasped. "That's not possible! The City was . . ."

"Run," Soh'shoro whispered. Because the Mists did not cease. Instead their tendrils struck out, in jagged lines like willow branches snapped by a storm.

He baited this trap.

"Run! We've got to run! Tell everyone! Now!"

All at once, the Outside army realized its ruin. Black Cloaks scattered, abandoning supply trains and powder stores. Roils surged from the City's doming Mists like arrows, or spouted from their heavenly veils like lightning bolts. Each bank smashed silently, smothering the Outsiders with apocalyptic quiet. In the blink of an eye, Soh'shoro watched an entire regiment vanish, the husking all the more horrific for its stillness.

His gaze snapped to the Mausoleum, now invisible behind the swirling Mists. He imagined the Onan'ji beyond those veils, wired into his terrible Throne, rotted eye glassing with fury as he called forth the Qu'en's magic. A single gesture of his fetid hand, and another hammer fall of Mists struck, silencing a full battalion.

Soh'shoro fell to his knees. There seemed no point in running. Here, so close, would be his end.

Except.

Except the Voice continued screaming. As it had only once before, its cries became impossibly clear and firm. It commanded him as a parent to a child, needling him into understanding, just as it had beside the Qu'su temple, a lifetime ago.

Trust the Mists, his mother whispered.

Hunting plumes pulsed with her invitation, spiraling for Soh'shoro hungrily, as if anticipating his entry.

I survived their embrace once. He remembered tumbling through their veils as a boy. How he had found both terror and strange comfort in those moments, as he crossed into his mother's memories. *I can endure the Mists again.*

Soh'shoro had been born apart from the Valley's magic. Perhaps that power would protect him now. Perhaps he might use his nature not merely to bring Death but to cross it.

As the last Outsiders were routed in terror, chased by whirlpooling veils, Soh'shoro alone strode toward their siren song. Confident and unblinking, trusting the Voice's calls.

This is my purpose.

And it must be. He had no other choice.

He imagined setting the powder bag. Searing apart the Emperor's Throne. Silencing the Onan'ji's final breaths, as his brief rule died alongside aborted rot. He took one more step toward that vision, risking everything.

And then at last, Soh'shoro walked into the Mists.

CHAPTER TWENTY

MISTS

The Mists' coiling embrace consumed him. With each pace, their veils darkened, the weightless tides tricking sight like inks streaking beneath rain. Motions skewed, as if glimpsed through ill-treated glass. Senses overlapped and blurred.

Their greatest art was of time itself. The princess's words came to him unbidden. *Contorting distances and abstracting relations.*

Instinctively, Soh'shoro grasped his mother's blade. Guided by her Voice, he strode on into the endless gray.

Now his thoughts filled with recollections. Gradually, his mind woke to every touch he had ever felt; every taste he had ever savored; every beauty he had ever witnessed. He held the princess, again and for the first time, in the very same instant he fitted the grasses of her burial shroud. Yei'an kissed his chest, over and over, even as Kenwu ruffled his hair with salt-stained hands.

And Soh'shoro stalked deeper.

Soon the pace of memories increased, building alien dissonance as their intensity compounded. Blades rainbowed brilliantly through his flesh, as the Onan'ji's lurid smile flashed above An-go'yi'ki's flaring pistol. Slops of Obajen-mahoe's mutations wedged a broken blade deeper into Yei'an's throat. All at once, the Mist became a conflagration of experience, simultaneously blending joys and sufferings. The ghostly memories reverberated against each other painfully, like stitching callously pulled.

Is this the secret of Rebirth? Do the Mists contain memory itself?

His mother's Voice called again, both anchoring and baiting him deeper into the spiraling amnesia of his mind. With its cries came new remembrances, both discomforting and dissonant.

Because they were not his own—

"What if there are more?" The question hung before the chirurgeon like a balanced blade.

"There are no more. Those that did not fail were purged."

A deep winter night, thick with snows. He puffed a narrow pipe with his mother's lips, its fumes heady with mercury and poppy.

"But not erased," she replied, her eyes running to the Misty peaks of the Valley. The veils seemed strangely new, too thin and barely settled. "Ours may be the last survivor. But elsewhere their works still linger. Their relics yet remain."

Is this the deep past? Soh'shoro wondered. *As the Valley was being made?*

"Exactly." The chirurgeon tapped her bearded mask, unlike any Soh'shoro had seen Outside. It was not avian but feline, its mouthguard swept into a tiger's grimace. "It is our kind we must fear now."

"And yet I fear my works the most," his mother replied regretfully. "The flaws in my design. The locks that might loosen. The unbarred ways to cross. The fading freedom of each coming cycle." She spat as the drug congealed unpleasantly on her tongue.

"Even such mistakes are still your brilliancies. For they twist into temptations." The chirurgeon reached for the pipe, taking a deep puff herself, eyes glassing. "It always needs a vessel. To break free, it must tame one of your puppets."

His mother rolled her head back, gazing into the snowy heavens. Her breathing came shallow and sweet with the opiate's haze.

"If only we knew its true nature. If it fought for its kind." She hesitated. "Or for their end."

Flakes fell heavily across her clouded eyes.

"On this we now disagree." The chirurgeon exhaled smoke over his mother's face, washing away her senses with its steaming anesthetic. "Whether worse or wondrous, eventually it must enflesh. We need only wait for Eternity to make it our own."

He felt his mother's tension, cracking the drug's euphoria. Almost reflexively, her hand rested atop the ringed pommel of her unbroken blade.

"And if we're wrong?" she protested, her voice bleeding into the bright burn of the drug. "We betrayed our Order together to seek sanctuary, not ascension. Remember our oath's warning—"

The power of its hand is invisible.

She did not speak those words aloud. Instead, the vow's refrain echoed through the mind she shared with her son, even as its snow-swept secrets bled away beneath the poppy's soporific smoke.

Soon.

And Soh'shoro felt the monster in the Mists now, slipping closer, lured by his mother's memory. Lazily and cruelly, the Qu'en came—its bone-bright fingers blotting out the heavens. He tried to focus on its danger. To run or to vanish from the skeletal elongation stalking toward him.

But sight slipped; terror twisted. He held no mastery of his own perception then. Because his mother's thoughts once more overcame his own—

A man held her close, his newly veinless hands a ghostly gold beneath summer's sunset. Heat curled with kisses into the lazy trails of their overcast heavens.

"What you have asked of me . . ." The Onan'ji's voice trembled.

But in his mother's eyes, he was not the mad monk Soh'shoro knew. Instead, he sparkled with the twinned vitalities of passion and hope. Even the shimmer of his veinless skin seemed not sinister but stunning.

"I am not asking," she pressed. "I am tired of Rebirth after Rebirth. Of stealing the future to sustain our past." She swallowed, blinking away tears. "That is our Valley's true nature. The clue I refused to accept."

"Like you refuse to accept us?" The monk reached for her, stroking her with genuine tenderness. "You said yourself you don't belong here. Why not then to me?"

"Because I can't abandon my purpose." In her hands now glimmered the crane-bright ossuary. When she half drew the sword, its shattered silver flared rubicund with sundown. "I broke this blade burying my mistakes. But I should never have let it stay sleeping. Not while I have more to redeem."

"And if you fail?" The monk's eyes welled. "If this, too, is what it wants?"

She shivered.

"Please, Soh'shoro." The Onan'ji whispered his mother's name like dew settling on fresh grass. "An Eternity alone is not paradise but punishment. I can't endure that. Not without you. Not forever." He gazed piteously into her eyes. "You are my joy." He caressed her, deeply and truthfully, his golden lips warm as a winter's fire.

"But we did not make the Valley for love."

Still she kissed him back, savoring his spidering touch with her son's own skin, whispering the strange syllables of his forgotten name, so thin on her lips even Soh'shoro could not hear them.

The prince recoiled in disgust. For at last he understood the secret sorrow of the Onan'ji. Why he shed tears at the mention of his mother. Why his tutelage blended cruelty and caring together. Why he could never forgive nor forsake both parent and child.

Only I am of Death. Only I could take my mother from him.

And the Onan'ji had always loved her.

Soon.

Like sunlight through a screen, the creature's wings unfurled from the memory, multifaceted and jagged as the limbs of a leafless tree. His mother's tryst was wiped away beneath those cocooning pinions, cradling Soh'shoro just as the monk caressed her vanishing ghost. And the prince could not even cry out before such revulsions.

Because the Qu'en descended upon him.

The demon did not move so much as unwind. It did not have form so much as resist existence. Glimpsing its unjointed angles and dipolar symmetries burned the sight, like staring directly into terrible radiance. Soh'shoro could only perceive it in pieces: massive, spindly legs, reversing with each pace; elongated arms of hollow bone, knifing into netlike fingers; a chest that curved outward, emaciated yet grotesquely muscled; a face that hung from the neck, featureless and flat, smothered by smooth sheens of veinless skin; and glorious wings that painted the heavens with pale flesh, as if fanning the world itself.

The creature looked directly at him. And that sightless stare exsanguinated thought, feeding an inferno of recollections. In one instant every single memory of the Mists woke within Soh'shoro, and he touched what others had touched; loved what they had loved; feared rapturous need and indolent desolation; dreamed cravings unspoken and satisfactions unfound.

He screamed a soundless scream, his suffering just another Voice. His mind burned beneath overstimulation. *Husking me.* He clutched his head so hard blood ran from his temples, as if mere physical pressure might contain that unbearable omniscience.

Soon.

The Qu'en stepped inside of him, stretching his body over its own like an ill-fitting robe. Every sensation exceeded agony, as Soh'shoro suffered pure and utter presence, so extreme he felt nothing except all of time itself, collapsed into this sorrowful singularity. His very existence snapped. He crumpled to his knees.

But the Voice cried one last time. And this call was different. Its whispered pain pulsed with genuine empathy, slicing a crack in the creature's control, leaking perception alongside the monster's will.

Again came his mother's memory. Her last, as blood rivered her stomach and spasms strained her heart.

"No!" he screamed with her voice. "Don't let them touch me!"

"But the birthing courtiers can still save you!" begged Obajen-mahoe. "Please! We both know this child is Death."

"Then let me die!" she cried. "Let me die so my son may live!"

All Soh'shoro felt was love. How his mother cared for him, even if she would never know him. How she wished so much to give him life, she would gift hers in return. And with a final, desperate madness, the original Soh'shoro snatched her husband's hand.

"Promise me." But already her words weakened, as her heart thundered out. "No matter how wrong, you will . . ."

"Don't ask me this," Obajen-mahoe interrupted, his voice cracking. "Not for this anathema. Not when his birth risks our Valley." His tears caught the candlelight in rings of gold. "Not when his life takes your own."

"Then because of it!" she pleaded a final time, blood flecking her pallid lips. "Promise me. Before it's too late."

Obajen-mahoe cradled her both lovingly and miserably,

running her frail fingers between his own in tortured indecision. Twice he opened his mouth to speak. Twice the answer died on his lips.

"Promise me!"

But she never heard his reply.

Because a final spasm swam across her sweat-slick skin. Because her head fell feebly against the birthing charms. Because her gaze, still searching, became lifeless and cold, even as a child cried out into the swirling vicissitudes of the Mists.

And at last Soh'shoro understood.

This was the source of his separation. Why his birth lay unchained by Eternity. His mother's love escaped even the Valley's prison.

This was your choice, he whispered to her ghost. *I was your choice.*

Now as her final memory faded, the Qu'en consumed with even greater fury, setting all its exsanguinating thoughts against that glorious revelation. But even as its husking remembrances ravaged, they strained against their limit: Soh'shoro's newfound joy.

Nothing could diminish her love. Her sacrifice.

It must not be in vain.

So Soh'shoro rose, like a titan from its slumber, fighting off the hollow spirit as if sloughing dead skin. Still its distended shape resisted, leaching the ancestral blot of its encephalic secrets, setting all its alien power against his mother's martyred purpose. And as the full might of the Qu'en broke over Soh'shoro, its own thoughts spilled alongside it. In one twinning moment their minds fused in terrible trickery. And though Soh'shoro could not comprehend the aberrant relations of the Qu'en's unnatural intelligence, still he glimpsed its hidden horror. Its monstrous, incalculable truth:

The creeping no-place, atramental and empty as the unbeating heart of a discarded doll.

He beheld this vision for only the briefest of moments, in an infinitesimal slice of pure and utter dread. That was enough. His mind glassed. His body jerked and spasmed. He fell flat and febrile, fracturing against himself.

This was the Qu'en's secret. What their kind feared and fought and fled. The grandsire of Death.

The end of time itself.

Must this be my purpose?

Because killing the Valley's Qu'en meant far more than merely defeating the Onan'ji, or liberating his home, or even protecting the Ang'soon princess. In vanquishing that demon, Soh'shoro would extinguish the only answer to life's entropic ultimatum. For he understood now. The Qu'en were truly Eternal. They had conquered time itself. And the Valley's Corpse was the last of its kind. By snuffing its spark, Soh'shoro erased existence's sole hope of enduring into the void. Condemning that very last immortal consciousness, however alien, to cease.

Must this be my choice? His mother had sacrificed everything for love. Would his be for oblivion?

Still, he knew his answer.

Because a world without end can never truly begin.

So Soh'shoro drew himself up to his full height, the Qu'en and all its masquerading memories falling from him like shattered glass. Still grander and grander Soh'shoro towered, surpassing statures unimaginable beyond the Misty veils. The creature cowered before him, driven cold and callow to the ashen ground. And higher still he rose, tall enough to touch heavens and quake earth, his mind rushing back to him with renewed clarity.

The Qu'en was nothing more than Eternity itself.

And I am Eternity's Blade.

Soh'shoro took his first step now, not remembered but real. The Mists fled from him like clouds spiraling in a tempest. Another pace, and their niveous wake tore wide, bleeding sidereal brilliance. The Qu'en slithered back, driven beneath its gray dominion, the pulse of its uncounted lifetimes impotent against such certainty of self.

And Soh'shoro raised his head.

The heavens split beneath his splendorous gaze as if lanced by sunlight. The last of the Mists vanished in a vacuum burst of preterition. With them, the shape of the Qu'en shivered completely apart. But somehow, the demon's dissolution did not seem like defeat. To Soh'shoro, its banishment felt merely like a shrug—of complete and utter indifference—a retreat into the ghostly patience of its skulking certitudes.

Soon.

And Soh'shoro stood alone, gasping for breath, transcendent in his majesty.

He did not know how long he had been lost in the Mists. His throat was parched, his feet were bloodied, and his muscles quivered with excruciating exertion. His chest heaved the choke of the grave. Through overstrained tears, Soh'shoro blinked back both dust and sleep, staring breathlessly beyond.

The City stood before him. It rose fetid and feracious, beneath the jagged spar of the moonlit Mausoleum. Within it the Onan'ji loomed, a chimera cocooned in his chrysalis of rot.

And gripping his mother's blade, Soh'shoro felt its hilt as her hand, girding him with grave-born strength. At last he knew himself. He was not merely a fallen prince or stolen assassin. Not heir to the Valley or demon of Death.

He was not even the real Soh'shoro.

He was more.

Within her selflessness lay the apotheosis of Soh'shoro's stain; the brightness behind his sin. His mother had shown him the truth. Death need not be dark but could be noble. If its majesty was not inflicted upon others but given of one's self.

Sacrifice.

And anchored by that love, the prince strode fearlessly toward the waiting assassins.

CHAPTER TWENTY-ONE

QU'SU

"Come for me," Soh'shoro whispered.

For above him they flitted atop eaves and lantern strings, coalescing like maggots on a corpse.

The Qu'su.

Still he strode uncaring, past prayer strips and funeral flames, working his way ever deeper into the City's heart. The last of the Mists' alien perception slipped from him. Time snapped again into its natural stretch. His breathing steadied, even as his heart quickened with the coming violence. But the shadows merely stalked him, as if waiting.

Soon the outer gates of the Palace lay before him, eerily ajar. Beyond, temples smoldered epoxy fumes into the starry night. Without hesitating, Soh'shoro stepped into the vacuous smoke, passing priests mindlessly worshipping salt pyres and Traders soundlessly miming benedictions to the Mists. None moved to stop him. Only the assassins circled, like crows for carrion.

Baiting me, he realized, kicking through the gateway to the Palace's second ring and the inner gardens. *Luring me beyond escape.*

Once courtiers clustered beneath tarps here, as ethereal fireworks rioted with the Gi'en's revelry. Now the sculpted paulownia boughs loomed vacant and haunting, mortuary decorations weighing their defoliated limbs to the briny earth. Ponds mirrored the blackened lantern light like bleeding wounds. And over everything hung the haze of salt: smoking inside funeral braziers, leaking from cartonnage lamps, burning in decocting fires of sweet grass.

"Soon." Soh'shoro watched the Qu'su flit through the wildwood, pressing on. "It will be soon."

He reached the Palace's final ring. And slashing through its corded gate, Soh'shoro stared across the wide courtyard surrounding the Emperor's tomb. Once he had danced above this curtilage on lantern strings, the shrines of the Gi'en gyring beneath him. Now the Qu'su settled atop the abandoned pagodas, flocking numberless as stars, ranking themselves in legions of dark flesh.

Fury quaked within Soh'shoro like a warming fire. He gazed up at the assassins, raising his mother's ancestral blade.

"Leave now and you will live."

But they poured from the eaves like a ghostly tide, their shurishi hissing through the salt-sick night like glittering fireflies. Soh'shoro slid beneath the first volley, weaving his ri'shou'an in quick, defensive arcs that splintered needles into rain. More shurishi flew, and he dodged fluidly, deflecting the ceaseless torrents with both his sword and the back of his free hand.

The Qu'su slithered close in veins of shadow, driving him toward the Mausoleum doors. And Soh'shoro killed then, beyond even the Voice's whispered instinct. For he no longer needed to listen.

Splitting an assassin's ri'shou'an in half, he fountained warm flesh as a child might pull at festival streamers. Another leaped for him, and he struck the blade so hard it torqued the man flat in the air, shattering his shoulder where he crashed against the cobblestones. Soh'shoro knew only the rough hilt of his ri'shou'an, its golden seams and dark stains of spilling blood. He fought, trailing bodies that bled as silently as the Mists themselves, reaching the hulking maw of the Emperor's tomb. Its alloyed gates were cast open, pouring lily petals into the night.

He retreated into that obsequy-strangled beyond. The Qu'su followed, turning the Mausoleum into a killing ground of brine-stained silks. Blades sang into waiting shadows. Shurishi whispered past ancient veils. Soh'shoro slid impossibly flat, answering with his own slash that spat crimson over rotting paper. Tangles of his hair were cut free, and rounding, he took the attacker's ankle, ri'shou'an spraying the falling body like foam churning atop the sea. More came and more fell. He weaved a wake of Death, gifting corpses to the copestone black even as he struggled deeper toward its rotted heart.

As he battled up the helix staircase now, its once-brilliant enfilade flared coldly in the radiance of sparking blades. Bodies tumbled like trundling ornaments, slickening the steps with gore. Catching a Qu'su off balance, Soh'shoro snatched the man's own ri'shou'an, knuckles flat against the metal as he reversed the weapon. In moments he scissored the assassin open with both swords. Railings snapped, and the Qu'su tumbled into the cavernous shadows below.

They fought now into the grand rot of the upper corridors, before the waiting horror of the Emperor's Throne. These halls were a maze of cobwebbed silks and mold-sick shrouds, illuminated by funeral lanterns of glass-woven bronze. Soh'shoro's two ri'shou'an flared through their ruddy light, slicing men in half as though folding courtly fans. He spun each strike into the next, metal scything bodies with brilliant flashes like heat lightning. And still the Qu'su came.

In desperation Soh'shoro hurled his spare blade, spearing an assassin through the throat. But he turned too late to his next attacker, barely parrying the strike with the ringed pommel of his sword. The Qu'su stepped into the blow, jarring Soh'shoro's wrist and sending his ri'shou'an clattering to the ground. Disarmed, he fought desperately, locking joints to keep blows away, weaving toward his fallen blade. He lifted it with his foot, kicking through a monk's throat in the same strike, catching the weapon and scything it through another's stomach. On he battled into the heartwood brilliance of the final antechamber before the stairs to the inner tomb itself, where salt braziers smoked out a haze of choking purity against strings of beaded jade.

Here Soh'shoro's ferocity was unmatched. Stepping beneath a cut, he knife-handed an assassin, snapping his soft bones like trees breaking under snows. Thinking him off balance, a second Qu'su struck too eagerly. Soh'shoro shattered the man's elbow and drove its broken tip through his throat. The last of the horde circled. Soh'shoro could not remember anything then except the cold glamour of steel, the winking spark of reflecting blade light, and the thinly pealing notes of finishing counters.

At last, he shouldered the final assassin to the ground. His gold-kissed ri'shou'an followed, lancing crimson through the man's chest. Gasping for breath, steaming blood and fury, the prince looked out on what he had done.

Gore washed the lacquer walls like an inked landscape. Corpses trailed into distant shadows, charting a path to the very doors of the Mausoleum itself. Born against Death, here that silent Order of assassins returned to it at last.

Soh'shoro gazed up the ancient stairs to the waiting sanctum of the Emperor.

"Eternity's Blade."

The words echoed over the ghostly patter of still-spraying blood.

He caught those same veinless hands, glinting like a cat's eyes through the distant salt smoke, luring him into that beckoning beyond.

"Your world is poison," Soh'shoro stated. His murders, his scars, his sacrifices—they all ached then, cruel weights begging to be put down. "I have nothing to live for but this."

"Come then," his master called from the Throne room.

And Soh'shoro followed into that tombstone dark.

CHAPTER TWENTY-TWO

FEAST

Death smoldered everywhere. Lily-cloth bindings wove like rotted webbing through umbrae thick with graven relics: arabesque talismans and calcinated braziers. Salt mists smothered the Emperor's dais like poison, seeping between mechanical veils. At once fantastical and luminous, the dead heart of man waited, shrouded by shadows and stained dawn red in the effulgent light of its grave lanterns.

"See it," the Onan'ji whispered. "See what I have done for the Valley."

For at his feet lay scattered the copies of the princess. Countless in number, discarded like rice husks after polishing. They lay strewn atop each other, some completely naked, others blanketed by petaled shrouds. The Onan'ji cradled the freshest in his arms, its skin still blue from sleeping in its Shard. And lovingly, he licked the rot from the clone's eye. Its face remained static and empty, as if no thoughts animated the mind beneath.

Still, the orb blinked.

"More," he urged, almost to himself. "The more I take, the more I change."

Already regal wings strained against the Qu'su's skin, ready to burst out of his flesh. Black rot streaked from those pinions, climbing neck and face, flowering his dead eye into a rich, lumpy iris like newborn skin. Fetid tubing speared the tumorous phage, trailing the Onan'ji's motions like a gossamer cloak, siphoning his rot up horrid cabling into the hideous hum of the reforged Throne. Its once-jagged metals now gleamed smooth, flaring lights that caught the chamber like perpetual fireworks, endlessly mirrored in the empty eyes of the clones.

"You are without feeling."

"I am only feeling," the Onan'ji replied. Wiping his mouth with the back of his hand, he flinched as he forced himself to swallow. "All else has been worn away with time, Soh'shoro. All the years of misery and sadness winnowing away everything except my purpose." His eyes flitted to a body. "I never enjoyed this. I have done only what I must."

"To make the Qu'en's power your own?"

"You think I am so shallow?" The Onan'ji shook his head in disgust. "This has nothing to do with my power. It is about hers." He tensed his lithe muscles, like a falcon stretching before its dive, popping the relic's tubes free in sweeping jerks. Dark liquid leaked from their limp ends, spilling over the princesses.

"I learned from her death, Soh'shoro. Eternity gives us certainty and control. But it also condemns us to suffering. To the cruelest finality of all. Living without those we love." Idly the Onan'ji drew a lily shroud over his feast's mute flesh, hiding its frailty. "That is what the Qu'en realized, I think. This is the madness that drove them to challenge oblivion itself. Or to embrace it." He slid forward, picking his way over the doll-like forms, like a pregnant spider awake to its winter laying.

"Is it worth it?" Soh'shoro sneered. "To spread the Mists? To blot out an entire world? Is the gift of Eternity really worth sacrificing all else's present?"

And the Onan'ji laughed. A hideous, distended sound, like wet glass cracking. "You still think this is about Eternity?"

"That's what you're doing, isn't it? Spreading the Mists? Making the entire world part of our Valley?"

The Onan'ji nodded. "But why?"

Only now Soh'shoro realized: The Onan'ji was never like him. Whatever motivated him to end the world, it could never be noble. His quest must come from no one but himself.

"Her," Soh'shoro whispered. "This is about my mother."

The Onan'ji's subdermal wings shivered eagerly.

"She died, Soh'shoro. But that only means she was Reborn again. Somewhere Outside." He unfurled his arms, casting them wide as if to engulf the entire world. "Do you not see? She abandoned the Valley. So I will bring it to her, wherever she fled." He swallowed. "We will be together again." The Onan'ji uttered the terrible truth of that potential: "You could be with her too, Soh'shoro. She could return to all of us."

"Madness." The prince shook his head. "She'll be obliterated by the Mists."

"Did you think only you could cross?" the Onan'ji taunted, stepping closer, his foot mangling a doll's unflinching face. "She came from Outside, Soh'shoro. She created the Valley. I know you glimpsed as much in the Mists. Just as I know she passed that power to you, through her love."

"She'd never want this." Still the prince hesitated. "Even if I could see her again, I would never help the man who murdered everyone I ever loved."

"Did I?" the Onan'ji hissed. "Or was it your hand that took each life? And I who saved them? Allowing each to wake Outside, protected by the Cult. I rescued your brother. And your bride." At the mention of the Ang'soon princess, Soh'shoro's eyes flitted pityingly across the tangled, lifeless dolls. "You are like me, now," the Onan'ji continued. "You need to preserve her love, don't you?"

Soh'shoro could only reply: "Yes."

The Onan'ji smiled so widely his jaw seemed to disjoint. "Then I can give her to you. There are so many copies, Soh'shoro. Some in whom the rot refused to take . . ." He licked his lips thirstily. "Why not Rebirth your princess in a more perfect shell? Why not share more than a single, sickened life? When you could join together for all Eternity? With your mother. With me."

The prince stared into the eyes of the dolls. Each empty duplicate waited, unwoken, in layer upon layer of his lover's endless flesh. More than anything in his entire life, he wanted to accept them. To believe that, somewhere in their voids, a spark of her still smoldered.

But no matter how he imagined, these silent simulacra could never be the same. Not after what they'd shared. Not with what they still might, however fleeting.

"When I finish you," Soh'shoro replied, rejecting the monk's temptation, "I will do more than destroy the Valley and its machine. I will free the world from the Qu'en's curse once and for all." He still carried the powder bag, its black bands nestled safely beneath his robes. Now he lowered it among the dolls, settling it among their broken husks like earth upon a grave.

"Fool!" the Onan'ji spat. "How long will this world of yours endure? When its every grandeur must fade, even the greatest loves, even the vastest passions? If you measure Man by his wants, then you need only wait long enough to judge his life meaningless." The Onan'ji stalked closer, his rotting eye flowering hungrily through the salt haze. "I have given you every chance. Because I love you. But if I am forced to choose"—he shuddered ferociously—"I love her more."

The Qu'su stretched before Soh'shoro now, blood trickling

down his spine and pooling thickly over the dolls' empty faces and into their mouths agape, even as wing nubs strained farther through the Onan'ji's flesh.

"I know your secret." Soh'shoro smiled wickedly. "I don't need her Voice anymore. I will kill you by my hand alone."

"Then you condemn her, and everyone else you love, to the slow Death of time." The Onan'ji's mouth contorted wider still, a tiger's smirk of malice. "Tell me, my child: Can you end Eternity itself?"

Soh'shoro's smile twisted too, mimicking his mentor's. "Of course."

"Then show me."

With the hunger of parched earth in high summer, Soh'shoro struck. In one smooth motion he cut, splitting the darkness of the chamber in scattering shadows of coruscating azurite, the Onan'ji shivering out of focus beneath the blade. Then the Qu'su was gone—a ghost into the salt haze. Instantly Soh'shoro rolled aside, a shurishi burying itself in the lacquer floor a hair's breadth from his throat. As he rose, their swords met with a quaking note that reverberated through the brine-specter dark like the timorous echo of chimes.

Soh'shoro rounded low, knocking the Onan'ji off balance and shouldering him against the hard stone of the Emperor's catafalque. The Qu'su rebounded with astounding speed, sliding beneath a slash as he locked his feet through Soh'shoro's, tripping him to the ground. The monk's ri'shou'an streaked the blue of a harvest moon.

But Soh'shoro caught a copy's reflection in that eclipsing arc. And this time its eyes smoldered with the princess's true brightness. Her tears, her scars; eyes pitch-black tombs he could never bear to close, perfect and familiar in their misery. Walled away from the world, she was a puppet, brought into it a creature of fading twilight. The taste of her blood mingled with brine tea; the falls of her hair tangled into an ageless darkness, consuming even the sweetness of her lilied skin. She smiled, then. He felt the sting of her lips parting, searing like deep winter's cold, goading him into motion. Still gore splattered against his face, unfeeling where it caught the ghostly memories of her mask.

And Soh'shoro spilled down the far steps of the Emperor's dais, his side split wide. Crashing through silken screens, he broke back-flat against a terrace doorway, tumbling atop another heap of her. As Soh'shoro struggled to stand, he felt the copies' hands lifting him up, his blood washing their pale palms clean.

The Onan'ji was already upon him, bursting from the alkali haze like a falcon from a cloud, blade spearing before him. Instinct alone let Soh'shoro catch the weapon, ri'shou'an sparking down the length of the monk's sword and snapping its guard aside. The Qu'su leaped then, vaulting his knee into Soh'shoro's chest, butterflying his other leg and cracking Soh'shoro's head against the terrace frame. They split through its sliding door in a shower of veils and tinted paper, streaming as wings unfurled onto the Mausoleum balcony. Soh'shoro crashed hard on his torn side, blood lacing the boards where he slid.

"I am doing this for her," the Onan'ji confessed, flicking gore from his blade as a cat might paw at string. He stood framed by the shattered screen, the flames of a spilled salt brazier rising into the night behind him like cinder fireflies.

Gasping through blood-flecked lips, Soh'shoro spat out his answer: "I am too."

And the Onan'ji felt it now: the gash where Soh'shoro's blade had split cleanly through his ri'shou'an's narrow guard. Already blood trickled down his veinless forearm, pooling crimson.

"So close." The Qu'su's fetid eye flashed. "I trained you well."

Soh'shoro watched his mentor advance toward him, calmly

and inevitably as shadows drawing long at eventide. There was a majesty about him unseen before, an ease of consequence both simple and terrible, like water filling the lungs of the drowned. He was not the man Soh'shoro had faced once before, in that other life bound by the limits of the Mists. By the taste of his princess, he had become far more: a force of nature, purposeful and cruel, like rot finding pleasure in savaging the dead.

Soh'shoro forced himself up to face him, ancestral ri'shou'an held low and askance, the roughness of its hilt binding pressing faintly like a lover's silk.

A keening wind scoured the balcony, whipping up the voluminous dust of spilled salt. They vanished into the cloud as they charged. Cuts woke like heat lightning in a summer storm, Soh'shoro skidding past the Onan'ji's furious counter. Effortlessly the Qu'su stepped with him, locking Soh'shoro's wrist and wrenching against his momentum. The prince hurtled against the balcony's railing, only reflex keeping him in motion as he struck. And as he hand-vaulted atop the balustrade, its pillars splintered beneath him with the Onan'ji's cut.

Two steps along the rail and Soh'shoro leaped free as the banister collapsed under his weight. Blades met midair, sparking starlight. Soh'shoro skidded back onto the balcony, rounding in a wide slash that caught the Onan'ji's sword against its grain. He felt metal chip beneath his fury, teething deeper as he stepped into the cut. Soh'shoro threw himself forward then, smashing them both through the railing and out into the night.

The upper ponds of the waterfall gardens waited below, thick with lily flowers that poured through their sunken glass into subterranean cascades. Soh'shoro had first glimpsed her in those leaded waters. He beheld her again now, drowning within the crystalline coldness of her submerged cells, begging to be saved. And his blade sang in answer.

Swords met mid-descent. He caught the Onan'ji's next lunge through the ringed hilt of his blade, torquing it free, then twisting for the killing blow. But the strike sang seconds too late. And the pond fountained petal-laced waves as both master and student meteored into its shallows.

Soh'shoro's ankle wrenched against muck-slick glass. He felt its crystal crack with the force of their fall, and he stumbled sideways from the fracture. A shurishi sailed past amid weightless arcs of foam. Off balance, he turned awkwardly into the next blow, the Onan'ji cross-stepping his guard and sweeping his legs from him. Soh'shoro's world bled silent as he splashed beneath the suffocating cold of the waves.

Instantly the Qu'su clambered over the prince, holding him below the churning flow. As they struggled, the Onan'ji's phage-stained eye flared, distorted through the waters like a gibbous moon. In its fury Soh'shoro found his measure, relaxing suddenly into the depths as the Onan'ji overstrained. Scissoring his legs, Soh'shoro twisted the Qu'su down alongside him into the shallows.

Now they grappled, starlight filtering their motions through the pond's glass basin and scattering shadows over the leaden fonts beneath. Overhead the balcony's railing tilted loose, swinging down as the entire structure sheared apart. The Onan'ji flipped Soh'shoro, striking him twice and trying to push him beneath a falling beam. But the prince evaded the blow, rolling away from the timber as it speared through glass in whirlpools of foaming shards. The entire basin gave way. And like shooting stars they fell, plummeting with sprays of lilies into the cleansing ivory of the waterfall gardens below.

His princess shivered through that cascade, her perfection burning away its avalanching waters. Somehow this was the house they had shared collapsing now, amid the weights of flames and snow and silence. He reached to her in tears, his touch cracking her mask into streaming ribbons of liquid starlight and fevered softness, their world bursting wide like a nova amid the rotting heavens.

And the prince and the Onan'ji crashed against the banks of the sunken gardens. Breath vomited from Soh'shoro's lungs; his weapon clattered to the ground. Dazed, he moved only because of her love, shifting from the dented marble just in time. In the fractious light a blade glimmered, as the Onan'ji hurled his own sword. It split cleanly through Soh'shoro's arm, pinning it to stone. Unhesitating, the Onan'ji dashed for the kill, snatching up Soh'shoro's ancestral ri'shou'an, dead eye flaring through the waterfalls' foaming haze. But the prince tore the Qu'su's sword from his own flesh, spilling a cloud of sparks and blood into the cascading heavens.

Blades screamed as they scraped past each other. But Soh'shoro felt the weakness in his mother's weapon: the golden inlay that repaired its ancient cracks had chipped free. So he threw all his weight behind the next strike, swords catching in a razor bolt of scything brilliance. A clean note fell, buttery and soft. And the ancestral ri'shou'an split like corded timber, the Qu'su's remaining eye fountaining wide beneath Soh'shoro's unyielding cut. The Onan'ji stumbled back. The prince turned his sword one final time.

Soh'shoro sliced downward for the killing blow—but he understood too late. The Qu'su fell to his knees beneath the cut, palms clapping the blade overhead, fingers lacing the weapon and wrenching it free. Soh'shoro's wrist snapped, overbalancing him into the waters beside the broken tip of the crane-bright ri'shou'an. The Qu'su flowed with him, snatching up the golden blade's other half, lancing its jagged hilt for Soh'shoro's throat. They froze in their final struggle: the Onan'ji clasping Soh'shoro from behind, choking the lower shard of his family sword into the prince's neck. Only Soh'shoro's weakening hold on its ringed pommel held the killing gold away.

"It ends here," the Qu'su whispered, dead eyes unmoving as the ancestral ri'shou'an burrowed deeper. "Goodbye, my son."

Amid the cascading heavens, Soh'shoro watched a form coalesce, a ruined idol made from ash and Death. But this was not his princess but his mother. A ghostly recollection of her, awoken now as in those memories of Mists. In lilied torrents she laved herself to divinity, ensorcelled by crystal and petrified in foam, a perfect image of time ensepulchered. The world above opened in a yawning maelstrom, and he caught the full chaos of it: rotund stars like fire consuming the world, echoes of that passionless dark drinking heat and color and life and leaving nothing untainted before the expansive misery beyond Death's dreaming.

He remembered her sacrifice. So now he made his own.

Soh'shoro reached for the upper half of his mother's broken blade, glinting beneath the waters. His palm seared as he grasped its naked edge. Then he knew no more pain, even as he drove the golden tip through his chest; even as the cool scarlet of his innards spilled into the shallows. The Onan'ji screamed too, his cries not real but a last escape of the Voice, draining all intention away. And Soh'shoro held his mother close, as if both understood what the other had chosen.

Sacrifice.

"Of course," the Onan'ji gasped into his ear, as wings burst free from his flesh at last. Blossoming into spans of otherworldly white, their rotting skin stretched farther and farther. They held for one moment, framing the unfurled Qu'en with empyrean perfection. But then the Onan'ji coughed, gore flecking his phage-black lips. "You can choose to die." And the wings wrapped themselves about Soh'shoro slowly, folding into a pearlescent veil.

Because the blade Soh'shoro had driven neatly through his ribs had caught the Onan'ji completely off guard as it burst through them. Pierced through the prince's upper back, the vicious tip had continued into the monk's chest. There it had lanced deeply into his heart, spearing silent forevermore those flowering beats of the Qu'en.

And the Onan'ji fell away now, pulling free of the sword's length and collapsing into the frothing waters.

"I wanted to give this to you," the Onan'ji gasped, sightless eyes rolling vigorously, ice clear and beyond any pain. His hand, pure and smooth as worn stone, rose as if pulling back a curtain. "Life Outside the Mists is only regret and sorrow and endings."

In answer, Soh'shoro wrenched the broken ri'shou'an from his own ribs, hemorrhaging warmth into his ragged lungs. "Then that is the price of potential," he forced out. "Death."

"No." The Onan'ji blinked his sightless eyes one last time. "It is its only reward."

The waterfall gardens continued their slow collapse, glass and metal shearing free, fountaining over the unleashed angel of the Onan'ji. Fragments cracked the dolls' ovoid cells, bleeding lily scum inside, filling the lungs of any remaining silent sleepers. And the newly risen Qu'en bled out into their cold, staining the floating lilies crimson with his dying divinity.

Everything after tasted of ash.

Soh'shoro relaxed his grip on the broken blade, revealing a palm sliced to the bone. Then he kneeled painfully, fishing the sword's twin from the bloodied waters. When he returned both shards to their ossuary, the final click of steel to sheath resounded like a funeral charm.

Now he waded to the watery banks, gasping for breath and trailing gore. His wounds were deep and vicious, and he doubted he could survive them. But he was no stranger to pain. And one final task remained.

Before the helix stair, priests chittered amid the shadows in horrified supplication. Soh'shoro caught the eldest among them, even to the end praying through stitched lips for his cemetery of angels. He broke the man's throat with a single punch, spewing blood like steam from a kettle. None moved to protect their master. Because none dared confront the murderer of the Onan'ji: Eternity's Blade made flesh.

Unchallenged, the prince ascended the Mausoleum, his vision swimming, his footsteps heavy. In that hideous peak still hummed the machine, and its aberrant tangle of wires and glass and bright metal. Beneath it lay scattered the broken graveyard of silent dolls. But Soh'shoro knew nothing here mattered. Certainly not the mute faces, and their row upon row of beauteous potential. Because they were never his princess.

Eerily, the Voice stirred one last time, with animal anticipation.

Soon.

He lit the powder bag. Then he ran as fast as his ravaged body would let him, leaping from an outer balcony and snatching its lantern strings. And the great heart of the Valley detonated behind him, in miraculous fireworks of cerulean and sapphire and scarlet.

He did not remember limping to the terraces of his House. But it was here, at last, he chose to rest. Leaning his head against their wooden railings, somehow still smelling the sweet grass of his childhood pillow, sight swimming beneath the sparkle of Obajen-mahoe's iridized robes as he imagined his father's arms once more sweeping wide the wondrous world. From here he watched it end: the waterfall gardens crumble; the Palace blaze; the Mists unravel until their last ethereal tendrils vanished beyond the mountain peaks. All fell to ruin, until even the alien Mausoleum melted into glimmering gold, its molten wreckage mirroring the silver starlight.

And still the conflagration spread. Across ponds and streams, over tributaries and river basins. For the fire fed upon the lily petals blanketing the Valley's floor. Like the trails of shooting stars, the perfect seas of white vanished into celestine smoke. So the Valley's heart beat free its veins of flame, vanishing alongside its perfect choke of lilies.

Ending Eternity at last.

EPILOGUE

QU'EN

He awoke to clouds.

Blinking in disbelief, he raised his hand to dim their fustic light. Then he struggled upright, grasping the terrace railing as he simply stared heavenward. For the Mists no longer blotted the Valley's sky. Instead a vivid dawn spanned empyreal and aureate, shimmering the grasses and streams of his homeland into iridescent golds.

And beneath those piercing rays, Soh'shoro imagined the coming world they warmed:

Qu'su temples rotting in the hills, their subtle knives now mere fireside secrets. His own rise from obliterated royalty, returning to rightful rulership over a Valley reforged. A new court for council, welcoming both chirurgeon and commoner. And the City rebuilt with stone, bathed beneath fireworks bursting on foreign powdered wings. The day yawned with such furious and fantastic potential.

He took one small step toward that future, as if mere motion might hasten its approach. But instead, Soh'shoro's injuries screamed. Collapsing atop the terrace's knotted wood, he could only watch his own blood clot against the boards, reflecting the dawn's miraculous rays a rotted ruby. And now that cerise sunrise seemed only to belie its countless coming darknesses: pain and futile perseverance; famine and disaster and disease; skirmishes against splinters of the Cult; War against seditious Salt-born; Black Ships beyond the foreboding seas of the chirurgeon's blotted cartographies; and something worse. A sibylline design secreted within the encephalic horror of the Voice's vanished whispers.

What happens now?

Soh'shoro had no answer. He could not guess which dream was real: the bright or the broken. All he knew for certain was that by freeing the Valley, he had also unleashed forces upon it he barely understood. He had been strong enough to deliver this future to his people.

But am I strong enough to lead us into it?

After, Soh'shoro sutured his ravaged body with scavenged epoxy and discarded silks, his stitching accompanied by no Voice except cicada calls. Thus he found her final gift. For the wound of his self-impalement stung with eerie familiarity, its scabbing completing still-older scars. As if his mother had shown him with An-go'yi'ki's first death how to survive his own.

You taught me so much. Soh'shoro winced as he poulticed salt and rice wine over the wound. *But not enough to understand.* Because if the Onan'ji had spoken the truth, his mother was still out there. *So why not return? What keeps you away?*

What do you fear?

He contemplated that question for days, as his injuries set well enough for travel. He knew he needed to rally his people; to reconstitute his court; to reunite with the Black Cloaks and chirurgeons. But all these obligations, and every other he must face as last of the Valley's lords, would wait.

First, he needed to hold her again.

So he dreamed feverishly each night, as he journeyed beneath the unmasked stars, of his love. Of the princess's body purified by surgery, like an autumn dream made flesh; shimmering in pulchritude and splendor, shuddering against him with bloated softness; as bones fattened and pocks receded; as shoulders ceased to stretch and any final stains stalled beneath eager chirurgical knives.

He almost felt her suffering.

You can be more than your darkness. The words were Yei'an's final warning, whispered as her winter bur and honey fled for the seas. But the sidereal price his selfish passion forced the princess to pay suggested otherwise. *You do not have to choose Death.*

But he had.

Then that morning—

Soh'shoro rose early to summit the Valley's peaks, hiking verdant snow lines knifing into ancient places he'd once wandered with the Onan'ji, beside Qu'en Shards suddenly silenced and nevermore marking the limits of the world. Soon his eyes kissed Outside, sweeping its amaranthine plains and cerulean swells, its cream-cored clouds like polished glass, contemplating that new Eternity: a horizon undefined.

Here, at the edge of both Valley and vastness, he drew his mother's blade. The shards slipped far too easily from their ossuary, as cranes failed to catch their tempered gold. A lonely lily petal, desiccated and quiescent, clung to the sword's cracked spine, still caked with Qu'en blood.

Now he polished the blade, using only what he had: the sleeves of his robe and coarse salt for abrasion. A thin skim of lily juice completed the brightening paste, bled by the petal pulling free. Soh'shoro worked lovingly and carefully, cradling the steel as if it were his mother's hand, treasuring its ancestral touch, marveling as its silver sacrifice sparkled ever more vividly with each purifying pass. For the first time, though he now knew it measured, he dreamed only of peace. As all the blood of the past washed away, until only the broken beauty beneath remained. So bright and bare, the prince could see it:

The creeping no-place, atramental and empty as the newly beating heart of its discarded doll.

The power of its hand is invisible.

And again and again Soh'shoro called out for her, as he realized what it was he had done.

ACKNOWLEDGMENTS

This book would not have been possible without the tireless help and support of so many wonderful readers, editors, and friends.

First I would like to acknowledge my parents for encouraging me to write starting in elementary school. And in particular my mother, who printed out dozens of copies of my first completed manuscript to encourage me to fearlessly share my work.

Next my incredible wife, Nahoko, who provided endless inspiration for *Eternity's Blade*. Many ideas and entire plots in this book are the direct result of her clever thinking, from kintsugi to cranes, and all have vastly enriched the novel's world.

To my incredible friend Manoli, who listened to me discuss this book for countless hours and read its many drafts over many years. (I'm sure you'll be surprised by how much has changed!)

Next to my agent, Tim Wojcik, who first took a chance on my nonfiction with *The Book of Esports*. Tim believed enough in my writing to double down by representing *Eternity's Blade*, making this manuscript his first foray into literary fantasy.

To my editors. First Francine LaSala, who previously edited *The Book of Esports* and who gave *Eternity's Blade* an amazing first pass to sharpen it for publisher submissions. Then to Diana

Gill, who provided some of the most incisive, thoughtful, and structurally smart feedback I have ever received on my writing. Huge improvements to the core narrative and its thematic arcs can be fully credited to her.

Furthermore, I'd like to thank my publisher, Blackstone, and their senior acquisitions editor Daniel Ehrenhaft for publishing *Eternity's Blade*. I truly believe they are as proud of this novel as I am. Here's to many more books together!

Lastly, countless others helped shape this novel in myriad ways. While I can't thank them all, I would like to specifically mention Peter Olson, Lee Child, Bree Barton, and my Japanese language and literature professors, including Wako Tawa, Trent Maxey, and—perhaps most crucially—Patrick Caddeau, for his incredible *Tale of Genji* scholarship. While the world of *Eternity's Blade* is obviously not Heian Japan, I have tried my best to capture some of the wonder and beauty of Genji's court.

An acknowledgment section is by necessity always too brief. To all those others who helped sharpen *Eternity's Blade*, thank you so, so much.

William Collis